Clive's Christn

Susan Willis www.susanwillis.co.uk

Chapter One

'I can't believe it's nearly a year since we first stumbled into each other in The Shambles, can you, Clive?'

I shake my head and whistle through my teeth. 'Neither can I, Barbie, it's flown over,' I say and hug her close while snuggled into the sofa. She's just come out of the shower, and I can smell her fresh clean hair. It's still a little damp and I know she will head upstairs shortly to blow dry her hair and makeup. So, I make the most of having her by my side. I slide my hand under her bathrobe and tickle her ribs. 'It was the luckiest day of my life, that's for sure.'

My girlfriend's name is Barbara, but since the day we met, I've called her, Barbie. Now, she giggles and squirms while I tease her.

'Thank goodness for that burst carrier bag and wayward tin of baked beans knocking against your ankle on the pavement,' I say and rub my chin on top of her hair. 'And of course, your kind and helpful aid to a perfect stranger.'

Barbie twists slightly and looks up at me. 'Well, you looked to be in a right old pickle running down the street rescuing your loaf of bread and vegetables. And what's a spare carrier bag between friends,' she says and grins. 'I would have done the same for anyone in a calamity.'

I nod knowing she would do just that. Her kindness and generosity are just two of the things I love about her. There are hundreds more, I think, and cannot resist her smooth soft skin. I stop teasing and begin more of a caressing movement which she obviously appreciates and moans softly.

'Have we time for this before you go off to work, Clive?'

I kiss down the side of her neck. 'There's always time for us, darling,' I say then all rational thought leaves my mind.

***

Making love to Barbie has always been a delight and not something to be rushed. However, now I'm almost running through the streets to the travel agency where I work to get there on time. My house is on Victor Street which is a small quiet terrace of houses with only a pedestrian access through an old York arch way.

In January when I'd returned to work following the furlough scheme, trade had been slow. And although holiday bookings have risen throughout the year, I had been reduced to working two or three days a week.

The city is busy this morning with workers climbing on and off buses. With seven weeks to go before Christmas Day, shoppers are waiting outside the big department stores to buy their gifts. However, I'm a fast walker and dodge in between people while pulling up the collar on my wool coat against a chilly wind. I take short-cuts weaving through the side streets until I reach the office and stop outside to compose myself. Phew, I think, only two minutes late and breeze inside calling, 'Morning.'

***

My two female colleagues are taking off their coats and I join them. We settle into the chairs at our desks and sign-in to the computers. Jane, who is the longest-serving member of the team and in her mid-forties, gets up and heads to the shop door then turns the closed sign to open. It's only a small room with light-grey walls that have posters advertising places to travel on holiday with their iconic images, bridges in Venice, canals in Amsterdam, and The Eiffel Tower in Paris. Next to my desk hangs my favourite poster of a beach in Bali. I look at the turquoise-blue sea, white sand, and glorious sunshine knowing I can only dream of lying on that beach.

The three of us chit chat about weekend happenings.

Jane asks, 'Did you do any of the ghostly-ghoulie tours this weekend?'

As well as working in the travel agency, to boost my income, I also work for a York tour company as a guide showing people around our city. The tips can be quite good especially on the night-time tours telling spooky stories in the dark. These tend to be the most popular as York's alleyways lend themselves to mysterious happenings.

I shake my head. 'No, not this weekend. Me and Barbie went up to Edinburgh to visit my grandfather in the care home. He hadn't been too well and it's difficult shouting our conversation on the telephone because he's deaf. We thought it easier to go up instead.'

'Wow,' Jane says. 'Isn't it amazing that you found him again after all these years?'

'I know, and it was all down to Barbie, really,' I say. 'She was the one that found him simply from an old address on a card. Last New Year, we wandered the

Edinburgh streets talking to neighbours until we were pointed in the direction of a care home, and Bingo, there he was.'

Jane sits back at her desk and sweeps her black hair over her shoulder. 'She's a lovely lass, your Barbara.'

Both my colleagues have met Barbara socially and I smile. 'She certainly is,' I say. 'It's nearly a year since we met and I'm wracking my brains trying to think of something special to do for our anniversary.'

Tina, sitting behind my desk claps her hands together and exclaims, 'Oooohh, how romantic! We'll get our heads together later and come up with something that'll blow her socks off!'

I spin around in my chair and smile at the starry-eyed look in her eyes. At nineteen, Tina is a stunningly beautiful blonde who is presently dating three different guys. I grin. 'Yeah, Tina, you can think of some things that men have done for you which will give me ideas.'

Jane gets up and wanders through to the small staff area next to the money exchange bureau and switches on the kettle. She reaches our three mugs down from a shelf and spoons coffee into them then turns to face me.

She raises her pencilled eyebrow. 'Well, Clive, you could always make the ultimate gesture and buy a diamond ring for her finger?'

My mouth drops open. I hadn't thought of marriage at this stage and stare at her.

She shrugs her shoulder. 'Well?'

I gulp then smile. 'Okay, so that is certainly something to think about,' I say. 'Thanks, Jane, and yes, as you say, it would be the grand gesture.'

Jane pours hot water into the mugs and talks more to the wall than me. 'That's if you do want to be her husband of course and be with her for the rest of your days?'

I nod and feel my face flush at her direct questioning then swing back around to my computer as a tinkle alerts me to an email. I glance at the sender of the email and decide this can wait for an answer.

I feel Jane's hand upon my shoulder as she places a coffee mug on the corner of my desk. 'Sorry, I sort of put you on the spot there and it's got nothing to do with me,' she says. 'But in my opinion women like Barbara don't grow on trees.'

My mind is in a whirl now at the thought of marriage again. I'd been married when I was twenty-two. It had lasted for six years until my wife, Sarah ran off to America with a basketball player called, Chuck. A flash memory of the pain and upset after she'd gone comes into my mind which makes me shudder.

'You're cold,' Jane says and removes her hand from my shoulder. While passing the desk she reaches up the wall to the thermostat and turns the heating up higher. 'And do remember, Clive, I'm speaking from a woman who is the same age as Barbara. At forty-seven the security that marriage brings could well be in her mind for the future.'

She places Tina's mug on her desk who is typing quickly but thanks her without looking up, and Jane returns to her desk.

Out of the corner of my eye I can see Jane is now sipping her coffee and reading something on her screen.

I take a deep breath of relief that the focus, for now, has shifted away from me. But know I've a lot of thinking to do about the subject of marriage.

A customer enters the office and I look up at an elderly man then plant a welcoming smile on my face.

***

At lunch time I saunter through the shopping area and buy a warm pasty from The Cornish Bakery. I often go to a pub for lunch but I'm trying to spend as little as possible on a daily basis. I wander up towards York Minster deep in thought. The pasty is warm and comforting. I eat it quickly savouring the meaty flavours then scrunch up the empty paper bag and toss it into a waste bin on the corner of Petersgate.

I look up at the main doors to the minster which was built in 1472 after several centuries of building in light Yorkshire stone. Even though I've been here countless times over the years, it still takes my breath away at the sheer size and beauty of the old building.

I remember meeting Barbie here on our first dinner date together. The memory of seeing her hurry towards me in a new red dress makes me smile now. The fact that she'd made such an effort had given me hope and I'd prayed Barbie felt the instant attraction.

I shiver with the chilly weather but not wanting to go back to the office, I wander inside and sit on the end of a pew. A group of school children are in front of the big rose window while their teacher explains about the fire in 1984 and how rebuilding in parts of the minster had taken place. The children all look up to him spellbound. Although the group and teacher are too far away to see clearly, I can tell his words have the kids hooked into the story.

That's impressive, I think. As a writer I appreciate how the effects of well-chosen words can captivate an audience or a reader. I smile thinking of my first novel which is selling quite well on amazon. I don't think I'll ever make six figures in my royalties but the amount, along with travel agency wages, and tips I make from the York tours, all adds to the monthly coffers.

Barbie, bless her, keeps telling me that it doesn't matter, and she can keep us afloat financially and give us a good Christmas. But I don't want that. I sigh and look down at my hands clasped together. She paid for our first Christmas together last year when I'd been furloughed so it doesn't seem fair to take money from her savings now. Plus, I would like to think that in twelve months of a year I had made progress and was in a better place financially.

Barbie runs her own food technology business and can travel for work anywhere in the UK but tries hard to make it home every weekend. Her mam and family live in County Durham, and I have got used to sharing her with them on flying weekend visits.

It was only last Friday that she'd arrived home from Leeds after completing a six-week contract. I had only seen her at weekends, so I've been cock-a-hoop to have her close to me 24/7.

I'd wrapped my arms firmly around her relishing in the knowledge she'd be home with me until the New Year at least. She had been wearing her old jeans and a white woolly sweater which brightened her impish face.

Her small grey eyes had shone looking at me and I'd felt myself melt inside.

'Oh, Clive,' she'd said in her soothing voice. 'Money doesn't matter between us and who pays for what isn't important to me, being together is what counts!'

But I'd taken her hand in mine and squeezed it firmly. 'And Barbie, that's amazingly generous of you, but it does matter to me,' I had said. 'It matters an awful lot.'

She'd snuggled in close and sighed with pleasure. 'Let's not have the usual tussle about money on my first day home,' she had whispered in my ear.

I had squirmed in rapture as she'd made advances towards me with her cuddly inviting body but determined this time not to be persuaded by her wily ways. 'Barbie, you know that I love you very much,' I'd said. 'And I find it almost impossible to deny you anything you ask for, but I'm quite resolute about this.'

She'd cooed and giggled whilst undoing the buttons on my shirt and I'd known I was on a losing wicket. Her small but steady hands had worked their way inside my shirt as she continued, 'I mean, if I do pay for most of Christmas again just think of it as rent to live here with you. If I were a lodger, or if it were the other way around and you were living with me in my place it would be the same,' she'd said. 'We're a couple now and building our future together, so what's the old saying, what's mine is yours and what's yours is mine!'

And that's when all discussions had flown out of the window. I look down at the alter now. The teacher and schoolchildren have left but I think about her comment.

Building our future together were the words she'd used and sharing what we have.

Hmm, I muse, maybe Jane is right, and Barbie wants, or needs to feel secure. I wonder if she has ever thought about marrying me then take a deep breath knowing marriage is a monumental step. I must be certain before I pop the question.

Chapter Two

The house is quiet now as I sit at my desk in the spare bedroom which is my office. I sigh with relief that Barbie's family have gone. Her sister, Jenny and brother-in-law, Geoff had stayed in The Middleton Hotel as a treat which is only a five-minute walk away, but the two children stopped overnight with us.

I know since moving in here with me, Barbie has missed her family who she was used to seeing on a weekly basis. And she's always been close to Jenny. So, I want to get along with them all and try my best to accommodate her family. However, I sigh, with no family of my own, other than a distant grandfather, I try to join in at family gatherings but sometimes it doesn't go as smoothly as I'd wish.

I like Geoff, he's a good guy, but Jenny often seems a little tense around me. It's as though, even after all the months Barbie and I have been together, she is still sizing me up to see if I pass muster. I clench my jaw but know I must keep trying until they accept me as her partner because no one could love Barbie more than I do.

Libby and Jack were excited to sleep on an airbed downstairs especially because Barbie had made it into a tent-like feature. They're lovely kids and obviously adore their aunty Barbara, as she does them, but I had no idea how much noise children actually make. I guess living alone before Barbie moved in, and then with just us two in the house, I'm not used to such hullabaloo and frenetic activity. Especially this morning at breakfast.

The radio had blasted out Christmas songs. Cereal and toast had been made then an argument had broken out which seemed to ricochet in my head at a thousand decibels.

Libby had shouted, 'Aunty Barbara, Jack took up most of the airbed and kept kicking me!'

Barbie had smiled leaning against the red kitchen worktop. 'I'm sure he wouldn't have done that,' she'd said. 'Jack wouldn't be that unkind to his little sister.'

Jack, being the elder by three years was red in the face and hotly denied it. 'I'm sick of her making up stuff to get me into trouble,' he'd said then jumped down off the tall stool at the breakfast bar where they'd been eating.

'He did!' Libby screeched. 'He kicked me twice!'

The screech had made my ears ring and I had shaken my head slowly. Jack had sloped back into the lounge, and I'd winked at Barbie then followed him. Sitting next to him on the sofa I'd found the sports channel on TV to watch the football. I've never in the least been interested in football, but I knew Jack was. I'd watched his shoulders slump and the heat leave his face. Unsure of what to say I simply squeezed his shoulder.

He'd turned to look up and I had seen sadness in his eyes. His despondency reminded me of my own childhood and the traumatic years I'd spent with a drunken mother and drug-dependant father. In those days, I believed that pushing others away was the best thing to do before they'd had a chance to hurt or leave me. And although I knew Jack was loved and cherished by all his family and wasn't in the same situation, the fleeting sorrow in his eyes had reached down into the core of my gut. I'd simply tutted, 'Girls, eh?'

He'd smirked and snuggled back into the sofa then had taken the remote control from my hand. I'd known all was well again but couldn't help wishing when I had been his age that a kindly uncle had been around to pacify me and my troubles.

Jenny and Geoff had arrived back to us at lunchtime bringing pizzas which was a lovely gesture but only added to the racket in the house.

I sigh now as the document opens on the screen and smile relaxing back in my computer chair. I've started to plot my second novel. The brief notes in chapters appear from where I'd left it two days ago.

I yawn and stretch my arms above my head feeling tired because I hadn't slept well. For some reason knowing the children were asleep downstairs had worried me, and I'd tossed and turned for most of the night. Barbie had slept soundly without moving but as she has been babysitting them for years it obviously didn't bother her.

However, the responsibility had certainly lain heavy on my shoulders. I'd worried in case there was a fire upstairs and we couldn't get downstairs to them. I'd worried in case one of them was ill and choked on their vomit. I'd worried that if a burglar broke in through the rickety back door the children would be in his first sighting. With all these ludicrous notions racing through my mind I'd been glad when it was eight o'clock and I could get out of bed.

I sip the coffee Barbie brought before she headed outside into the back garden. She has offered to tackle the wilderness that hasn't been touched for years. Gardening is another subject that I have no interest in whatsoever. However, she reckons we can make it into a nice place to sit in the summer. So, with a clipboard in her hand she is outside now designing the space.

'Wouldn't it be a better idea to leave it until Spring,' I'd said.

She'd shaken her blond bob and gave me a determined look. 'No, Clive, I'll get wrapped up warm and draw out my ideas now then we can shop online for the bits we need.'

I drain the coffee and push the thought of how much these bits will cost from my mind and look around the room. I'd painted it grey just before my ex-wife, Sarah had left to designate it as my own personal space.

Although the whole house is mine now, at the time it had given me a lift to decorate and arrange the room to suit me. And only me. I remember thinking that grey was a trendy colour because I had seen it on man-cave photograph.

Now, I grin and decide it had been a good choice because it's a relaxing classic colour. A non-descript colour that doesn't jar with anything else in the room. My desk and filling cabinet and vinyl flooring are also a dark grey and I sigh in satisfaction at a blended scheme that I pulled together.

I begin to read the chapter notes I've written when my mobile tinkles and I groan at the interruption.

I read a message from Tommy Sanderson, the tour company manager. 'Apologies for the short notice, Clive, but we wondered if you could step in and do the ghost trail this evening?'

My shoulders slump. I'd hoped to have the afternoon and early evening free to write, but I think of the tips I could make and reply, 'Yes, that's no problem at all.'

I close the chapter document and quickly check the weather forecast. Dry but cold, it tells me, and I work out the trail accordingly. If it rains, I try to organise places under cover and shop doorways to talk to the customers and tell them my stories. But this won't be a problem tonight and I smile.

I click onto the tour website to re-check the details of the trail while remembering an old saying from a fellow author. He often says, 'People do love a good story.'

It's a while since I've done this tour called, 'Silence in York Shambles' and I need to know that the pick-up and finish points haven't changed. I read the details confirming everything remains the same.

It's described as York's Mystery Trail. People can either do the route self-guided with information sheets or tag along with me in a group. Younger visitors like to do their own thing and work out the clues for themselves, but others, thank goodness, enjoy the guided tour by yours truly.

The particulars also explain that it is a walking tour which navigates past the best historical landmarks that York has to offer. It has the perfect route plotted-out to make sure you see all the highlights inside the city walls. York Minster, The Golden Fleece Inn, The Shambles, and more hidden gems.

Ye Olde Starre Inn is the oldest pub in York dating from 1644 in Stonegate, which I love. It's one of the places where it is ideal to stop and talk in the rain because the Inn is at the end of a long stone passageway lit with fairy-lights. Everyone can huddle together while we discuss the clues on the murder mystery trail, but I always start by warning them about the uneven flagstones underfoot. 'However,' I usually state. 'There's not much I can do about them as they were laid in the 1600's!'

This often gets a whistle of admiration from the men, and I boast about the marvellous food and roaring fire inside. In the summer I let everyone know at the back of the Inn is a great seating area to eat outside.

The tour website also tells us that the trail is flat and there are refreshment stops and photo opportunities along the way. It states, 'York is a city with Roman roots and a Viking past, thirty world-class museums and contemporary shops and eateries. York is the original city for adventure, and it is considered Europe's most haunted city with its cobbled streets and snickelways.'

The start of the trail is at St. Helen's Square, and it has three stars. I reckon this means that people must have a modicum of intelligence to complete the clues and follow the trail. It takes 2.5 hours and is 1.2 miles. The walk is on pavements and cobbled streets which is classed as easy. It is also wheelchair accessible which is great because it means people with disabilities can join in the tour and enjoy my stories.

As a writer, I find it easier than most to make up stories suitable for the trail and entertain people. I love seeing customers rapt and interested in our beloved city and its history. Instead of just stating facts I make up little scenarios and characters to tell the old tales.

One of the great places to stop is, York Ghost Merchants. This is at number, 6, The Shambles. The shop is full of history from 1780. It looks spooky with myth, heritage and legend overlapping to create an intriguing effect. Even the shop assistant, an older man, dressed in a shirt and brown herringbone waistcoat with a big hessian apron tied around his waist, creates the old-world atmosphere. The customers purchases are packed in boxes with a crossed swords emblem and the description stating, 'From the City of a Thousand Ghosts.' People love it and often return to buy ghost memorabilia during their visit which is good trade for the shop, so it's a win-win situation.

At this stop I often explain that at one time, The Shambles had twenty-five butcher shops and the meat was laid out on the front wood plinth all day or hung from hooks above the doorway. I always point the hooks out to everyone and explain how they are still there to this day. My joke about there being no such things as food safety standards in those days sometimes gets a laugh.

Next, I point out how close the windows are at the bottom of the alley. And how, if a person opened the window on the right and leant out, they could clasp hands with a person leaning out of the left-hand side window.

I usually say, 'Can you imagine the conversations they must have been able to overhear especially in the summer if the windows were wide open. And what tales they'd be able to tell?'

If I have their attention and see them nod in understanding I tell my make-believe story about a butcher and his wife.

'So, our big jovial butcher, Richard is devoted to his glamorous wife, Mary. And although Mary loves her husband, she also likes other tradesmen, especially ones who don't smell of raw meat!' I usually pause here and wait for laughter.

'In particular, an inn keeper, called James who lives directly opposite. Mary makes an excuse to Richard one night about visiting her long-suffering mother. The butcher nods in agreement even though this has been the second time in one week. An hour later Richard goes upstairs to find something in the bedroom and opens the window wide in the stifling heat. And yes, you've guessed it, he hears James whooping and groaning as his old headboard hits off the wall in the throes of shall I say, pleasing his woman. Richard laughs wondering who good old James has upstairs tonight?' I pause here again to let the women giggle shyly and the men nudge each other knowingly.

I often lower my voice at this stage especially if other people are passing by us in The Shambles, then continue, 'Richard gingerly moves closer to the window to eavesdrop. He wants to hear more, and the name of the woman, so he can tease James about it the next day. But suddenly, James shouts at the top of his voice, "Mary, do that again to me, you're driving me wild you wanton hussy!" Richard staggers back when he hears his wife's voice crying aloud and making the strange little noise he knows so well.'

This is when I look at my tour group because their eyes are usually as wide as saucers and willing me to continue with the old tale. I put a menacing tone in my voice and usually pace backwards and forwards on the cobbles.

'The big butchers knees quiver and he staggers over to the bed. His bed. The bed where he sleeps with Mary. His whole body is infused with anger and a hatred he cannot control. He thunders down the narrow staircase and grabs his meat cleaver from the shop counter and runs across the cobbles. He looks and sounds like one of the cattle he slaughters and charges up the staircase to find his wife with her long legs wrapped around James neck. He brings the cleaver straight across James throat then slices his head and Mary's feet clean off in one fell swoop!'

The women frequently gasp as if they are horrified but lean towards me at the same time desperate to know what happens. And that's when I know I've got them in the palm of my hand. By this stage I don't mind admitting it gives me a thrill that I can entertain a crowd of people in this way. I suppose it's how readers feel when turning the pages of my books desperate to find out what happens next.

I usually end the story by saying in an eerie voice, 'They reckon Mary's screams and howls could be heard over by the minster, but she lived to tell the tale by moving around on her knees for the rest of her days. The stumps of her legs were covered with soft socks as I suppose there weren't any slippers in those days. Mary, or her ghost is often seen floating, not walking around The Shambles in a long red dress soaked in her blood…'

Then I give a long theatrical bow from my waist to loud applause and that's when I can tell if I'll receive good tips or not.

Now, I close the website down and look out of the window. Barbie is in the front garden, and I lean over to open the window wide so I can call out to her. She is pacing with one foot closely in front of the other in her blue ankle boots trying to measure the length of the old vegetable patch. I smile. My insides melt just at the sight of her and automatically feel a stirring which makes me shuffle in the chair. She's had this effect on me since the first day I met her. I grin in the hope that it will never leave me.

'Hey, Barbie,' I call.

She swings around then looks up to the window.

'I'm going out at seven to do the ghost tour tonight because someone has phoned sick.'

Her little face fills with disappointment and she puckers her lips comically. 'Oh, no,' she calls back. 'And I thought we could have a cosy night in now the kids have gone and we're on our own?'

I grin. ‘True, but it’s only a couple of hours and I’ll be home before you know it.’

I lean out a little and look up and down the terrace of houses making sure no one is in sight. ‘Hey,’ I say. ‘If you’re looking for things to measure, come up here with me. I think I’ve got something that’s a reasonable length!’

She hoots with laughter and covers a hand over her mouth hissing, ‘Ssshh, someone might hear you!’

But I know she can’t resist me as much as I cannot resist her. Clutching her clipboard, she hurries down the path until she’s under the window then calls softly, ‘I’m on my way, big boy.’

I grin. Maybe, I should buy her a large measuring tape along with her diamond ring.

Chapter Three

Tim Robbins is sitting with his head in his hands. At the age of twenty-seven, he knows he should have more in his life to be cheerful about, but the walls in their restaurant seem to be closing in on him. The newly decorated walls that he has spent all their savings on in a major renovation.

He can hear his Italian wife, Rosa in the kitchen of the restaurant clashing pans about on the new range that has been installed. Tim lifts his head up to look at the trendy steampunk pendant lighting which cost a fortune. He rests back on one of the grey leather high-back chairs and traces his finger along the smooth retro-designed table. They all look beautiful but unfortunately are empty. They haven't had a customer through the door for three days now and he is fraught.

People may say it was foolhardy to do a major refit during the pandemic last year, but the restaurant was, and still is, family owned. And if truth be told, Tim has always been a little afraid of Rosa's two burly Italian brothers. They had recommended the contractors to do the refit works and once the ball was in motion, he'd had to brave it out and go with the flow.

The final bill when it came was nearly double the original quotation and he had felt physically sick knowing once it was paid it would wipe out all of their savings. Rosa had reassured him that once the restaurant was packed every night the profits would soon come rolling in, but this had not happened. It hadn't been an easy year for people and the hospitality businesses that survived pandemic restrictions didn't pick up as quickly as foreseen in a widespread slump.

Rosa's parents had signed over the restaurant to them three years ago when it was making a tidy profit and he'd had great plans. But now, he thought gloomily he couldn't see a way out – other than trying to sell.

A friend had told him. 'Tim, I think you've got this all wrong. You've made the place into a trendy urban eatery which doesn't work with Rosa's Italian home cooking.'

He'd gulped hard and nodded understanding his friend's words. He had spelt out the problem in a nutshell. But Tim hadn't known how to say this to Rosa without hurting her feelings and had avoided the issue for over a week. He loved with all his heart.

This morning he'd tried. 'Look, darling, why not change the menu and try some different upmarket dishes?'

She'd fumed at him. 'Oh, so now it's all my fault and my cooking isn't good enough for you!'

Rosa had slammed the old menu card down on the table and stomped through into the kitchen. He had followed her and there'd been a huge row. Rosa has the typical Italian fiery temper, which when he first met her, he'd loved. But now, not so much. She wouldn't speak to him, and he didn't know where to turn next.

He bites down hard on his bottom lip now thinking of the kids and how they've been promised a new bike and an iPad for Christmas. His hands tremble and he clasps them together in desperation knowing he doesn't have a penny towards buying either of them. He has no idea where this money will come from and has looked at loan sites online. But he's heard so many awful stories about loan sharks that he clashes the laptop shut.

Chapter Four

I've dragged myself away from Barbie and the soft squashy sofa and am walking fast up to St. Helen's Square. I head for Mansion House which is where all the people booked onto the tour will meet. The house is not easy to miss because of the pink and white façade around the huge white pillars. I smile appreciating the beautiful early Georgian style building. It was built in 1732 for the Lord Mayor to entertain visitors and holds the cities silver and gold collections alongside civic treasures.

There are a collection of people standing together and I pull up the collar on my brown flying jacket while walking across the flattened cobbles. It's colder than I thought and wished I'd worn my big coat, but I've had this jacket for years and I smile. It's so familiar I just seem to have grown into it. The jacket seems like a part of me somehow.

I'd been wearing it the day I met Barbie and remember how she'd later described my look as trendy yet casual. Not that I was aiming for that, of course, because I don't know enough about fashion and clothes to class myself in a certain look. But it had bolstered my confidence and I often ask her opinion now when choosing clothes.

I sweep my thick brown scarf further around my neck and snuggle into the softness. Barbie's mam bought it for me last Christmas and I love it. Not just because it is a great scarf but more that in her house at Christmas there'd been three parcels under the old tree with my name on the tags. One from Barbie's mam, one from Jenny, and another from Barbie's close friend, Linda.

I'd never had so many gifts before and had felt slightly overwhelmed by their generosity. 'They're just little gifts, Clive,' Barbie had said. 'Just scarf, socks, and aftershave, nothing expensive.'

And I'd nodded. But it wasn't the monetary value that dumbfounded me it was the fact that these people cared enough to choose a gift that they thought I would like. The sight of beautifully wrapped parcels and glittery tags with Happy Christmas, Clive, written on them had been exciting even at the age of twenty-nine.

It was something I've never had before in my childhood. When I was little, I only ever had a Christmas present from my gran up until she died when I was eleven. My parents had spent every penny, especially at Christmas time, on their drug and alcohol fixes. Aged seven, my mam gave me a fiver and told me to buy myself something but that hadn't been the same as glittery wrapped parcels with exciting surprises inside. For a while I'd been under the impression that if I achieved enough at school, I would be worthy of my parents love but this hadn't happened. I had been the first to get my swimming certificate and I got an A mark for my history essay. But none of my achievements had made any difference to them.

I shake the thoughts away and stride up to the group of eighteen people who have booked the tour. They look like the usual crowd of people in different age groups ranging from late thirties to an oldish couple in their mid-seventies, I guess.

I introduce myself and give everyone what Barbie often calls, my winning cheeky smile.
'Okay, everyone, let's get going on this thrilling journey around the city,' I say and sweep my arm dramatically around in a circle. 'So, here we are in the square where in a few weeks' time the Christmas lights will be switched on and we always have our beautiful big tree. In the 1700's this square was the main departure point for two stagecoaches to London, so I guess it was their early bus station!'
There's a slight snigger from the women but I know at this stage the group are singular in their interactions and won't begin to communicate with me, and each other until later when we head through the city.
I usher everyone forward along Stonegate to walk up to York Minster. A couple sidle up to my left side while we walk, and I can tell as soon as the man speaks that they're American. I chat easily with them while keeping my eye on the older couple at the back of the group to make sure they can keep up our walking pace.
I stop the group halfway along Stonegate and explain, 'So, everyone has heard of Guy Fawkes, who tried to blow up the Houses of Parliament, haven't they? Well, he was born in one of these houses in 1570. His father, Edward was a church lawyer and a prominent protestant in the city, but he died when Guy was only eight years old. His mother remarried a catholic and they moved to Knaresborough.'
Everyone nods and I point out Guy Fawkes Inn. 'So, the ghost story here, is that in this pub one night a woman saw a black-hooded manly figure skulking in a

corridor but as she stepped towards him, he disappeared through a door!'

I shrug my shoulders and say, 'Believe that if you wish while we continue.'

We reach the outside of the minster and I turn to everyone as they gather around me in a circle.

This is one of the things I like about being a tour leader. I'm surrounded by a crowd of people who look at me to help and instruct them. It is one area of my life where I am in complete control. I am the boss and their leader.

Older men might say that I should be in command at home but when I think of Barbie, I know this isn't true. To use an up-to-date phrase, we share responsibility and manage our lives together at home. But to use an older phrase, I know who wears the trousers in our relationship, and it's not me. However, I grin, she does look great in a tight pair of jeans, so, who's to argue, certainly not me because I'm more than happy to take the back seat.

I speak up loudly now to make sure everyone can hear. 'Well, here we are outside our glorious York Minster. I know many of you will have been inside during your visit to our city, so I'm not going to bore you all with facts. You've probably read it all in the pamphlets,' I say. 'But I am going to tell you a little ghost story.'

I can see everyone lean in towards me and I lower my voice trying to make it sound creepy. 'In the 1820's tours of the minster were conducted, and two women decided to join in. During their tour, a tall man wearing a neat naval uniform approached the two women, whispered into one of their ears and then incredibly disappeared into thin air before their eyes!'

I hear the older lady at the back of the circle gasp and know I've got them with me, so I continue. 'One of these women recognized the man as being her brother, who had died while serving in the Navy in recent times. Rumour has it that this sister had made a pact with her brother while they were both alive. They had agreed whoever was first to pass away would return to the other still living sibling and give them definitive proof that there was an afterlife.'

The older man pulled the peak of his cap further down over his forehead as though he was saluting the sailor. 'I was in the navy myself,' he said. To which, the other men in the group nodded in respect. 'But, not in the 1820's of course!'

Everyone smiled and I grinned at the old man. 'Thank you for that, Sir,' I said. 'And where was that?'

He told us that it had been in Portsmouth during the second world war and a general buzz went around the group. I knew I had to get them back on track and said, 'So, do we think this woman received some pretty compelling proof from her brother that he is still around and floating in and out of the minster?'

A louder discussion takes place with the men dispelling the idea of an afterlife and a naval ghost in the minster. However, I can see the scepticism in their faces as though they aren't one hundred percent sure. Two of the younger women are colluding with each other and telling their own spooky happenings in other places they have visited.

I raise my voice again. 'And now we are off to The Golden Fleece Inn, which was built in the early 16th century and claims to be the most haunted public house in York.'

The women ooh and ahh while holding their husband's arms and we set off again along the street. This time I purposively walk alongside the older couple and chat to him about his naval career. Not particularly because I'm interested in the navy but because we have a couple of busier roads to cross, and I want to make sure they're safe.

The pub is situated on the pavement straight opposite the opening to The Shambles and when we reach the Inn, I tell them, 'The Golden Fleece was mentioned in York City Archives as far back as 1503. And the back yard of the inn is named, Lady Peckett's Yard, after Mrs Alice Peckett, the wife of John who owned the premises as well as being Lord Mayor around 1702. And I don't know if you watch it, but the Inn was featured in, Most Haunted, a television series about supposedly paranormal phenomena?'

The group chatter about the programme while I take a photograph of Mrs America in front of the inn with the recognisable golden fleece sign hanging above the door.

'Jeez, it's so quaint and traditional,' she says. 'I wish we'd been staying here instead of The Hilton!'

Her husband grumps. 'Well, I surely don't – it looks tiny in there.'

I explain that the small frontage does not represent the size inside as it is exceptionally long and narrow.

I ask everyone to look at their printed trail leaflets and we work through a couple of the challenges so they can solve the mysteries of wicked witchcraft and stories of buried treasure.

I declare dramatically, 'But which suspect is behind these sinister events? Never have your detective powers of deduction been so baffled as this is your spookiest challenge yet.'

I smile then say to the group, 'Now, look out for the alleged twenty-three cat statues guarding the walls and rooftops in York. Let's call out as we go and hopefully no one will spot all of them because if you do the saying has it that you'll be cursed for the rest of your life!'

The crowd laugh then I walk everyone across to The Shambles and begin my well-rehearsed story about the butcher and his wife. I know it off-by-heart now and can go onto automatic pilot.

I finish the story to a loud round of applause and know it's going to be a good night for tips. Mrs America asks me about my fictional story, and I explain that I'm an author. Never being someone to look a gift-horse in the mouth, I pull a business card from my jean pocket and hand it to her.

'I'm, Clive Thompson, and you might like to read my novel on amazon.' I say then hear her husband tut from behind me.

Moving swiftly on, I think and steer everyone around in a circle back to Stonegate to the last inn on the trail, Ye Olde Starre Inn. As we walk, I ask, 'Can anyone navigate the labyrinth of snickelways in York?'

The group shake their heads and I smile. 'Well, neither can I but I did look up the word snickelways and this is the definition. They are alleys, ginnels, snickets and lanes, many of them ancient that run between the streets in York,' I say. 'They were first coined by author Mark W. Jones in 1983 and snickelways are often hidden and require some effort to discover. And, boy-oh-boy is he right. I've never been able to fathom them out and I have lived here for years now.'

We stop outside Ye Olde Starre Inn and while the old couple amble towards the rest of the group I wait before speaking again. I can tell they are weary now.

I can't pass this pub without remembering how I took Barbie here on our first day out together. We had a great lunch in front of the roaring fire and that's when I knew. I knew she was going to be someone special in my life and thankfully she's been just that. I hadn't even kissed her then. We'd had long and lingering looks into each other's eyes, and I'd been aching to make the first move but had been scared that I would frighten her off. However, I needn't have worried because the following day in Harrogate, after a couple of passionate kisses she'd made the first move and invited me back to her hotel room.

I shake myself back to the here and now when the old man huffs and puffs reaching my side. 'Clive, is the last point on the tour?'

I place my hand on his shoulder and can feel his thin muscle underneath the light-weight jacket he is wearing. 'Yes, Sir, but you can leave whenever you want to. I can try to call you a taxi?'

He shakes his head. 'Oh, no, we're okay, it's just the missus gets tired easily.'

I see his wife tut and shake her head. She looks much more robust than him. I can tell it's the old boy who is tired but he's using her as an excuse to cover his own fragility. Which is endearing and I wonder if Barbie and I will be like this at their age.

I turn back to the group. 'Okay, everyone, we are now outside Ye Olde Starre Inn which was built during the English Civil Wars from 1642. The cellar was used as an operating theatre for injured soldiers. The entrance is through a passageway down there,' I say and point with my finger. 'This opens into Star Yard which has a well, and at one time it was claimed to be the only source of pure water in the area.'

There are loud signs of appreciation and I call the tour to an official end. 'So, I do hope you've enjoyed our tour around the city tonight. Are there any more questions or anything I can help you with?'

Some people shout, well done, and most of them tell me how much they've enjoyed the trail which makes me feel happy and satisfied especially when I receive a big round of applause and I give them another bow.

One by one they all come up to me shaking my hand and pressing notes into my palm which is the subtle English way of tipping appreciation. There's only Mrs America who gushes and makes a display of pressing a £20 note into my hand while smiling around at the rest of the group as if to shout, we are giving the most.

However, I'm very grateful and thank everyone as they slowly call goodnight, and all make their separate ways though the streets.

***

I pull my collar further up around my neck as the cold is seeping into my shoulders and neck then hurry down one of the snickleways to head for home. I stop underneath a streetlight and arrange the notes in my hands then count £110.

Grinning, I shove the notes into a small plastic bank bag and tuck in the little flap then push it into the back pocket of my jeans. I figure this money will make a healthy contribution to Christmas presents for Barbie's family this year and I'll be able to exchange gifts with a clear conscience.

I'm rushing further down the dark street when I feel a blow to the back of my head and fall forwards onto the cobbles. I'm lying spreadeagled on the ground.

My head is spinning, and I can smell blood. I hate the smell and manage to lift my hand to my forehead where I feel a gash. I ease my fingers away and stare at the red sticky blood. I feel sick and dizzy. When I look ahead all I can see is a pair of brown leather shoes and the dark trouser legs of a man.

I can smell a thick woolly-coat material mixed with another strong aroma. I realise the mugger is leaning over me with his coat trailing over my shoulder. I feel a hand rummage in the pocket of my jeans, and I want to cry, get off, I've just earned that but I'm too scared to utter a sound. The words seem lodged in the back of my throat.

I moan and lift my head a little then grab at the tail of the coat, but I see his hand reach down and yank the material out of my hand. And that's when I see it. A tattoo on the back of his hand in the shape of a black spider.

I hear someone shout, 'Hey there, leave him alone!' And I know someone is coming to help.

I hear footsteps running away which I figure are the muggers and then two sets of footsteps coming towards me.

'Are you okay?' I hear a young lad's voice ask.

I manage to lift my head further up, but the pain is thunderous, and I slump back down again.

Then I hear another voice, a young female saying, 'I'm going to ring the police.'

I feel the girl's hand gently rubbing my shoulder and there's a slight flowery perfume filling the air space around me.

'Just stay still,' she whispers close to my ear. 'An ambulance is coming and the police.'

I'm managing to lift my head and shoulders up when a paramedic and police officer help me to sit upright. I lean my back against the wall. My vision swims a little, but I can feel the paramedic cleaning the blood away from my forehead.

Once again, the smell of blood fills my nostrils. The smell is mixed with my own fear from childhood memories of the house in Doncaster. My mam had been crying because dad had hit her, and blood poured from her nose. She'd tried to cuddle into me, but I'd been terrified and crawled away to hide under the table. I had never felt safe there.

My vision clears and I can see the paramedics bright ginger hair. 'Well, I can feel a lump on the back of your head where he's hit you but the gash on your forehead is from hitting the rough cobbles,' he says. 'We should take you to hospital because you might have concussion.'

I try to shake my head but decide this isn't a good idea when pain surges through my scalp. 'No, I'll be fine,' I say. 'I just want to get home.'

The police officer takes all our details and I thank the two young people who have come to my rescue. A thick warm blanket is draped around my shoulders and absurdly tears fill my eyes at how kind people are.

***

Within the hour I'm safely ensconced at home on our soft squashy sofa with Barbie fussing around me like a mother hen. She is white-faced with shock and in her pink bathrobe that she'd pulled on hurriedly when I'd turned up at the door with the police officer.

Barbie had eased the flying jacket from my shoulders before lying me down on the sofa and thanked the police officer in the hall then shown him out.

'They're coming back in the morning to take a thorough statement,' she says and kneels on the floor next to me.

I nod. The aftermath of being mugged is slowly sinking into my brain and can't believe it happened to me. Was it a one-off attack? Or something more calculating from someone that knows me? But if that's the case, then who and why? I'm just a normal guy living in what I've always thought of as a safe and beautiful city. With this thought in mind my stomach lurches - what if the mugger knows where I live? And what if they come looking for me again. I have Barbie to look after and take a deep breath to steady myself. I will not be a victim again, by God, I won't.

'Barbie are the doors locked,' I ask. 'Both back and front?'

She nods miserably. 'Yes, and both the cats are in.'

We have two cats, Spot and Stripe. They're my cats really, not hers, but she loves them as much as I do now.

'That's good,' I say and lie back on the cushion.

Her little face crumbles. 'Oh, Clive, thank God you weren't seriously hurt.'

I nod thinking how true this is and know she's right. 'I'm okay love and yes, it could have been a lot worse.'

Tears fill her eyes, and she grasps hold of my hand then squeezes it tight. 'I love you so much the thought of losing you is just too much to bear.'

I can see the love and concern in her face and know I'd feel the same if I came anywhere near to losing her.

She begins to cry and has a faraway look in her eye. I know she is thinking of her husband who at the age of twenty-two was killed by a drunk driver in a horrific accident. They'd been schoolyard sweethearts and she'd often said, 'One minute he was here and the next he'd gone.'

I can tell this is bringing it all back to her and I sigh. I cup her face with my hands and kiss the tip of her nose.

'I'm okay, darling. It's just a bump on the back of the head and a gash on my forehead,' I say touching the dressing. 'Which if it wasn't for our beloved cobbled stone paths wouldn't have happened.'

She sniffs onto the sleeve of her bathrobe and nods.

I need to reassure her and make her feel safe. 'And Barbie, I'd feel the same if it were the other way around. I couldn't bear anything happening to you either, but I'm not going anywhere. I wouldn't even go to the hospital. I'm staying right here next to you.'

She sighs, 'It's just when you hear on the news about stabbings and guns, well,' she shivers.

I nod and tremble myself. 'I know I've been more than lucky, although the pain in my head doesn't feel that way,' I say and groan.

She jumps up and scurries off into the kitchen then returns with painkillers and a cup of hot sweet tea. I lie still letting the tablets work and half-smile at her. 'And all of this when I've had such a good night. I got £110 in tips! That would have paid for a turkey and all the trimmings at Christmas.'

Barbie shushes me, 'Now, don't worry about the money, Clive, it's not important. As long as you're okay that's the main thing.'

I sigh, 'I know but it's such a waste!'

She puts her hand onto the other side of my head to stroke it but then quickly pulls her fingers away. 'Yuk, your lovely blond hair has got blood in it. I'll wash it in the morning for you.'

The frightening events of the attack begin to wane, and now I feel angry. 'I mean, how could someone attack me like this? I've never done anything to deserve such aggression. I was only working!'

'Ssssh, don't wind yourself up,' she soothes. 'It'll make your headache worse.'

Spot jumps up onto my side and snuggles into the sofa with me. I tickle her ears and she meows loudly. Stripe sits next to Barbie looking up at her as if to ask what's wrong and I smile for the first time since I'd felt the blow to my head.

Later, we switch sides in bed so I can lie with my forehead on the opposite pillow. She lies facing me and plants a kiss on my lips. 'Oh, those big blue eyes look so sad,' she says. 'But don't worry it'll all seem better in the morning.'

Chapter Five

Tim is sweating. He tugs at his shirt collar which seems to be choking him. He's sitting in the restaurant in the dark fearful of switching on the lights in case he can see what he has become. Rosa is at home with the kids, but he knows he can't return yet until he has calmed himself down.

Staring down at the spider tattoo on the back of his hand he tuts and shakes his head. He'd been on his stag night with his mates when filled with drunken bravado he had thought the spider looked amazing as if it had been crawling along his hand. Rosa had been less than enamoured on their wedding day.

He pours himself a large measure of whiskey from the optic behind his bar and takes a big gulp. The last hour of his life tumbles around mercilessly in his mind and what he has done.

He'd been wandering along Stonegate deep in thought after pricing the bike and iPad online and reckoned he needed to find at least £300 just for their Christmas presents alone. Tim had seen the tour manager outside Ye Olde Starre Inn collecting money from people who'd given him a round of applause. It had looked like a decent amount of cash, and that's when he'd thought, why not?

In an expensive flying jacket, the manager didn't look as though he was short of money and at least he had a job, he'd pouted. He wasn't a bankrupt restaurant owner trying to buy his kids presents for Christmas.

Initially, his plan had been to knock the tour guy over and grab his money. He certainly hadn't meant to hit

him so hard, but his leather shoe had slipped on the wet cobbles and in shock his hand had come down heavier than he'd intended while holding his bunch of keys.
He had run a few steps then looked over his shoulder. The tour manager hadn't moved on the ground. In a moment's hesitation he'd wanted to turn back and go to his aid but had been terrified and kept on running.
He drains the whisky from his glass and takes another deep breath. Opening his mobile, he scans local news reports to see if the mugging was recorded and if the tour manager has been admitted to hospital. The word, mugger settles in his mind. Was that what he's become? A mugger?
Were the man's injuries serious and had he killed him? He'd heard stories of people dying from massive brain injuries by just one blow. The whiskey regurgitates in his stomach, and he puts a hand over his mouth. And all this mess was simply to buy his kids presents for Christmas. He wonders if the tour manager has a family and kids, and they'll wake up tomorrow fatherless.
Tim runs through the restaurant and throws up in the toilets. He wipes his face with a paper towel then looks in the mirror and gasps. His usual thin face looks gaunt and the pupils in his grey eyes are huge. Sweat is standing on his upper lip, and he sighs, Rosa will know with just one look that something is amiss. He thinks of his beautiful wife now and knows that if he is arrested, Rosa will leave him for good.
At twenty years old, he'd fallen straightaway for her huge dark brown eyes, black wavy long hair, and

generous curvy figure. Who wouldn't, he thinks? And she's just as beautiful now even after having the kids, if not more so.

His thoughts go to the children, and he cringes, what will become of them if he goes to prison? He knows they'll be bullied at school then swallows hard thinking of Rosa's two big brothers. Italians are notorious for good family values and this shame would never be forgiven. His life, as he knows it will be over, that's for sure.

Chapter Six

I'd jerked awake in the night a couple of times and pulled Barbie safely into my arms. On the second occasion I had sat bolt upright and knew suddenly what the other smell had been. The mugger's coat had smelt strongly of garlic. Relieved that I'd remembered I drifted back to sleep and had a weird dream about thousands of spiders running across the cobbles.

When I stagger downstairs later Barbie is in the kitchen wearing a red T-shirt and jeans. I tease her, 'You're blending in with all the red cupboards and work tops!'

She giggles and hands me more painkillers and coffee. Before Sarah had left, she'd had the bright, and I mean, bright red kitchen installed which I've grown to hate over the last three years. I know Barbie doesn't like it either but she's too nice to moan about the colour and has agreed it is on our home improvement list.

My head is throbbing, and I eagerly swallow the painkillers then gulp at the hot strong coffee.

'Clive, the police have rung and are coming at ten,' she says. 'So, I'll help you wash your hair in the shower.'

'Great thanks, although I think I could manage but I'm always happy to have you in the shower with me.'

She laughs and I drop two slices of bread into the toaster. While Barbie is tidying the lounge, I crunch into the toast and recall my thoughts from last night.

Was it a one-off mugging? Or could it be someone who'd known me back in Doncaster. I'd had, as Barbie often says, a troubled upbringing and at the age of fourteen I had nicked stuff to buy booze. At first it had been for my mother and then I had got to like the effect when I drank it. The alcohol took me away from all the crap in the house, and it had also impressed my mates. I'd got mixed up with a bad crowd although at the time I had been pleased to be accepted into their gang. It had been better than being left alone to fend for myself and at least they'd wanted to spend time with me which had been more than my parents had. However, I'd ignored warning after warning from social workers until I had ended up in a young offender's institution aged fifteen. I had spent three years there and was released on my eighteenth birthday. One of the team leaders had called it a short sharp shock and it had worked. It had made me want to change my life and never be that horrible person again.

And, I muse now, I've done just that. Never again have I drunk more than a single glass of wine or beer, and although I wouldn't admit this to other men because it's not macho, I don't particularly like the taste anymore. When I first met Barbie last year, I hadn't told her about my past but when it all eventually came out, she'd forgiven my transgression and given us a second chance. Thank God, she believed in us, or shall I say, in me.

When I remember the petty thieving, I wonder if the man who mugged me could be someone from back then? Does this person want to seek revenge? But the rational side of my brain kicks in and I shake my head. Who would remember the theft of a CD player or £20 stolen from a kitchen windowsill? Or indeed, would want to go on a vendetta after fifteen years?

I decide this train of thought is nonsensical and it must have just been a one-off mugging. I'd simply been unlucky and in the wrong place at the wrong time.

The fresh-faced police officer sitting opposite me on a dinning chair at our table agrees when I tell him this. He has rosy chubby cheeks and kind soft eyes when he smiles.

He nods his head. 'We don't often get much of this in York,' he says and fiddles with the small flip notebook in his hand. 'We have other criminal offences on the rise like parking and drunken behaviour, but not mugging.'

Barbie offers him a coffee, but he refuses and spreads out photographs of spider tattoos on the table. 'There are a couple of lawbreakers operating in York but neither have tattoos on their hands,' he says. 'And I know you didn't see his face so, there's no point in showing you mug-shots, but do you recognise any of these spiders which are quite common designs?'

I stare at the photographs and shake my head. 'Well, to be honest all spiders look alike to me, and it had been just a brief glance because I was dizzy.'

I don't feel much help to him, and I shrug my shoulders. I sign the statement I'd given last night, and he files it in a black folder.

He rubs the side of his chin and nods. 'That's okay, Mr Thompson. We'll continue to make enquiries and have statements from the young couple who came to help you but unfortunately, they didn't see him either in the dark.'

Barbie interrupts. 'Is it possible to have the couples address because I'd like to send them a card and flowers to thank them for helping Clive.'

The police officer shakes his head. 'I'm afraid not. All details are data protected now. But when I speak to them, I'll pass on your thanks,' he says. 'Maybe tomorrow I will go into the tour office to warn all your colleagues to be on guard and advise them, as well as yourself, how to keep your tips more secure in body wallets.'

I nod and thank him as he gets up to leave. 'Take a few days to rest up,' he says. 'And if you remember anything else or have flashbacks then do get in touch. But for now, be alert and observant especially when you do go back to work.'

I make a pot of tea while Barbie shows the police officer out and think about what he's said.

She comes into the kitchen and wraps her arms around my waist resting her head on my shoulder. I melt at her touch and swing around to hug her tightly.

The policeman's words come to my mind. 'Look, Barbie, I don't want you venturing out again after dark, and I'm not letting you go anywhere on your own.'

She smiles. 'Well, that might be a little tricky as it's dark at six now, but I know how shaken up you are after this and it's your way of being overprotective,' she says. 'Which is nice but don't worry I will be careful.'

Barbie sets her garden design drawings out onto the table and sips her tea while I gesture that I'm heading upstairs with my cuppa.

I sit at my desk and boot-up the computer then dial the tour office number and let them know what has happened. It's a lengthy call with Tommy, and I explain everything to the smallest detail. He agrees to immediately alert all leaders who work both day and night-time tours. I end the call agreeing to join them in the office tomorrow when the police visit.

My next call is to Jane and Tina. I'm not due back into the travel agency until the weekend but want to let them know what's happened.

'Oh, but Clive, you must rest,' Jane says, and I can hear Tina picking up the extension.

We share a three-way conversation and I take a selfie close-up of the dressing on my forehead then send it to them. I'm not worried about staying off sick if needed because I've never missed a day at work since I started.

Tina ends the call saying, 'Just let Barbie take good care of you for a couple of days and rest.'

I smile thinking of their faces and the gossipy chat they'll have now that I've hung up. Usually, I'm part of this office natter and sigh missing them already but distract myself scrolling through emails from other author friends online. I wonder if I should broadcast the mugging on social media to warn other people living in the area. Deciding it can't do any harm, I post my selfie onto Facebook and Twitter with a heading, 'Mugger is loose in our city.'

Within minutes messages of disbelief and support pour in and I absorb myself with all the shocked comments.

I think of my new novel and the research I've done about crime. Surely, if I can work my way through scenarios that I have created then I can find answers to my own mugging. An author friend has been writing a story about a murder-mystery weekend going horribly wrong and Sherlock Holmes using his powers of deduction.

I smile knowing all I need to do is use Sherlock's analyses, however, there's not much to go on but I list the few things I do know.

1, It was totally unexpected so it couldn't have been a premeditated crime

2, Someone must have been watching my movements. Was this from Ye Old Starre Inn? Or when I added up the money under a streetlight in the snickleway?

3, It was a man with a heavy enough hand to deliver the blow to the back of my head. However, I can't blame him for the gash on my forehead that was the way I'd fallen flat on the wet cobbles and lain spreadeagled.

4, He had been wearing dark trousers and brown leather shoes. I remember these distinctly. They were a two-tone brown colour and smile knowing they were shoes I'd choose for myself.

5, The coat he'd worn had been thick material, and once again this wasn't a thin cheap fashion-coat that a young person would buy online. It too, had been good quality with a damp woolly smell.

6, And Garlic! There was a definite strong reek of garlic when he reached over me and grabbed my money. His coat must have been open to trail over me. Had this smell been off his clothes underneath? Does garlic hang around on material?

7, Spider tattoo. This is the only concrete piece of evidence I have because although the other points could be construed as conjecture, I definitely saw this.

I sit back from the computer and consider my list. It's always helped to write my thoughts down. That's the writer in me saying that if I can see words in black and white on a screen then it makes more sense.

I think back to when I moved up here to York with one of my friends from the young offender's institution. His father had allowed me to stay with them in their big house and I'd studied at home while working as a labourer to gain my English and Maths A' levels. I had been in my element and felt for the first time in my life that I belonged somewhere. Feeling safe and secure in these surroundings I'd managed to relinquish my old belief that someone better would come along to take my place.

Encouraged by my friend's father, I had applied and got the junior team-member job in the travel agency and started an evening study course in writing. Which is where I met Sarah, who was doing an English course. She'd believed in me and dispelled the fears I'd built-up through my childhood. She made me feel worthy to be loved and accepted in our relationship. I'd let her in without fear of being hurt and managed to stop being suspicious of people in authority and parental figures.

I shake my head now thinking how long ago that seemed, but really, it was a mere ten years. A shiver goes up my back to think that someone has been watching my actions and whereabouts. Was it just a man who had seen me collecting my money from people on the tour and it was simply happenchance?

I decide that although Sherlock's deductions have helped me on the trail to discovery, I would much rather understand the person who did this and why they stole from me in the first place. I know these weren't the actions of a young homeless person and the theft was done through a different kind despondency. This mugging doesn't have a reasonable explanation like the usual street robberies occurring in big cities.

Reading the seven points again I make more notes next to each one. I sigh and remember how I'd stopped under the streetlight to add up the money then folded the notes and put them in that old plastic bank bag. How stupid was that? It's not as if I don't have a wallet to keep my money in because Barbie bought me a brown leather one for my birthday. Although I suppose he would have grabbed a wallet just the same as he had the little bag. But it was careless, and I reprimand myself shaking my head. I've always had this blasé attitude to credit cards and money. It drives Barbie mad who is the opposite and very methodical.

I scrunch my eyebrows and try hard to remember the shoes. I decide they'd looked expensive good-quality leather so obviously the mugger wasn't destitute. But there again, he could have bought them from a charity shop for a fiver.

Was I mixing up the smell of garlic and wool on the coat? I'd had the stench of blood in my nose which had always made me feel sick, so now I'm not a hundred percent sure about the smell. Barbie will know if garlic is strong enough to hang around on clothes and material. I think it will be but will double-check with her first.

And now, the spider. I remember it had been on the back of his hand but higher up towards his wrist. I imagine lying flat on the cobbles again and how his feet were in front of my face. So, if he leant over me to grab the money which was in my right-hand side pocket then surely, he would have used his left hand? And don't most people wear their watch on the left wrist? He mustn't have been wearing one because it would have been over the spider, and it wasn't.

I'm pleased to see that I've remembered some aspects of the assault and have convinced myself that it was just a happenchance mugging.

However, I remember those gates to the institution and how I had robbed people myself. I know Barbie and other well-meaning folk would excuse these crimes as the result of a dreadful upbringing and my reaction to rejection and neglect. I cringe and shuffle on the chair. Although I'd never coshed anyone over the head or been aggressive when I stole, it still doesn't excuse my actions.

Now I know how it feels to be on the victim's side and it's not a good feeling. It is the invasion of my privacy that annoys me the most. The fact that a stranger has been in my personal space and had his hand in my jeans to grab the money. It was someone that I didn't know who felt he had the right to do this.

I wonder if the people I'd stolen from felt like this. I sigh heavily knowing if there was a way to go back and return the small amounts of money and CD player that I had stolen, I would happily do it to salve my conscience.

***

Within a couple of days, the lump has gone down on my head and the gash on my forehead has practically healed. Thankfully, it hasn't left a scar.

'We can't have it spoiling your good looks,' Barbie teases and I hug her close. With staying at home together we have celebrated this time with long relaxing baths, even longer love-making sessions, great food, and enjoying each other's company more than ever.

We're lying on the squashy sofa wrapped around each other with Spot at the top and Stripe at the bottom. 'Those flowers that Jane & Tina sent me are lasting well,' I say.

Barbie had arranged them into a vase and smiles. 'Yeah, they're gorgeous. Maybe I should be jealous that two women are sending my man flowers, but I know it's because they think the world of you.'

I slide my hand along her thigh and tickle her. 'Ah, Barbie, you've no reason to be jealous of other women,' I say. 'There's only one woman for me and I've got her right here.'

I think of my last morning in the agency and how Jane had suggested marriage to Barbie. And the more I think about it, the more I like the idea and know it's the next logical step. Not only would it give her the security that Jane thinks she needs, but it would also make me feel more assured in our relationship. Barbie has been so loving and supportive since my attack that I know I wouldn't have coped as well if she hadn't been here. If I'd been living alone in what I think of as, pre-Barbie days, it would have been difficult to say the least, and a shiver runs up my back.

I never want to be without her. I don't want to live in this house even though it's my home, or anywhere else without her. So, I can't think of a reason not to pop the question. But I want the occasion to be special and have my plans in place.

She says, 'I'm so pleased you seem to be getting over the attack, Clive, it was awful to see you so shaken up by it all.'

'Well, I'm still upset in a way,' I say. 'It's just that I can't bear the thought that he's got away with doing this to me, let alone the money! And if the police could find and arrest him then it would be one less lawbreaker on the streets in York. I can't believe this happens in our city now because I've always loved living here.'

'Hmm, I know,' she says. 'So, are you going to do anything more about it?'

I grunt. 'Other than walk around York looking at every man's hand for a spider tattoo or sniffing them for garlic I'm not too sure what else I could do?'

She giggles. 'Well, all I know is that if someone says garlic to me, I automatically think Italian food.'

It feels like a light is switched on in my brain and I reach over Barbie for her iPad on the table. I begin to Google Italian restaurants and eateries in York and save them onto a list. 'Hey,' I say. 'You might have something there.'

A plan forms in my mind about what I could do to help. I'm by no means a maverick and remember how I'd been too scared to speak when the mugger wrenched the money from my pocket. But if I could trace him and let the police know then I might get some type of justice.

My mobile rings and I pick up knowing it is Tommy from the tour office. We have a long discussion about safety on the streets and how he's warned everyone to be on their guard. He's taking further advice about keeping money safely as we work. But in the short term it might be worthwhile for another leader to join in at the end of the tour for moral support. Although the police have reassured him that my attack is probably a one-off, Tommy has suggested a rota to cover shifts especially the evening tours and asks if I'd be interested.

Without hesitation I agree and plan to join one of the female tour leaders tonight at Olde Starre Inn when she collects her tips then walk her to the car park.

It's only when I click my mobile off and explain to Barbie what I'm going to do that I feel my stomach flip with alarm. Is this the best idea I've ever had? I frown but know I must do something to help and if it means returning to the scene of my attack then so be it. It'll make me feel better. I pull my shoulders back and determine that if I do see the mugger again, this time I'll definitely man-up.

'Oh, be careful, Clive,' Barbie wails. 'I can't bear it if you get hurt again.'

I wrap my arms around her and cuddle her tight. 'Don't worry, it'll be fine. I can't think for one minute he'll try again so soon after robbing me, but in a way, I feel responsible for all of this and need to help out where I can.'

I jump up off the sofa. 'I'll pop in the shower and get changed to leave in an hour.'

Barbie follows me upstairs. 'Clive, this isn't your fault,' she cries. 'But if you're going then so am I.'

I swing around to face her at the top of the stairs. 'No, Barbie, you must stay here where it's safe. Dear God, can you imagine your family if they knew I'd taken you along with me,' I shout. 'They'd never forgive me!'

She sets her lips into a determined pout. 'We'll do this together, Clive, or not at all,' she says. 'We'll both walk the tour leader back to her car and I'll take you to the first Italian restaurant on your list to look for a man with a spider on his hand!'

I hoot and chase her into the bathroom.

***

I can't help remembering that first night, although I've done another five companion shifts now. The office has started calling them this and I quite like the phrase. Instead of thinking of myself as a bodyguard which is ludicrous, being a companion to someone is rather nice. Especially to our two female tour leaders, and our elderly gentleman, Charles.

It hadn't been easy returning to the place where I'd been mugged on my first companion night, but Barbie had been a great help and support.

We'd met the female tour leader, Pamela, outside Ye Olde Starre Inn. We had been in our jeans, but Pamela was dressed in a blue suit with a long camel coat. Barbie had whispered, 'She seems very professional looking.'

I had sighed. None of us dressed in a profession manner like this and were more casual which, of course, was weather dependant. I'd nodded and admitted that I didn't know Pamela well and that so far, she'd seemed quite aloof. When Pamela had finished her tour, I'd walked towards her and introduced us both. She'd taken my hand and shook it briskly like a man would and I had seen Barbie wince when she had done the same to her.

Pamela had pushed her tips into a big handbag then slung it onto her shoulder. Her long blonde hair wafted in the wind, and she'd tutted in annoyance as it caught under the strap. Barbie had chatted easily with Pamela about her lovely designer handbag then suggested a small body-bag across her chest rather than the trendy big bag on her shoulder.

Probably, if I'd suggested this, Pamela would have taken offence, but nobody could take umbrage with Barbie. She was too friendly and approachable in her kind attitude which was obvious from first looking at my girlfriend.

As we'd walked up towards the car park and along the snickleway the hairs on the back of my neck had stood up to attention. I'd relived every moment of the attack from how I had crashed to the ground and smelt blood on my forehead. The personal invasion when the stranger had grabbed money from my jeans. The choking words in my throats as I'd been too scared to say anything in fear of more violence.

My lips and chin trembled when I had stared down at the exact spot. I had felt my shoulders tighten and my palms sweat with memories of how frightened I'd been.

Barbie must have sensed this and took my hand firmly in hers. She'd whispered, 'Coming back here is what they call a trigger so it will bring back horrible memories of your mugging, but don't worry, you're not alone tonight and it's all going to be fine.'

I'd nodded and had been glad of her hand as we'd followed Pamela to her car then breathed a sigh of relief as she drove off without mishap.

***

Now, I've done another five companion shifts alone and all without incident. We've also eaten Italian meals every night since.

Only yesterday, Barbie had complained, 'I'm sick of pizza and pasta, and even though they're only take outs, it's costing us a fortune!'

During last year's lockdown most restaurants survived by offering takeout meals and even now have kept the service going. So, every night when I collect our takeout in the restaurant, I make an excuse and nip to the toilets then look at every male hand in sight hoping to catch that elusive spider tattoo.

I know that I'm going to have to give up on this theory soon because Barbie is right when she says my mugger might not even live in York. But there are only three left on the list, and because I am thorough, I want to tick these off.

I sigh wishing I could catch him. It's not vengeance for taking my money that I want, but more for disrupting my carefree life and the way I've always lived in York. Now, it feels filled with insecurity and wariness at street corners which I have never felt before. York is not classed, nor ever has been, as a dangerous place to live, and I don't want it to become that.

Chapter Seven

There have only been two customers in the restaurant for three days and Tim reckons it's not worth putting the lights on now. He is sitting in his usual chair by the window in the restaurant while Rosa stands in the kitchen doorway with her hands on her hips.

She grumbles. 'I just don't know why this is happening, I mean the couple who came last night have always loved my lasagne!'

He shrugs his shoulders but doesn't comment because the last thing he wants is another argument. However, he'd heard the woman huff at her husband saying, lasagne again. It was the word again which made him cringe. These were people who had been coming to their restaurant for years.

They weren't new customers enticed inside by the up-to-date décor nor the younger set of people he had hoped to attract. He wants to rage at Rosa. So, why not cook something up to date, but Tim stays silent in his despair following that dreadful night.

For the first two days he'd jumped every time there'd been a knock on the door thinking it was the police coming to arrest him. If his mobile rang with an unrecognisable number on the screen, he dreaded taking the call. He had hardly slept and when he had cat-napped his dream held visions of people in a circle around him shouting, it's him – that's the mugger.

He hadn't eaten much but drank strong cups of coffee throughout the day. He'd longed for his nightly glass of whiskey which usually helped him sleep but this hadn't worked. All it had done was raise his levels of anxiety, not decrease them. The children's excited chatter about Christmas aggravated him beyond belief. He had found himself continually snapping at them until Rosa had intervened and managed to reinstate their usual happy family environment.

The flashbacks to the tour guide lying on the ground motionless had been terrible. But as the days passed and there'd been no reports on the local TV news and newspapers, he figured the man must be okay. And, that he wasn't a murderer, just a thief.

Rosa stands in front of him now and raises her eyebrow. 'Look, I know you're worried about money and the business, but is there something else bothering you?'

He shakes his head and picks at the skin on his thumbnail.

Tim can almost smell her warmth and slight flowery fragrance when she bends over towards him. She strokes his cheek and for a split second he wants to bury his head in her chest and blurt out the whole ghastly mess. But this would only make her worry more and knowing Rosa, she'd probably make him return the money and apologise to the man.

Which, Tim thinks, has crossed his mind, but Rosa has more of a conscience than him and he's already spent the £110 on groceries to feed the family. The rates are due, and he still has no money for the bike and iPad.

'Look, we haven't been out of this place for ages,' she says. 'How about we go over to my brothers tomorrow and have a big family meal?'

Tim thinks of walking around York and shudders. He's already decided to stay close to home in case he sees the tour guide again in the streets. Tim also wants to avoid her family at all costs in case the mugging is discovered.

'No, I'm not really up for that and I know we don't usually open on Sundays, but I think we should just in case a whole bus full of tourists turn up!'

He was being ironic, but Rosa takes it the wrong way and flounces off into the kitchen. Tim watches her big hips in a tight red skirt swaggering from side to side and he melts. He wishes his life were back to normal and he could chase her around the kitchen like they used to do and end up writhing about on the floor.

Instead, he looks out of the windows at shoppers passing by and thinks of the £110. He didn't know the tips on tours were so good but figured that the guides did not get a huge wage from the company and their tips made up the shortfall.

It certainly seemed more lucrative than the position he was in paying rates and bills for a property that wasn't making any money with a family to support. Tim knew he was blaming others for the mess he had created and was wallowing in the depths of despair, but he couldn't help himself.

He sighed. An honourable man would accept the responsibility of the wrong decisions he'd made and the fact that he was too much of a wimp to stand up to his two brothers-in-law. He had always thought of himself as a decent man but not now.

Tim decides there's no point in racking his tired brain for ideas to raise the ready cash because he'd exhausted all the possibilities weeks ago. He frowns, there was nothing else to do but give it another try. This time, however, he would just grab the money and run. He determined to be more in control of himself, and in charge of the situation. He gulps, knowing he mustn't make another mistake.

Chapter Eight

I'm just finishing my shift in the agency with Jane and Tina on Saturday. We've had a good day of sales and I spent my lunch break daydreaming about the customers holidays that I've booked to jet them off into the winter sun abroad.

When I close my computer down and get ready to leave for the day, Tina asks, 'Hey, Clive, have you given anymore thought to a gift for Barbie on your anniversary yet?'

I haul my winter coat off the stand and give it a shake. It got soaked this morning when I walked into work, and still feels a little damp. 'Em, not really with the mugging last week and everything else I haven't had time.'

Jane smiles. 'I bet Barbie is simply glad you weren't seriously hurt and probably couldn't give a toss about anniversary gifts, and the like.'

I nod knowing she's right. Jane's black hair is tied up tightly in a bun on the top of her head. I think it makes her look too severe like a school headmistress. 'Yes, she's already said that Jane, but I still want to do something,'

Tina grins. 'Well, most of the big hotels have Christmas special weekends advertised but they'll be full of noisy work parties which I suppose won't be very romantic.'

Jane tuts at Tina and shakes her head. 'He doesn't want to be buried amongst all the Christmas razzmatazz. They won't be able to hear each other speak let alone whisper sweet nothings to each other!'

I push my arms through inro the coat and wrap my scarf around my neck. 'That's true,' I say and smile at Jane. 'But I have been thinking about your suggestion of the grand gesture.'

Jane grins and Tina shrieks. 'OMG, are you going to propose?'

I shuffle my shoes together and look down onto the vinyl floor. 'Well, let's say, I'm seriously thinking of it.'

I head towards the front door and hear Tina hoot then yell, 'Oh, its' soooo exciting!'

I grin closing the door behind me and step out onto the pavement knowing I've left them both is a state of flux.

***

I head up to The Shambles to be companion to Charles at four o'clock when he finishes his tour. There's a bitterly cold wind which seems to blow in circles into the opening of the old, cobbled street. I've ditched my flying jacket today and worn a big thick coat but still have my favourite scarf wound around my neck. When I'd gashed my head last week it had been splattered with blood, but Barbie has managed to wash it all out.

I can see Charles shaking people's hands as they give him tips and thank him profusely. It's obvious they've loved his tour which I know everyone does. He's a dapper old man and I'd hate anything to happen to him because in his mid-seventies he'd be an easy target. However, Tommy has insisted that he only does the daytime tours now.

Charles has a certain way of relating facts in his quiet educated voice that hooks everyone in from the start.

He doesn't make up stories like I have to do to gain interest and he knows an amazing amount of old York history that lures customers into his world. He is the font of all knowledge.

I know I'm in a good place to champion him and that Charles has spotted my whereabouts. He hasn't waved or spoken but has given me a nod of his head and a wide grin above his neatly timed grey beard and moustache.

At six weeks before Christmas it's dusk now and while I wait for Charles I look up to the signage, Little Shambles. The streetlights have been hung and the shops decorated but it is too early for carol singers and the usual Christmas hype.

The little cobbled area is filled with ordinary looking shoppers walking up and down then stopping to look in the speciality shop windows. There are no big department stores in The Shambles because the streets aren't big enough to house these. I muse, everyone seems to be looking for that perfect special gift.

Last year when I first met Barbie, she'd dragged me into our famous Christmas shop where I'd bought a beautiful decoration for her tree. She had said, 'I've collected baubles from all of my travels but don't have one from York.'

I suppose I could buy her another bauble, but it doesn't seem big enough as an anniversary gift although I know what ever I give her she'll be delighted with. That's another thing I love about her. She's not materialistic in any shape of form and appreciates the small meaningful things in life. I smile just thinking of her and long to be at home.

Loud singing and laughing makes me swing around to see a group of young women on a hen party. They are in fancy dress and look very drunk. I smile. York is getting a reputation in the North East as a party town which I know residents reckon has its advantages and disadvantages.

I shiver and stomp my shoes on the pavement in a futile gesture to keep warm. I remember reading a quote related to what I'm doing as a companion. It said, being brave is about facing and doing something that fills you with fear.

I think about these words and decide that I'm not as cagey as I'd been on the first night with Pamela. However, I still feel a little uneasy even though there's been no more reported muggings in the area. I wonder if it had been just a one-off and the mugger is long gone, never to strike again. But what if he's still around and keeps mugging people on the streets and is never caught?

I know this time; I'll be brave enough to tackle him and won't cower away because if I don't, we'll all feel victimised again. And I can't let that happen. I don't want to live in fear and be vulnerable when walking these streets of the city I love.

I think of another popular saying. A man who fears nothing loves nothing. The image of my beautiful Barbie comes to my mind. Knowing how much I love her means that I can't allow myself to be frightened of something that happened in the past. I must be able to protect her.

I think of her this morning all sleepy and tussle haired when I'd left for work and kissed her. I'm aroused just at the thought of her and remember her complaint about pizza and pasta. I decide to treat us to Indian food tonight for a change and collect a take-a-way when I've safely seen Charles to his bicycle near the train station.

I whistle between my teeth. How cool is that to be still riding a bicycle when you're seventy and see him walking towards me.

'Good evening, Clive,' he says. 'It's a pleasure to see you although I'm not sure it's a total necessity.'

I shake his hand. 'Well as the saying goes, it's better to be safe than sorry,' I say. 'Did you have a good tour?'

I watch over his shoulder as he puts his money into a small body-bag strapped underneath his tweed jacket. It's a smart jacket which matches perfectly with his checked deer-stalker hat, and I smile. I wouldn't mind this traditional look - it's smart and casual.

I hear a woman calling across the road.

'Helloooo, Clive!'

I swing around and recognise Mrs America from my last ghost tour/ I grin and greet her warmly. 'Hey, are you guys still in York?'

She is wearing the brightest pink wool coat I've ever seen and a white Russian-style furry hat which makes me smile. She'll never go unnoticed, I reckon, and decide Mrs America would make a great character in my next novel.

'Oh yeah, we leave t…tomorrow,' she gabbles. 'But I just wanted to tell you that I've started to read your novel and I'm loving it!'

This is, and always will be, like music to my ears. I can't help puffing out my chest at her flattery and kind comments. I thank her but notice out of the corner of my eye that Charles has begun to walk ahead to the side pavement.

And that's when I see him come from almost nowhere.

Although it's nearly dark the man is standing near enough to a streetlight for me to see his long black coat and the stealthy way he moves. It must be a sixth sense because I don't know what the mugger looks like but the swish of his thick coat and the way he circles around Clive makes my heart begin to pound.

I hurry away from Mrs America and feel sweat form on my top lip. I'm at Clive's side in seconds just as I see the mugger raise his arm as though to push him over.

I yell at the top of my voice. 'Get away from him!'

I can't let him hurt Charles, he's an old man and needs my help. My mouth is dry, and my heart is racing but the outrage I'd felt last week consumes me. I pull my shoulders back then pounce onto the mugger knocking him to the ground.

Mrs America screams.

I force my knee onto the mugger's chest to hold him at bay and see people rushing over to us. The mugger is flaying his arms around and kicking out with his feet, but I'm determined to hold him down.

Charles springs into action and puts his polished black brogue over the mugger's wrist to stop him thrashing. The initial fear I'd felt is now replaced with unease in case it's not the same man from last week and I've made a terrible mistake.

And that's when I see it. That is when I see the spider tattoo.

Mrs America hurries over shouting, 'Someone call the cops!'

I smile at the Americanism while Charles calmly takes out his mobile and does just that. He doesn't seem scared at all, and his blue eyes are crinkling with amusement. I think he's enjoying it all. Two middle-aged men come to help hold him down.

My hands are trembling a little but the relief that floods through me is immense. I want to hoot with delight that it's the same guy.

I punch the air and shout, 'I've got him!'

Charles claps me on the back and grins. 'You certainly did, Clive,' he says. 'Well done, it was an impressive citizen's arrest!'

I look down at the mugger. His whole body has gone limp as though he's given up fighting and has nothing left. The man looks around my age but is bigger and bulkier than my slim physique. I look at his thin face and grey eyes that are deadpan now. I know for certain that I've never seen this man before which dispels any theories of him knowing me from my past in Doncaster.

Bending forwards, I inhale the lapels of his coat just to reassure myself that he is the same man. The whiff of garlic fills my nose and I nod in satisfaction.

I hear sirens in the distance and know the police will be with us soon. I need to know why he did this and stare at his face. 'You knocked me to the ground last week and stole my m…money,' I stutter. 'Why would you do that to me?'

The mugger is staring up at me and shakes his head slowly. 'I'm sorry,' he whispers. His lips hardly seem to move, and he's spoken so quietly that I lean further towards him. I see a big tear well up in the corner of his eye when he says. 'I don't have any money to buy the bike and iPad.'

The same young police officer charges towards us as I think the mugger looks like a beaten man.

Chapter Nine

I've just arrived home and although I rang Barbie earlier to tell her briefly what has happened, she now wants to know every tiny detail. I'm still pumped full of adrenaline and hurry into the kitchen behind her.

'Can I eat first,' I say and hug her tight. 'My stomach is groaning, and I've just been through everything with the police.'

We are in the kitchen with bags of Indian food on the countertop. She spoons our favourite pilau rice and butter chicken onto plates while I tear off a piece of naan bread and dip it into the sauce.

She smiles. 'Okay, let's eat because I'm starving too.'

We sit next to each other on the sofa with trays on our knees and I try to smile reassuringly while wolfing down my food. I drain a whole glass of water and then sigh licking my lips. 'Oh, that's so good. I don't think I've ever been as hungry.'

Barbie clears away our trays while I sit patiently then ease off my shoes and wriggle my toes. Immediately, Spot jumps onto my feet wanting to play but I lift him off and gently shoo him away.

Barbie joins me and sips her glass of wine. 'So, has Charles gone home?'

I nod and pour another large glass of water. 'Yeah. I know he lives alone, and I'd wanted to bring him here rather than him return to an empty house. But he refused stating that he intended calling to his brother's house for supper,' I say and smile. 'I can just imagine him there now telling the tale of how we'd caught the mugger.'

I shake my head at these words and still can't quite believe what happened, but I tell Barbie all about the arrest. She is understandably full of questions which I try to answer methodically because I know it'll help me process the happenings and my thoughts.

She takes my hands in hers and raises an eyebrow. 'I remember how spooked you were revisiting the place where you were attacked, so were you scared tonight?'

I look at her and nod knowing only the truth will do because she'd know if I was lying. And I don't want to beef myself up into a hero because I wasn't.

'Well, yes, I was at first when I saw him edging his way to Charles. My heart was thumping, and I was sweating but when I saw him lift his arm to push old Charles over, all the temper from last week blew up inside me and I just threw myself at him!'

She squeezes my hands and I continue. 'Then once I'd pinned him to the ground and saw others coming to help, I'd panicked at the thought that it might not be the same man,' I say and whistle through my teeth. 'I suppose if it hadn't been him and he'd denied attempting to push Charles over then I could be in trouble myself for being a vigilante?'

Barbie grins. 'I don't know exactly what that word means, but you are definitely my hero,' she says and kisses me full on the lips. 'I'm so proud of you I could burst!'

'Well,' I say. 'The definition is a self-appointed doer of justice.'

She throws her head back and laughs. 'I love that! Clive, my tour leader companion and doer of justice.'

I shake my head but can't help twitching my mouth at her vocabulary. 'Anyway, as soon as I saw that spider tattoo, I think I yelled aloud, I've got you, or something like that and flooded with relief that he was finally caught and won't trouble us anymore.'

Barbie claps her hands together. 'Bravo! He deserves everything he gets for wanting to rob innocent hard-working people like you and Charles.'

My cheeks flush at her praise and adulation. The adrenaline has diminished and I'm back to my usual placid self. I yawn feeling tiredness sweep through my body. Emotional upset always has this effect. I don't know why, but all I want to do now is go to bed. I take her hand and pull her up from the sofa. 'Do you fancy coming upstairs to bed and showing me how proud you really are?'

***

I sleep long and deep then wake late which is usual for me on a Sunday morning. Barbie is downstairs and I can hear the radio playing in the kitchen. I stagger down and she greets me by throwing her arms around my neck.

'How's my local hero this morning?'

I smile and kiss the side of her face. 'Aww, give over, Barbie,' I say. 'I'm not a hero. I just did what any other guy would do when an old man was at risk. I was more than lucky that it all ended well.'

She let's go and pours cereal into a bowl. 'Well, I don't care how bashful you are, I'm really proud of you.'

I sit on a stool at the countertop and much into a bowl of cornflakes then sip my hot coffee. The memory of the policeman's words comes to mind. Although he'd praised my instant actions, he had also reminded me that criminals often carry knives and guns now-a-days and how in future I should always ring the police first before jumping into an unknown situation. I smile, supposing it's not in their remit to approve of have-a-go-heroes.

My mobile rings and it is Charles who says, 'Morning, Clive, I hope it's not too early to ring?'

'No, it's fine, I've been up for ages,' I say, which is a little fib, but he sounds bright and breezy, and I don't want him to think I'm lazy.

'I'm still at my brother's house and he wants to speak to you if that's okay?'

I talk to his brother who thanks me for helping Charles. 'I don't know how I'd cope if anything happened to my twin,' he says.

I smile. 'Oh, I didn't know you were twins, are you identical?'

'Yes, we are,' he says, and I can almost see the same smile on his face that Charles has.

He continues, 'I doubt you'd be able to tell us apart. Not many people can but thanks again, for looking after him, Clive.'

Charles and I talk more about the arrest, and I explain certain happenings that we hadn't had the chance to talk about last night. Just before we end the call, he says exactly what I've been thinking.

'Well, Clive, not that I know what muggers look like, of course, but this guy just didn't seem to fit the brief, as it were.'

I agree and click off my mobile then finish my now soggy cornflakes. While I gulp my warmish coffee, I think about his comment. I remember how the mugger had given up fighting against us. How he'd seemed to crumble into submission. Was this the actions of someone hell-bent to wreak havoc on innocent people in their desperation for money? I shake my head knowing this wasn't something that spider tattoo man was used to doing.

My mobile rings again and I answer the call from Tommy. He thanks me so profusely that once again I feel my cheeks blush at his complements and tribute.

I wonder why I feel uncomfortable accepting praise and thanks from people? Perhaps it's because I've never done anything in my life to warrant this and don't quite know how to handle it all. I haven't been outstanding in anything I've done not like police and firefighters who do this on a daily basis. They'll be used to praise for their bravery and commitment to the public. As are the NHS workers especially during the pandemic with their endless efforts to save lives.

Tommy and I talk the event over and agree that even though we should still be cautious there was no need for companion shifts any more.

I head upstairs and stand under a hot shower feeling quite sad that I won't be a companion again because I'd really enjoyed meeting the other tour leaders and sharing their comradery. It has always been a solitary job where the only interaction I have is with my customers, but this event had brought us closer together in a strange way.

I can't call myself a people's person, but I've been pleased to help and enjoyed the new experience. I sigh deep in thought. Other than helping people to choose their holidays I have done nothing worthwhile in my working career. Or to use the popular saying, given anything back to the community. But I know in the future I'd like to get involved with something like this on a smaller scale. It feels good to help people.

Barbie brings us fresh coffee and sits next to me with her iPad on her knee. 'Oh, wow,' she grins. 'You are all over Facebook and Twitter, and Charles has posted a small piece about the arrest claiming you were like his own personal bodyguard!'

I look over her shoulder at a photograph of Richard Madden and cringe. But then I read Charles's articulate and well-meaning words. 'I am profoundly grateful and astounded at the kindness in people, and especially Clive Thompson. Who, with little regard for his own safety, aided me in my hour of need.'

I feel a warm glow inside my stomach spread upwards to my chest and can't help smiling at the thousands of re-tweets and likes.

Barbie's mobile rings and I listen while she tells Jenny about last night. I hear Jenny yell, put him on the phone, but I wave my hand in refusal.

'He's too embarrassed,' Barbie says and giggles.

I sigh but take her mobile and talk to Jenny. I can hear pride and appreciation in her voice that I've kept her precious sister safe. Maybe Jenny didn't think I could do this, and would cowardly leave Barbie open to attack?

Her husband, Geoff is a big burly man who is like Richard Madden, and obviously well able to look after his family, but I suppose I don't quite look the part. However, I accept the thanks and praise with jokey humour and feel closer to her when we bid farewell.

After lunch, I find Barbie talking on the landline and creep up behind her then put my arms around her waist. She giggles and tries to push me away.

'Yeah, it's him messing around,' she simpers with a love-struck look on her face. 'And yes, Jane, he is my hero.'

I realise she's talking to the girls at work and signal that I'm busy while taking yet another call on my mobile. It's a reporter who wants to do a small piece in the local newspaper, but I frown with indecision.

I'm not a particularly shy type of person but don't want to do an interview and be in the spotlight. I imagine the headline; local author captures mugger in citizen arrest. And although I know the publicity would be great for my book, I decide against this, and he leaves his number if I change my mind.

At night, I roll from side to side in bed listening to Barbie lightly snore. I can't get comfortable, and my mind won't switch off. There's something about the mugger that niggles in the back of my mind, and I decide it was the expressions on his face. His defeatism. His hopelessness in the act of being caught.

He hadn't looked like a nasty piece of work full of hatred. I know what thugs look like from way back in the institution and this guy wasn't. I remember the bullies and their vile expressions. The loathing and anger in their faces with their attitude that everyone owes them a living. But this mugger looked like an ordinary guy who was simply down on his luck.

He was well-dressed and obviously felt comfortable in his appearance. I could tell that he suddenly hadn't bought those good-quality clothes; he was used to wearing them. They were familiar to him as though he wore them every day and like me, he enjoyed the good things in life.

It was obvious that he wasn't used to begging for hand-outs and scrambling around for ready cash. This guy looked like he had a healthy bank account and worked in business. He'd had a proud swagger when I'd first spotted him under the streetlight as though he often strode through York with his head held high and shoulders pulled back with confidence. I couldn't imagine him cowering around street corners although this is what he'd done last week before attacking me which didn't add up and make sense. I drift off to sleep wondering why.

***

I'm not due into the travel agency on Monday and have no tours booked but feel charged and raring to do something. I settle at my desk prepared to write but struggle to clear my mind. I'm working on a new character and plotline for my second book but can't seem to detach myself from the last two days.

I decide to write about my own mugging and experience with Charles on Saturday. I start describing Mrs America in a character folder which is full of interesting people I've met. Their appearances, character traits, and quirky personalities. I'm just starting to get into the flow when my mobile rings again and am tempted to switch it off. I feel as though it's been glued to my ear for the last two days but decide to answer.

The call is from the police, and I listen carefully scribbling down notes when they tell me what to expect next. As I end the call, Barbie pops her head around the door.

'Come on, it's a lovely morning let's get wrapped up and walk along the riverbank,' she says. 'And leave that mobile here you could do with a break from it all.'

We do just that and head down the old stone steps on our end of Shekdergate Bridge. Although it's cold the fresh air is fantastic, and I drape my arm along her shoulders as we keep pace with each other along the riverside path. Even though I'm trying not to think about it, we walk past a man who is obviously returning from work wearing a suit. I sigh remembering the mugger again.

I tell Barbie, 'Well, the police have said the man has been charged with robbing and attacking me, and the attempted robbery of Charles. He's been given a charge sheet which sets out the details of the crime he has been charged with. They've decided not to keep him in police custody until he is taken to court for his hearing, and because he's admitted everything there's no need for further investigations.'

Barbie doesn't comment but nods in understanding.

I continue, 'Apparently, because there is now a time limit on bail, the police often prefer
to release suspects under investigation instead. And there are no deadlines so he could remain a
suspect under caution indefinitely.'

I kick at a pebble on the path with my trainer. I try to explain how I feel about this guy and how his appearance doesn't fit with being a mugger. I describe the misery and anguish in his face with deadpan eyes and how a tear had been in his eye.

Barbie turns to me and stops walking. She says, 'Well, he can't be that much of a decent guy if he intended knocking an old man over to rob him of his money?'

'I know,' I nod. 'But he'd simply looked like a desperate defeated man and when I saw the tear in his eye, I couldn't help feeling sorry for him. Which, considering what he did to me is crazy!'

She teases, 'Underneath your bodyguard image you're just a big softy.'

She kisses my cold lips and I enjoy the cherry flavour of her lip gloss then sigh knowing the writer in me wants to find out more.

Chapter Ten

Unable to sleep, the muggers face swims in and out of my dreams with his distraught look and the tear in his eye. His stuttering words, I'm s…sorry, repeat over and over until I sit up in bed and rub my eyes. What has brought this man to his knees? And why mention a bike and an iPad?

I get up and wander through to my desk then stare at the list of restaurants. There were three places left on the list that I haven't checked, and plan to visit them this morning. I want to find him. I need to know how he fits into these happenings.

We'd had a bit of an argument this morning because Barbie wants to come along. She's made excuses claiming that she needs to go shopping and wants to spend the day with me but I'm uneasy. If I do find this guy who has already struck out at me once, there's a chance he'll do it again. Although from his demeanour two days ago, I'm nearly sure he won't. I frown, where Barbie is concerned is nearly sure, enough?

I pull on my black trousers and blue shirt buoyed up with the fact that I can keep her safe. I smile because there is also the fact that I couldn't stop her even if I wanted to.

Barbie is standing at the bottom of the stairs waiting for me dressed in a blue wool skirt and jumper. Barbie looks so pretty that I catch my breath and kiss her. She's always complaining that she is putting on weight and looks peeved when I call her cuddly. Although I don't care what she looks like, she is simply my lovely girlfriend.

She takes my hand, and we walk down Victor Street and into the city centre. The crisp sunshine from yesterday has gone and its cloudy so I pull up the collar on my flying jacket against the chilly breeze. We stop in The Shambles market and Barbie buys small stocking fillers for Libby and Jack.

I feel a tremor of excitement looking forward to this year now that I know what their traditional Christmas entails and remember how much I'd enjoyed myself. Of course, when I was married, Sarah and I exchanged presents, but it was only ever one biggish gift placed underneath the little tired-looking tree. Often it was vouchers in an envelope or something for the house which we never wrapped.

Christmas stockings with little surprise gifts feature heavily in Barbie's family traditions. Last year she'd made me a surprise stocking and placed it on the end of our bed. I'd been overcome on Christmas morning. It was the first time ever that Santa had left me a stocking and she'd made me feel like a little boy. The small notebook and long pencil with a Scotsman on the top had been the best presents I'd ever received, and we'd eaten satsumas in between making love.

I smile now at the memories then tell her my plan and we find the first restaurant on my list which unfortunately is closed. I sigh and chew the inside of my cheek.

'Where's the next restaurant,' she asks and squeezes my hand. 'Come on, there's another two to go, don't give up!'

Using Google maps, we wander through the streets until we turn the corner and stand on the edge of the pavement at a big restaurant with two large windows. The signage in gold lettering says, Eat to Enjoy, and even though the blinds are down on one of the windows and I can't see inside, I can tell its upmarket high-end décor.

'He can't be here,' I say and sigh again feeling that it's a wasted exercise. 'Whoever owns this place can't be that short of money to warrant stealing £110? These fittings and décor alone must have cost a fortune.'

Barbie smiles. 'Yeah, but spider man could just work here. It doesn't mean to say he owns the place, does it?'

I nod knowing she's right and saunter along the pavement to look in the other window where the blinds are pulled up.

And there he is sitting forlornly at a table with his head in his hands.

I swing around to her and hiss, 'It's him!'

Barbie scuttles towards me and takes hold of my hand which is sweating now.

She looks up at me and raises an eyebrow. 'I'm not sure we should go inside, Clive, he could still be dangerous?'

I listen to her words but know I must take the chance. I need to speak with him and can't bear the thought of leaving without answers. But I'm conscious of her safety.

'Look, why don't you go back down to the shops, and I'll text you when I leave here.'

She clicks her tongue. 'Er, no way, like I've told you before, we're in this together.'

I nod and squeeze her hand. 'Well, he doesn't look dangerous to me,' I say. 'He looks as though he's had all the stuffing knocked out of him.'

Barbie shrugs her shoulders. 'If you think so then let's go for it.'

I open the door slowly and look around the gold leaf pillar to where he is sitting in the corner. I can smell garlic and cooking then hear someone moving about further down the large room where I figure the kitchen is likely to be situated. At least we aren't alone, I think and take a step forward.

'Hello,' I say quietly and lick my dry lips. I can feel Barbie standing close behind me and am glad she's there.

Suddenly, the man looks up and jumps to his feet. 'Ooooh, hello!'

He steps quickly towards me, and I hold both my hands up in front of me as if to say, I come in peace. My heart begins to pound, and I stare at his face. Memories of how frightened I'd been on the two previous occasions with this man makes a shiver run down my back. I take a deep breath to try and steady myself determined not to let spider man intimidate me again.

He smiles then stops still. 'It's y…you,' he mutters.

I can see the shock on his face and how he's bracing himself for my retaliation. But I haven't come for that and know if I do, I'll never get the answers to my questions. 'Yes, it's me,' I say. 'The guy you mugged last week.'

I can see him shuffling his feet together on the expensive floor tiles. His gaunt troubled face looks down at the floor and I can tell he's on the defensive. He begins to babble, 'Look, I'm sorry about that, I…I, well, I don't know what's happened to me lately and I shouldn't have done it,' he says. 'I…I've never done anything like this before. And I…I'm sorry. I didn't mean to hurt you; I was just desperate!'

I step towards him again and smile knowing I need to calm him down. 'Hey, it's okay, I'm not looking for trouble or revenge. I'd just like to talk with you if that's alright?'

He turns around and sits back at the table and I walk towards him. I introduce myself and Barbie who peeps around from behind my back and gives him one of her winning smiles.

There's a large cafetiere in the centre of the table with milk and two used mugs.

'Oh, right,' he says gesturing to the chairs.

I pull out a chair opposite him for Barbie then sit down next to her.

'Would you like some coffee,' he asks, and I can tell he is used to looking after his customers.

I grin. 'That'll be nice, it'll warm us through out of the damp weather.'

He turns behind him and gathers three clean mugs from the nearby table which is set with crockery and cutlery. 'By the way, I'm Tim,' he says.

I spot the spider tattoo on his hand. Although I don't need this to identify him now, all the same it's good to see it after days of looking at men's hands. I note that it isn't like the photographs of tattoos the police officer had. However, if what Tim has just said is true then he won't have a police record or criminal history. Unless, of course, he is lying and hasn't been caught until now.

I look around the restaurant. All of this could have been done with the proceeds of crime or it could be the front for a criminal enterprise. But there's something about his face and demeanour that tells me, Tim is not capable of this.

Barbie takes over and rearranges the mugs then pours milk into two. Holding the carton aloft, she looks at him and he nods his consent.

I begin to chatter and tell him about the lump on my head and gash on my forehead. And, how I've looked inside lots of restaurants in York and everything I could remember from last week about the incident with Charles. 'So, I've found you at last.'

I can see by his raised eyebrow that he can't understand why I'd want to find him. And neither can I. It's just a gut feeling that it'll make me feel better. I know now-a-days victims sometimes get the chance to meet their perpetrators with a view to closure of the incident.

I say, 'I simply can't understand why you picked on me in the street and I wanted to establish the fact that you didn't know me or where I live. I've wracked my brain wondering if we had met and maybe in the past if I've done something to warrant the attack?'

Tim shakes his head. ‘No, I don’t know you from Adam and this wasn’t planned. I’d simply seen you pocketing your tips on the street and in a split decision tried my luck.’

I relax my shoulders. ‘Okay, so that’s good in one sense to know that I was simply in the wrong place at the wrong time.’

His eyes look watery as though he’s going to cry, and I sigh heavily.

He sniffs into his shirt sleeve. ‘Yeah, well, I don’t know why you’d want to find a snivelling gutless coward like me?’

Barbie can obviously see his distress too when she asks, ‘So, is this your place and do you have a family?’

Tim relaxes and while we all sip our coffee he opens up like a floodgate and tells us everything from the make-over, his financial problems, lack of customers, to his children’s Christmas presents of a bike and iPad.

I’m gobsmacked listening to his tale and keep nodding and grunting but don’t comment. I still have resentment and mistrust raging through my mind. I want to yell at him, but this is no reason to steal from other people. You might be in a tough situation, but this doesn’t mean to say that my circumstances are any better.

In between his words, Barbie makes soothing comments, ‘That’s not an easy situation. Families can be hard work. You wouldn’t have known where to turn. It’s understandable the pressure you’ve been under.’

She’s showing him the understanding and sympathy that now I’m struggling to find. I look at her and realise how good she is at making conversation with strangers.

I know she is great at getting me to open up but didn't realise her skills also worked with outsiders. Although, I muse, within her job Barbie is used to meeting new people every day. Obviously, she has much better communicational skills than I have sheltered in a travel agency working alongside two women.

'So,' Tim says, 'I'm at home awaiting the court hearing where I'll probably get a community order and probation.'

Yeah, I think, my measly £110 wasn't enough to warrant anymore penalty. I stick out my lip and know I must look petulant. 'So, what about Charles because he's an old man? Was he picked at random in the street too or were you on such a high after grabbing my money that you wanted to repeat the mugging and stash his!'

Barbie raises her eyebrow at me and gives a slight shake of her head.

I notice Tim wring his hands together as they tremble. He must feel as though he's on trial in court with us asking him questions. But I want to get to know him so I can judge his character.

Tim sighs. 'Look, I know you reached me yesterday before I could rob Charles, but I wasn't going to attack him. I'd sort of learnt my lesson because I worried all of the next day that I'd left you lying on the ground,' he says. 'And I would never knock an old man down. I'd intended trying to grab his strap bag and hoped it would come loose.'

All I can manage is a tut and nod of my head.

'Of course, you weren't,' Barbies soothes.

Tim stares at me now. 'And I'm so sorry for hitting you hard, but my shoes slipped on the wet cobbles, and I sort of fell forward a bit. Plus, I had a bunch of keys in my hand which must have caused the lump on your head.'

We both lift our heads at the sound of whirling coming from the kitchen.

Tim says, 'That's my wife, Rosa in the kitchen using an old rotary whisk.'

I wonder what she's like and if Rosa knows about what he's done.

'She's not speaking to me now,' he says. 'And I don't blame her really. We've been arguing for weeks about the menu, but I can't get her to wake up and smell the coffee. It's obvious to everyone, except her, that the dishes she makes are not upmarket. Rosa is making the same old lasagne that she's been doing for years. And don't get me wrong it's amazing just like her mama used to make but it doesn't fit in with all of this.'

He waves his hand around the room. I can practically see Barbie's ears perk-up at the words, menu, and lasagne. I explain to Tim that Barbie works with food and is a technologist.

For the first time I see a slight glimmer of light in his eyes. 'Hey, I don't suppose?' he says. 'Nooo, I can't ask that, not after what I've done to you.'

Barbie leans forward. 'Yes, of course, you can,' she says. 'I'd like to help in any way I can.'

Tim scrapes his chair back. 'Okay then, come and meet Rosa.'

Barbie gets up to follow him and my stomach does a somersault. Although I now understand what drove Tim to mug me, would he still be a threat? Or could his wife be dangerous? I jump up from the chair and hurry along behind them to the kitchen door which now swings open. A woman appears drying her hands on a tea-towel.

Tim explains briefly that Barbie works with food and is interested in their menu while I appreciate the beauty of the Italian dark-haired woman.

Barbie immediately smiles and shakes Rosa's hand. 'Tim has told me about your famous lasagne, and I wondered if you always use fresh pasta?'

Rosa lifts her shoulders at the compliment. 'Of course! I make my own pasta.'

Within seconds I can see Rosa succumb to my girlfriend's charm. Barbie frowns. 'Oh, right, I haven't got a pasta-making machine, could you show me how to make it by hand?'

I grin at Barbie knowing she has practically invited herself into the kitchen. When the two women leave us, my stomach settles, and I walk back to the table with Tim.

As I sit down and drain the coffee from my cup, Tim begins another apology.

I look at him and know if I'm to move forward with this I must accept what he did and that he's learned a valuable lesson. I also need to make peace with him and myself.

'Okay, so now you've explained everything, and apologised, I'll try to let it lie,' I say. 'And I suppose the gash on my forehead was because of the rough cobbles.'

Tim sighs heavily. 'All the same I feel terrible that I did it to you. I'm really sorry, and if I ever get back on my feet again with money, I'll repay the £110 I robbed from you, I promise.'

We talk more and Tim tells me how desperate he'd felt. 'I know you don't know me but it's the first time I've stolen a thing in my life! I wasn't brough up like that and I drum it into the kids that they must never take anything that doesn't belong to them at school.'

I can see honesty in his eyes as well as the torment he's suffered. This is a man that people can usually trust. He is a family man. When I look at his whole demeanour, I appreciate his despair and feel a smidgen of pity for him. The mistakes he has made were through concern for his family and I know that I'd never cope with the responsibility of children.

I think back to Libby and Jack sleeping over in our house and how I had hardly slept imagining all kind of happenings that could befall them. I suppose if you're a full-time parent you must live with this concern daily and I shiver.

Tim snivels. 'And, I still don't have the money for their bloody Christmas presents because the cupboards were empty, and I bought groceries at Tesco with the £110.'

I sigh and nod realising this is just one of the repercussions which has followed the pandemic and the effect it's having on society. At least my money went to good use, I think which does makes me feel a little better.

Changing the subject, I look around the restaurant. 'Even though you're in hock because of all this, Tim, it is stunning! And I love the name, Eat to Enjoy.'

He pulls his shoulders back and smiles for the first time. 'We played around with names for ages, Not Just Pasta, and Eat Till You Burst, and finally the kids came up with it,' he says. 'But how on earth do I get people inside on seats to eat here?'

'Well, it's not my area really, but have you looked around other restaurants to see what they're doing? You could copy the way they are drawing-in diners on social media. And how about re-advertising and a new marketing program with an outlook to promote the food.'

I see hope in Tim's eyes as he lifts his head from the table and pulls across his tablet. Even though I still feel aggrieved I can't help throwing myself into his project and have always thought of problem solving as one of my better skills. 'Look, try Googling restaurant marketing strategies and plans,' I say. 'Not just here in York but look at what the big guys are doing in London for new ideas. And of course, we have The Ivy, and Betty's here in York.'

We pour over other restaurants advertisements, local newspaper articles, Twitter, Facebook, and Pinterest on social media.

'Hey, look at Betty's photographs on Instagram,' I say. 'They've lots of images and are asking for reviews on Amazon and TripAdvisor. And there's adverts on

TV asking people to go onto Google and support their local businesses by leaving reviews. That would be a fantastic way to spread the word about your new dining experience. Barbie and I could leave a review now to start you off as we have different surnames!'

Tim smiles. 'I see what you mean,' he says. 'I've never done anything like this before because without sounding big-headed, we've never had to with our usual loyal customers.'

'Yeah,' I say. 'But now you need a new band of customers, don't you? The younger crowd of people coming to York for weekend breaks all seem to have money to spend. And, if they can see rave reviews on social media, you might just be on to a winner?'

'We certainly do,' he says and rubs his jaw. 'And yes, it would be great to attract them in here, that's if I can get Rosa on trend?'

I grin. 'Ah, just wait until my Barbie has finished in that kitchen with her. If she can't get her trying out new stuff, then nobody can!'

***

Barbie has stepped into the kitchen and the first thing Rosa does is make a pot of strong coffee.

They sit on stools at a counter and Barbie looks around the kitchen. 'This is an amazing space to work in,' she says and grins.

'Yeah,' Rosa says and lifts her chin. 'I practically designed it myself because I knew exactly where I wanted everything when I'm cooking.'

'Very impressive,' Barbie says then explains her technologist job. 'But I've worked in factory kitchens which are smaller and much more outdated than this one and the chefs still create some amazing recipes.'

Rosa thanks Barbie then wrings her hands together. 'I suppose Tim has told you both about the mess we're in,' she says and whispers. 'But I haven't told the rest of the family about him stealing money.'

Barbie nods. 'Yes, Tim told us, and I can't begin to imagine what you've been through. It must be a huge worry for you?'

Rosa shrugs her shoulders. 'It has been, and it still is,' she says. 'And I'm sorry for what he did to your partner. Tim's not a bad man, you know, he's just out of his mind with worry and I've never known him steal before. Usually, he's as honest as the day he was born.'

'Men!!' Barbie says, 'It's a good job they've got us behind them steering them in the right direction.'

Rosa nods. 'When I found out what he'd done, I totally flipped - we were at home in our kitchen, and I threw two plates at him which narrowly missed his face. But when I grabbed the frying pan and advanced upon him, he cowered in the corner with his hands over his head. And before I could do any real damage he burst into tears,' she says. 'And that's when I realised what a state he was in, and we ended up cuddling and crying together on the kitchen floor!'

Barbie nods and while they talk woman to woman, she pulls out the iPad from her bag then begins to Google, on trend Italian pastas and pizzas.

Within minutes she has Rosa engrossed and her eyes are bright and excited. 'I don't mind admitting to you, although I wouldn't let Tim know, I've shied away from making changes because I'm not sure if I can do other recipes. I only know what I've been cooking forever, and what my mama taught me, which are homely dishes using basic ingredients.'

Barbie smiles. 'That's often the case and you're not alone. Lot of chefs and cooks hang back through a lack of confidence, but you've already got the skills and knowledge of using good ingredients.'

They pour over the recipes on websites.

Rosa cries, 'But these are all dishes I know! They've just been made to look different and don't have our traditional names.'

Barbie grins and knows that Rosa understands. 'Of course, they are, this is what you already cook but jazzed up a bit. So, why not copy the style and pattern on these images with your own dishes and give them names from different areas in Italy. Maybe, the small towns and villages where your family are from?'

Together they sit and plan a list of new recipes, Caprese Salad with Pesto Sauce, Panzenella, Arancini Risotto Balls, Pasta Con Pomodore E Basilico, Chicken Piccata with Lemon Sauce Cannoli, and Three Ways Lemon Gelato.

Rosa is bubbling up with excitement and scribbling notes on a pad and Barbie smiles.

'Now, Rosa, look at the photos again and tell me what else you can see compared to your dishes?'

Well,' Rosa says, 'the crockery is all white with much bigger wine glasses.'

Barbie nods. 'Exactly, so ditch your mother's patterned crockery and send it back home. Then use plain sleek white plates and serving dishes and much bigger wine glasses.'

Rosa cries, 'But we haven't any money!'

Barbie takes her hand and squeezes it tight. 'Well, hire them for six weeks until you get your first few bookings then buy your own,' she says. 'There's always ways around things.'

Rosa jumps up from the stool as Barbie makes to leave. She throws her arms around Barbie and hugs her.

'You've been like my guardian angel, thanks so much,' she says and grins. 'Now, away with you out of my kitchen I've got a whole lot of cooking to do!'

Chapter Eleven

I'm wearing my navy pinstripe suit which is the only one I possess with a new grey shirt and a blue tie. Already the tie feels tight, and I fidget waiting for Barbie in the hall. It's our anniversary today and we've swapped presents and cards earlier. She bought me a good pen and I bought her a bauble for her tree collection with a scene of the Ouse Bridge. We'd already decided not to spend much money and save it for Hogmanay up in Scotland.

I've chosen my card carefully and wrote the following words inside which sums up my feelings for her. 'From day to passing day, love brought us together and I pray it will hold us fast for all our years to come.'

Barbie walks regally downstairs, and I gasp. She looks absolutely stunning in a short black cocktail dress with tiny sequins. Her hair is shining, and her eyes are big and full of expectation.

'Ah, Clive,' she pouts. 'Tell me where we are going.'

I wag my finger at her. 'Er, no, I've told you three times already that it's a big surprise!'

She raises an eyebrow. 'You know I don't like surprises; can't you give me at least a hint?'

I grin. 'No, I can't. And the only reason you don't like surprises is because you're not in control. So, Barbie, for one night only, I'm taking the lead.'

She giggles and pushes her arms into a white wool coat then ties the belt snuggly in front.

I look at her black heels. 'Are you okay for a fifteen-minute walk in those or shall I call a taxi?'

‘I’m fine to walk. For One Night Only,’ she stresses and grins.

I throw my head back and laugh locking the door behind us. We set off to walk and I purposely manoeuvre us to Tim and Rosa’s restaurant in a different direction which I’m hoping will throw Barbie off the scent.

I’ve had a busy week doing two tours, and an extra day in the travel agency to cover for Tina’s holiday. I have also helped Tim via email and with calls while he made various posts, online banners, and adverts. Although my social media and IT skills relate to novels and writing quotes, I have made suggestions and altered his wording to grab attention using more vibrant colours. Tim’s friend, who pertains to be an amateur photographer, has taken amazing shots of the restaurant frontage, signage, and gorgeous interior images.

On Thursday, Barbie spent the day with Rosa in the restaurant kitchen. Rosa had cooked her whole new range of dishes and they’d tasted and tweaked until both women had declared they were perfect. Barbie had suggested new descriptions with enticing sensory terms and photographs were taken to display the range to its upmost advantage.

I whistle now as we walk. I feel so happy, I could burst. I remember how I’d told Tim that we’d leave a review on Google because we had different surnames. I look at my girlfriend and think of her being Mrs Barbara Thompson which makes me smile. Within a week my outlook has changed and while I hold Barbie’s hand, I feel blessed just to be with her. She’s so beautiful, and I hope that soon I'll be her fiancé after I've sorted out my special plans.

We turn the corner to the restaurant and Barbie exclaims, 'Oh, are we eating here?'

I grin and nod. 'Yep, we are going to, Eat To Enjoy!'

Tonight, is the grand re-opening of restaurant but I've asked Tim and Rosa to keep this as a surprise to Barbie for our anniversary dinner. We both stand still admiring the trendy metal and glass stand. Both blinds are now open, and I can see inside the well-lit room with people inside talking, eating, and enjoying themselves. It looks warm and inviting and I know they've cracked it.

Barbie reads down the newly created menu on the stand with stylish photographs. 'Wow,' she breaths out slowly. 'This looks fabulous!'

I whistle between my teeth. 'Yeah, they've done an amazing job in such a short time,' I say and take her hand.

I open the door to the restaurant. Tim and Rosa rush to greet us warmly. The women hug each other, and I shake Tim's hand. Rosa is dressed in a green velvet dress which emphasises her big eyes with a long black apron tied around her waist. Tim is wearing a black tux and they are both glowing.

I marvel at the change in Tim. He's gone from sitting at the table with his head in his hands to this upstanding, proud, and happy man. Which, I figure was how he'd been before fate dealt him a blow.

'Come in,' Tim cries. 'You are both our special guests for the evening, and I have a table all ready for you.'

He leads us across the room into the centre where the table is set for two and decorated with red heart confetti. Two big balloons which state, Happy Anniversary, are tied to the chairs.

Barbie gasps. 'Ah, Rosa,' she cries, 'how lovely. Have you done this?'

She nods and beams at Barbie.

Tim moves to the side and with a flourish of his arm shows us a bottle of Champagne in a gold bucket and stand. 'It's on the house to say thank you for everything you've done to help us,' he says. 'I don't know where we'd be now if you hadn't come.'

Tim takes our coats and I sit down opposite her. The women talk about their dresses, and I look around the room. There are five young couples at a long table down the side of the room and two middle-aged couples in the other corner.

One of the girls walks past us heading towards the Ladies. 'Try the Chicken Piccata, it's delicious,' she says excitedly. 'We're all raving about it!'

I look at Rosa who is grinning. She thanks the girl and I see her eyes are watery with tears.

Barbie clasps her hand. 'There now,' she says. 'What better recommendation do you need, Rosa. You've done it and I'm so proud of you.'

Rosa nods and squeezes Barbie's hand. 'All thanks to you!'

But Barbie shakes her head. 'No, all I did was make suggestions. You're the one who has developed and cooked all of the dishes on the menu.'

Tim hugs Rosa and says, 'We have eight new bookings for later tonight and six for Sunday lunch.'

Tim pops the cork on the bottle of Champagne and they all cheer then he fills four tall flutes.

Rosa says, 'Well, it's not a huge quantity but it's enough for now to keep us afloat.'

Holding up my champagne flute, I say, 'To us all and congratulations for turning this place around. You've done an amazing job in such a brief time. Well, done!'

We all sip the champagne and Rosa calls out, 'And Happy Anniversary.'

Tim heads over to the counter and till then returns with money in his hand. He passes a handful of notes to me and looks down to the floor then shuffles his feet.

'Here is the £110 I robbed from you. I can't apologise enough to you for what I did,' he says. 'Once again, I'm so very, very sorry.'

My heart swells with a mixture of pride and satisfaction. Pride because I feel like I've turned a bad situation around by helping these people. And I feel better in myself for confronting Tim. The mugging is not at the forefront of my mind and although I'm trying to forgive Tim's actions, I know I'll never forget his assault.

I shuffle on my chair and nod. 'Ah, keep it towards the kids Christmas presents.'

But Tim shakes his head and pulls back his shoulders. 'No, but thank you,' he says. 'I'll be able to afford their gifts now.'

Barbie takes his hand and Rosa's. 'I think the four of us are going to be friends now,' she says. 'And who would have thought that possible?'

I nod and smile at us all knowing she is right, or at least I hope so. I've still a smidgen of doubt in the back of my mind about Tim. And, as the saying goes, I don't think I'd ever put my life in his hands, but who knows? Over time, this may change.

When I'd been mugged, I had wanted retribution to stop me feeling like a victim and hoped that understanding the reason behind his attack would help to ease the emotional upset. Now I realise, any type of vengeance wouldn't have this desired effect.

To see the restaurant up and running with our contribution has helped me come to terms with the assault in a much better way. Retribution would not make me feel as good about myself as this has done.

Chapter Twelve

Barbie is working down in Nottingham this week, and by 11am on Monday morning, I'm missing her already. I am at my computer plotting the scenes for chapter one of my new novel but struggling to concentrate. I know she'll Zoom every night until she comes home on Friday but all the same her absence is acutely felt.

The house seems quiet. Although she's not a noisy person to live with I miss the gentle plodding of her mule slippers on the wood floors or the clickety-click of her heels if she is going out. I've got used to Barbie being away for work since she moved in with me last year, but I look out of the window and sigh. Maybe it's because I've had her at home for two weeks, and now she's headed off again, I'm missing her even more. Spot and Stripe miss her too because they're sitting at the front door looking expectantly around as if to say, where is she?

I smile remembering our great anniversary weekend with the celebratory dinner and how we certainly, Ate to Enjoy, at Tim and Rosa's expense. Although I'd only drank half a glass of champagne because I didn't like the dry taste, Barbie had drunk quite a bit of bubbly and giggled all the way home in the taxi.

Yesterday, we'd stayed in bed eating, laughing, and making love. I think it was the perfect weekend for two people very much in love. I like this phrase and jot it down to use somewhere in my story.

My first novel has a solitary detective as the main character who is divorced and embittered towards the women around him. It's time for a change, I think and decide upon a new protagonist who is happily married and loves his wife as much as I love Barbie. This should be easy to write, I think and begin to tap cheerfully away on the keyboard noting down many of the things I love about my girlfriend, soon to be my fiancé, I hope.

I'm so engrossed that when my stomach growls in hunger I glance at the clock and hurry downstairs remembering the appointment I have with Tommy in the tour office. He's called in all his tour leaders to discuss another problem. I sigh and pile baked beans onto pieces of buttered toast.

Tommy hasn't elaborated on his text, and I wonder if there have been more repercussions from the afternoon with Charles. Although, I frown, surely that issue has been sorted out. I hope Tommy's business isn't in trouble and we aren't going to be finished because the job is a good little earner which supplements my low wages in the travel agency.

***

I'm wandering down towards Museum Street where the tour office is situated. A weak winter sun is trying to break through the thick clouds, and I know Barbie would enjoy the walk. This is her last contract before Christmas, and I grin thinking of the fun we'll have making the festive preparations.

The streetlights have been switched on now and the city is beginning to look very Christmassy. I smile knowing I wouldn't have given this a thought before I met Barbie.

Sarah wasn't big on Christmas, and I'd thought I wasn't either. I can still hear my ex-wife retorting, 'It's all just commercial claptrap.'

But now, I find I'm looking forward to the hype. I grin remembering how I'd enjoyed it all last year and look up at the magical elves with Santa Claus lit up.

Shaking the thoughts from my mind I stop outside the small front window and door of the tour office. The door and windowsills are painted green and look a little tired as if they could do with a fresh coat of paint. I frown, hoping my earlier thoughts aren't going to come true. The office befits most of the old properties in these streets and at just above five foot ten I lower my head to go inside.

The office interior is smart and modern with new grey shelves around the square room holding all manner of leaflets and brochures advertising the different tours available.

An elderly couple are sitting at the small round Formica table which is in front of two desks where Tommy sits at one, and his assistant, Ms Willoughby, at the other. She is chatting politely with the couple about the weather, and I smile.

Miss Willoughby takes bookings for tours, payments, and generally runs the office. It's always clean and tidy, and I know she takes great pride in her work. She is a tiny forty year old lady with a bird-like face and pointy nose. Her rimmed glasses are always perched on the end of her nose making her look like a teacher. I'm not even sure what her first name is, but in the years that I've worked here, I wouldn't dream of calling her anything other than Ms Willoughby. I'd worry that she would take offence. She is, however, thorough, and meticulous in her organisation and I'm always paid on time with top-notch paperwork.

Pamela and Charles with another three tour leaders are stood in the far corner chatting and I wave at them.

I hear the door open behind me and an Indian couple enter the office. She is wearing a beautiful bright pink Sari and he is wearing jeans with a grey shirt and blue jacket. Immediately. I appreciate the style and quality of his jacket and wonder if it is Armani? He holds open the door for a young guy in a wheelchair behind him.

Negotiating his wheelchair around the turn into the office space, the guy smiles at us and I step to one side. Tommy jumps up and hurries to the table where he shuffles the small four chairs around to make room for the wheelchair.

Tommy Sanderson is a big chap in his thirties with lots of brown wild hair. He wears short sleeved T-shirts, winter, and summer alike with rock group images on the front. Although he doesn't look much like a business owner, Tommy is one of the kindest men I've ever met and cares passionately about his company, staff, and customers.

'Hellooo,' Tommy calls. 'Welcome to you all, and please make yourselves comfortable.'

Charles wanders over to me and raises an eyebrow as if to ask what's going on, but I shrug my shoulders.

'I'll just make the introductions to everyone and then we can get started,' Tommy says. 'This is Grace and

Henry Makepeace, Adhar and Binita Patel, and Matt Johnson.'

The five people around the table all nod at each other. My mind is whirling. What's happening? Who are these people and what have they to do with the problem Tommy mentioned on his text?

Tommy looks at the five people and waves his arm towards us. 'And, this is my assistant, Ms Willoughby, and as many of my tour leaders that I could pull together at short notice. Of course, some are out touring with customers and can't be here.'

I nod at the group around the table, and they all smile back.

Tommy turns to us now and says, 'Guys, I've asked these people to join us today because they've all had money stolen whilst on one of our tours. Grace, Adhar, and Matt have had their wallets and purses taken and have verified to the police that they definitely had them on their persons before the tours started and were missing afterwards.'

I gasp. This information is dreadful coming not long after my mugging even though we have an explanation for that now. I'd told Charles about Tim and Rosa on the telephone last week and extended their invitation for a complimentary meal in the restaurant as a small way of making amends to him. He'd been delighted to hear the genuine reason and apologies about his attempted mugging and had rung Tim to arrange a reservation.

I look at Charles now and he frowns then shakes his head. 'But this is shocking,' Charles says to Tommy.

Tommy nods. 'I know. We've always had a little petty pilfering in the city but three cases in two days means it's escalating. And the police have asked me to make you all aware of the situation.'

I step forward a little. 'I suppose because the mugging has been spread about on social media, pick-pocketers now think there are takings to be had between ourselves and our customers,' I say. 'Perhaps we are classed as an easy target?'

'Maybe,' says Tommy. 'But going forwards I want all of you leaders to be on watch out. We can't have theft increasing and if these good people were all robbed by the same person or persons then it needs to stop right now!'

I look at them and approach the group. 'I'm so sorry you've been robbed and especially on one of the tours,' I say and open my hands towards them in a gesture of goodwill. 'Were you all on the same tour on the same day?'

Grace is the first to speak then Adhar and Matt join in stating the days and times they were robbed.

Tommy says, 'So, I wanted to reassure everyone that as a company we are taking this very seriously and, to apologise that it has happened on one of my tours. I know it's not much recompense, but I've made arrangements in the café across the road for you all to have coffee with some cake treats at my expense.'

I nod at Tommy's thoughtfulness and digest the information then pull up a stool to sit beside Matt in his wheelchair.

I smile at everyone. 'So, we've got Adhar and Matt on the same day, one being in the morning and one in the afternoon then Grace on the next day,' I say. 'Therefore, I think the pick-pocketers had good takings in one day and decided to try again the next morning?'

Matt turns to me. 'Looks like it,' he says. 'I can't believe someone would rob me?'

This thought sickens me to my stomach. How any mobile and able-bodied person could thieve from a vulnerable young man in a wheelchair is beyond my reasoning. There are no excuses whatsoever for this and I tut. 'It's sickening to even think about it.'

The group and robberies have got my interest piqued and I look up at Tommy standing by his desk. I raise my eyebrow as if to make sure he's happy for me to take over. He nods then turns to the other tour leaders and talks to them while I continue with the group.

'Okay,' I say. 'I'm, Clive Thompson, and have been doing tours with this company for a few years now and as Tommy says we've always had one-off occasions of pickpocketing around the big attractions, but I'm concerned to hear about all of this.'

I notice Grace clutching her handbag on her knee and sigh. I know this defensive stance will be a direct result from having her purse taken and feel my heckles rise. Along with Matt being robbed, thieving from an old lady is despicable in my eyes and I want to help them all.

Both telephones on Ms Willoughby's desk begin to ring and two young students enter the office squeezing past us around the table.

Quickly I decide. ‘Look, how about we pop over to the café and get a coffee, it’ll be quieter in there and we’ll be able to talk more.’

Chapter Thirteen

Settled in the café around a bigger table with Matt's wheelchair comfortably spaced we all order coffee and cake. Around four in the afternoon the café is quiet now and after I've recommended the chocolate and carrot cake, and the helpful young waitress has scurried off with our order, I settle back into my chair. It's a pleasant room with a friendly relaxed atmosphere. The room is decorated in pink and white candy stripped wallpaper which I think Barbie calls, chintz, and the long counter has an array of large cakes ready-sliced. It had been a hard decision for me between chocolate, lemon cake, and strawberry gateau.

'That's better,' I say beginning the conversation. 'You know, I'd always thought that most people on my tours were visitors to York, but do you guys live here?'

Grace answers first. 'Oh, yes, we've lived here all our lives,' she says. 'We recently moved from our big house into sheltered accommodation near Nunnery Lane, which is handy for all the buses, but I miss our garden. So, we've been trying to take more exercise and walk around the streets and the park. And of course, Henry is a history buff, so he loves all the information that you guides give us about the city. We'd been listening to a ghost story at the top of The Shambles on the tour when it must have happened.'

I figure the couple look to be in their mid-seventies and pull my shoulders back. 'Well, that's great to hear you enjoy the tours and the history info that we give everyone. It makes me feel that it's all worthwhile. But, at the same time I'm saddened to think you weren't safer with us than sitting in the park.'

Henry speaks up and I look into his kind blue eyes. 'Our Grace worries about everything, Clive, and, before things even happen,' he says then chuckles but drapes an affectionate arm along her shoulders.

Grace pats her short grey hair into place on the back of her head. 'Well, you can't be too careful now-a-days, and I've been proven right!'

I nod and agree. 'So, if you don't mind me asking, how much money did you have taken from your purse?'

Henry tuts. 'The little blighters, whoever they are took £85.'

I nod knowing I won't be able to remember everything they all tell me, so I take out the small notebook from the pocket in my coat. All writers carry notebooks to jot down interesting facts and ideas.

'Do you mind if I take down a few notes from everything you tell me,' I ask. 'I've got a memory like a sieve some days.'

Henry laughs. 'Ha! Just wait until you get to our age then you'll know all about memory loss.'

Grace nudges him with her elbow and I smile at their togetherness.

She frowns and draws her thin grey eyebrows together. 'It's not really about the money, although out of weekly pensions that's a miss, but more about what I had in my purse that they've stolen.'

'Was it credit cards,' I ask. 'Because you can put a stop on them.'

She bristles. 'I've never had a credit card in my life! We pay for everything as we go and always have done, we don't owe anybody a penny.'

The waitress arrives with our coffees and cake. Once everyone has milk, sugar, and cake on their plates, I continue. 'So, what else did you have taken, Grace?'

I see her brown eyes water and hope it's the steam from her coffee and that she's not going to cry.

'W…well, our son was killed in a car accident after he returned home from Afghanistan, and I had his service medal in there. I know it was stupid to carry it around in my purse, but I just liked to know he was still close to me.'

The whole of my insides sinks. I feel sorry for asking because I don't know how to cope with upset elderly ladies. I wish Barbie were here because she'd know exactly what to say.

However, Binita stretches across to Grace and rubs her arm. 'I'm so sorry to hear about your loss,' she says.

Henry nods and smiles his thanks to Binita.

Henry strokes Grace's cheek. 'Come on, old girl, buck up,' he says, and she dries her eyes then sips her coffee. While Grace and Henry tuck into chocolate cake I turn to Binita and Adhar.

They look to be in their thirties and the sequins on Binita's sari twinkle under the strip-lighting. 'So, what about you guys, how come you were doing one of our tours?'

Adhar runs his hand through his jet-black hair. 'Well,' he says. 'Although Binita's spoken English is good, she is trying to improve her written language and is reading everything in sight. So, we were on the tour and in the graveyard at St. Mary's Abbey in the Museum Gardens. There were lots of people around and when we were bent over reading headstones and plaques, I'm sure that's when my wallet was taken from the back pocket of my jeans.'

I sigh. Here is another man like myself who is careless with keeping money in his back pocket as I'd done when I was mugged. As Barbie had already commented, it must be such an easy grab for thieves because the back pocket is open for everyone to see rather than the inside of a jacket.

Binita clicks her tongue. 'Such a stupid place to keep our money!'

I look at her huge oval brown eyes and big wide smile. Reading plaques in a graveyard would not be one of my favourite past times, but I think, whatever floats your boat.

I know the ruined Benedictine Abbey quite well and have done that tour on many occasions. The Abbey was built in 1088 and is Grade I listed located just west of the minster. I can imagine them both there and being surrounded by lots of tourists because it is one of the major attractions.

I think about Adhar's words. 'So, did you feel someone take the wallet?'

He shakes his head. 'No, afraid not. And I could kick myself because I had yesterday's takings from the business to put into the bank later.'

Binita frowns and shakes her head at her husband. 'Over £400 lost in one quick move. I'd worked and cooked day and night to make that amount in our take-a-way.'

My ears prick up at the mention of this and I ask, 'Oh, me and my girlfriend love Indian food. Which is your place?'

Adhar lifts his chin and tells me where it is and their name. I grin. 'But that's our favourite! We often order by phone and have it delivered. Barbie, my girlfriend, loves your butter chicken and I'm a prawn biriani man myself.'

They both nod and thank me. I am determined to try and help these people. I'm conscious of the fact that there's only Matt to ask which tour he'd been on, and I do so.

'Well, I had £55 taken and my wallet which was in my jacket hanging on the back of the wheelchair,' he says. 'Which, yeah, I know was a daft place to leave the wallet, but I never dreamt anyone would steal it?'

He moves his hands together over his legs in the wheelchair, as if to say, after all I couldn't run anywhere or fight back. I grind my back teeth knowing what I'd like to do with the people who had done this to him. 'Okay, so why were you on the tour?'

I'm scribbling in my notebook as he talks. He shakes his blond curly hair and I notice what a good-looking guy he is wearing his black leather jacket and expensive trainers.

'Well,' he says. 'I was at Exhibition Square taking photographs for a course I'm starting next week. And that's probably why I wasn't aware what was happening because I was concentrating on the camera and focusing the lens.'

Henry tuts and says, 'That's awful, and how did you end up in that wheelchair, Matt?'

Grace hisses, 'Henry! That's very rude!'

But Matt smiles. 'It's okay, Grace, I don't mind. I came off my motorbike three years ago and damaged my spine. So, I'm stuck in this now.'

I feel so sorry for all of them and drink my warm coffee as the group begin to talk together. I look around the room at the shelves holding varied sizes of teapots from large to small and a collection of teacups hanging from hooks underneath in pastel colours. I sigh. These are all decent ordinary people living in York and should feel safe in our streets. I decide to investigate to see if I can find out anything more about this person or persons who have stolen their money.

'Look,' I say. 'I'll work with the other tour leaders and if you give me a few days to come up with something maybe we could meet again?'

Henry nods. 'Well, the coffee and cake are good here. How about same time, same place, next week?'

Everyone agrees and I write down their contact telephone numbers in my notebook.

Chapter Fourteen

I've made a burger in a large white bap with melted cheese on top and hold it in my left hand. This allows me to use the mouse in my right hand to negotiate around the computer. I wolf down the burger and with greasy fingers I wipe them down my jeans.

I use the search bar on Google and type in pick pocketing.

The definition tells me that it is the action of stealing from a person's pockets. It has a sub note stating, higher levels of street crime and pickpocketing.

Hmm, I think, this fits Adhar having money taken from the pocket of his jeans and Matt's wallet from his jacket pocket but not Grace's purse from her handbag. So, our lawbreakers are not just picking pockets. They're versatile, I'll give them that.

I write up the points I've taken from my notebook knowing I have an hour spare before Barbie will Zoom from her hotel room. At the thought of her a memory pings into my mind. When we'd first met, we had been lying in bed together one night and she had told me about a trip to Barcelona years ago when she'd taken her mother. And how she had worried about her mam's safety because of what their holiday rep had told them going into Barcelona on the coach.

As soon as she pops onto the screen, I ask her to repeat the experience slowly so I can write it down word for word.

She tells me, 'The gang who was in Barcelona at the time were picking on elderly people to rob. They were refugees and not Barcelonians. Their plan entailed one person chatting to the elderly tourist which distracted them while another person crept up behind and grabbed the handbag. Then they ran off leaving the elderly person upset and bereft of their money, credit cards, passport, and in some cases, mobile phones.'

I nod and thank her. It's lovely to see her face again tonight and I tell her about our meeting in the tour office and the café afterwards. Barbie warns me to be careful when I tell her about my plan to survey the main attraction areas looking for dodgy characters. She commiserates with the two couples and Matt at the hands of pick pocketers. And is as shocked as I was at the fact that a person of disability has been robbed.

She apologises but signs out early to prepare notes for a big conference meeting the following day. I don't like seeing her look tired knowing she has more work ahead of her tonight, but she reminds me of the wages she'll receive then says goodnight.

'You're my own *Super Sleuth*,' she says and giggles blowing kisses onto the screen.

***

The next day on my lunch break from the agency I hurry up to Exhibition Square munching on a warm sausage roll. Could our pick pocketers be a duo? A two-person organised band, or just a solitary thief. Of course, in Grace's case they only took her purse and didn't grab the handbag itself. I shake my head and curl my lip. I hate this person or duo already knowing what they've put these good people through. Especially an elderly lady like Grace, it's shocking.

There's a chilly wind today although it's dry, so I keep on the move and wander around the square looking at the usual place where we stand to give our little talk to customers quoting facts and dates. I often tell people that Exhibition Square is where the open top sightseeing bus leaves from. It takes fifty minutes and has eight stops. It's a good way of seeing the city if you can't manage to walk around all day then you can hop off and on at the different stops. Our Exhibition Square was built in 1879 with a big hall, part of which now houses York Art Gallery.

I remember my own mugging and how I hadn't seen Tim's face, but I could recall sounds and smells which had helped in my quest to trace him. I write down in my notebook: ask Matt, Grace, Henry, Adhar and Binita if they heard any distinctive voices or accents. Were there any strong smells around them? Did they notice any solitary persons loitering around them without a definite purpose?

While I'm walking around watching people, I continue to make notes about people's characteristics. I smile knowing it's a good test of my powers of observation.

I categorise people as to what they are doing. There are professional people from work on their lunch breaks as I am, dressed in suits and big overcoats. I watch the shoppers looking for Christmas gifts with small department store bags and then other types of shopping with bigger heavier bags full of groceries.

Visitors are walking around the square pointing up and around while holding street maps as they trace the main attractions. I notice friends, both male and female, meeting for drinks and food in the nearby cafes and restaurants.

I note a group of schoolchildren with two teachers looking harried as they try to keep them in line. There are older students and young people heading into the Art gallery.

It's the last man I see heading into the Art gallery with a camera slung around his neck which reminds me of poor Matt. I sigh, did the pick pocketer notice his jacket on the back of the chair and wonder what was inside to pinch? I know I never could.

Even back in my youth I couldn't have done this because it's the lowest of the low, and no matter how desperate I was for money I'd never steal from people with disabilities. Although, when I remember my mam and dad and how desperate they'd been for their next fix, I can't put my hand on my heart and say they'd wouldn't have.

These pick pocketers mustn't have a conscience because if they had, they wouldn't sleep at night. It's an awful thought that one human being has so little disregard that they'd want to steal their dignity and the little money they do have.

Of course, I don't know Matt's financial situation and he could well have more money than I have, but even if this is true, I have something Matt doesn't have which is the ability to get up and walk away. Or run in the opposite direction away from a thief. I grind my back teeth and wish I could find them which might restore some self-worth back to the guy.

I think of Matt's inert legs and imagine myself sitting down in a chair which would make me on a lower level to people standing upright. Therefore, if someone was in front of him bending down to converse with him would this distract Matt long enough for the sidekick to rifle through his jacket on the back of the chair looking for his wallet?

I ring Matt.

'Hi, it's Clive, here,' I say. 'Hope it's okay to call?'

Matt answers brightly. 'Yeah, of course, how's it going?'

I tell him briefly what I'm doing and what I'm trying to achieve then ask, 'I just wondered, did anyone speak to you in the square? And if so, was it male or female, a young or mature voice, or a definite accent?'

I hear Matt pause. 'Nah, I can't think that I spoke to anyone other than the people like me on the tour and the leader at the beginning. I was too busy photographing the buildings, sorry.'

'That's okay,' I say. 'And did you notice any solitary people loitering around with no definite purpose?'

'Nope, sorry, Clive.'

'No problem,' I say. 'See you next week, bye for now.'

I continue my trail then perch on the end of a bench to turn over a page in my notebook. I write down people's appearances. Their hair colour and length, curly or straight. Their skin colour, white, brown, or tanned. The shape and colour of their eyes. I stare at people's glasses noting the shape, colour, and designer sizes.

Clothes are next and I note each image I can see to match their age group. Are they smart-professional, or casual-trendy? Is there a difference between casual and just downright scruffy? I look at men's height and their walk, do they saunter or rush. Is their gait normal or do they have a limp? Are they stooped or upright? Their size, skinny, slim, chubby, grossly overweight, or obese.

I watch the looks on their faces. Are they furtive, inquisitive, indifferent, happy, smiling, miserable, or angry? Then I do the same for women which are markedly different. I smile knowing all my observations will come in handy for writing character profiles in my new novel.

***

I head along to the Abbey and look at the ancient headstones in the graveyard beyond the church. St. Mary's Abbey was built in 1088 and begun by William the Conqueror to reinforce his hold on the north.

Usually when I tell do this tour, I tell my customers a little story here and start with the fact that the ruins we can now see are all that remains of one of the wealthiest and most powerful Benedictine monasteries in England. The abbey estate occupied the entire site of the Museum Gardens, and the abbot was one of the most powerful clergymen of his day. I describe the monks spending their days working in abbey administration, copying books, providing food and supplies for the monastery, and helping the poor.

In Exhibition Square there'd been a buzz of noise and activity but here it is quiet. There is an eerie reverent atmosphere. A few people are looking around the abbey but there's only one old man in the graveyard. I know when we do the tour at the abbey there are often big crowds of tourists to negotiate around when I'm speaking to my group. But Tuesdays are quieter than other days and, of course we are heading up to Christmas therefore most people will be down near the shops.

I look around the graves. This would have been where Adhar and Binita were bending forwards to read the old lettering on the headstones. So, does this mean the pick pocketer was behind them and the couple had their backs to them the whole time? Or, if it were a duo, would the other person have been facing them and leaning across the headstone distracting them with conversation.

I notice there are no walkways in between the rows of headstones. It is a grassy area but decide it would be possible for people to talk across the graves.

I think of Binita and Adhar strolling around here and sigh. I wonder if their race has a bearing on this robbery. It's shameful to think that they've been targeted because they are an ethnic minority. Sadly, minorities are treated differently by some people in our society. I've never done this. Everyone is the same to me no matter what colour their skin is or what language they speak. But I do know that not everyone holds my beliefs and attitude. It makes me wonder, is racism a big problem in York?

This prejudice hadn't made any difference to the pick pocketers. It could simply have been the case that his money was visibly protruding from his back pocket and the temptation was there.

I must ask Adhar if they've seen anyone hanging around the take-a-way premises, or if anyone would know that he'd be depositing their takings into the bank that day. Was this a weekly ritual that he did on the same day and time? If so, I figure a happenchance pick pocketer might not be to blame as in Grace, Henry, and Matt.

***

I walk home after work at five and pass down Nunnery Lane noticing the sheltered accommodation block. It is the only one in this area so I know Grace and Henry must live here. On impulse I ring their number and Grace answers the telephone.

'Oh, but you must come inside for a cuppa,' she says. 'We are at number eighteen.'

As I press their intercom button, I remember Charles telling me that Grace and Henry had been on his tour last week. And he remembered them, especially, Henry who asked him questions about dates in history at every main attraction.

I hear Henry's voice now, shouting, 'Come in, Clive.'

I step inside the hallway and glance around. It's a biggish flat with two-bedrooms and a reasonable square lounge area. Grace welcomes me into the lounge where she has a tray of tea on the small table. It is very warm in the room, and I slip off my thick coat then perch on the end of the sofa. There are two big armchairs on either side of the fireplace which Grace and Henry sink into.

Grace says, 'I was just making some tea, would you like a cup?'

I smile and nod.

I notice that Grace has a proper teapot, sugar basin, milk jug, cups, and saucers on the table. There are no mugs here, I muse then spot a plate of biscuits. Grace chatters telling me all about the move and how they'd had to downsize their belongings to squeeze into the flat. But how the advantages far out-weigh the big old house.

I look around the four walls which have framed photographs of their son in his army uniform. Some are of him alone but many with his regiment.

'I can see you were enormously proud of him,' I say pointing to the photographs.

Henry puffs his chest out. 'And we still are, Clive.'

Grace smiles. 'Our memories are very precious to us because it's all we have left of him and he was so proud of the medal they gave him for doing his stint out there,' she says. 'And now I've gone and lost it.'

I sigh and see the distress in her eyes. She feels as though she's let him down and I swallow hard praying she isn't going to get upset again.

'But I swear my purse was in my handbag when we stood at the beginning of The Shambles listening to the butcher story because I took out a handkerchief and saw the purse then,' Grace cries. 'If only I'd pulled the zip along on my bag, I'd still have his medal but now it's gone for good.'

I bite the inside of my cheek. Not if I've got anything to do with it, I think. But instead, I say, 'Grace, I swear

I'm going to do everything I possibly can to find your purse.'

Grace pours our tea and offers me a chocolate digestive biscuit which I gratefully take.

'Well, Clive,' Henry says and draws his bushy grey eyebrows together. 'If the police can't do anything, I can't see how you'll manage, but I do appreciate you trying.'

I nod, dunk the biscuit and crunch into it sighing in pleasure. 'So, I just want to ask you both a couple of questions and please think very carefully about your time in The Shambles. Did you notice anyone loitering about with no definite purpose? And I know this is a strange question, but did you notice any strong smells amongst the crowds of people around you,' I say then drain the tea from my cup. 'And lastly, did anyone speak to you in The Shambles, other than the people on the tour or Charles himself?'

I watch Grace close her eyes and sip her tea. It's obviously she is concentrating trying to remember. Henry gets up from his big armchair and begins to pace around the room. He also looks deep in thought.

Suddenly, he swings around to face me. 'Yes, there was actually, and I was irritated because I was missing some of Charles story,' he says and shakes his head. 'But it was a girl not a pick pocketer. She asked me which way it was to the market, and I told her then pointed my hand down The Shambles pavement.'

Grace claps her hands together. 'Oh, yes! I remember her now. I leant towards Henry wondering what she was asking him about.'

Bingo! I think and grin at them. Here was my first lead to the fact that it could be a duo working together.

I smile. 'Well, Henry, it's nice that you think a girl couldn't be a pick pocketer but believe me these days there's no difference between men and women. She could have kept you talking while her accomplice had their hand in your bag, Grace.'

Grace puts her hands onto her cheeks and murmurs, 'Oh no, how could they!'

Chapter Fifteen

Zoe is sitting on her bed in the hostel room. It's tiny with a single bed and small table with two shelves on the cream painted walls. But it is warm, clean, and compared to spending six days sleeping rough on York streets, it feels like a palace. The memory of feeling so cold day and night lingers in the back of her mind and she relishes being in the heated room.

It is far enough away from Blackpool where she would be recognised but not too far away if she ever did want to return home. Although that notion would never become a reality because as awful as it was being homeless, it wasn't as bad as living at home.

She squats on top of the bed and empties her money wallet out onto the checked quilt cover. Nervously, she glances over her shoulder in case anyone comes in then smiles with reassurance that the door is securely locked. Another blessing, she thinks. If only she could have locked her bedroom door at home to keep out her stepdad.

When she'd asked her mam for a padlock, she had tutted and shaken her head in bewilderment. 'Now, why on earth would you want to lock your door,' her mam had asked. 'What secrets are you hiding from me, Zoe? You're not doing drugs, are you?'

She'd cried, 'Of course, I'm not! And I'm not hiding anything, I just want a little privacy, that's all.'

Zoe had known that even if she had told her mam about the way her stepdad peered down her pyjama top, she wouldn't have believed her. In her mam's eyes, he was like a silver-haired God striding through their home keeping them all safe from harm. To her, he was a silver-haired monster.

Hmmph, she groans and empties the wallet they'd stolen from the guy in his wheelchair. It's a nice wallet and she wonders if it is worth anything? Although, she thinks, licking her lips, the money they would get from selling it wasn't worth the risk of being caught. Smiling, she flattens the money down into piles of ten and twenty pound notes. She begins to count and resists the urge to whoop in delight when she counts £55. She needs the money to pay for this room in the hostel. The thought of going back onto the streets in the cold makes her shiver.

The Indian man's money is rolled up with an elastic band around it which had been so easy for Jay to pick out of his back pocket. Slowly, she removes the band and flattens out the notes, once again onto the same piles. When she reaches £400 in her count, this time she does cry out aloud and jumps up from the bed to dance a jig.

There's a gentle tap on her door and in one swift movement she pulls back the quilt over the piles of money then stealthily crosses the room.

'Who is it,' she whispers.

She hears Jay murmur, 'It's only me.'

Zoe had met Jay on her second day in the hostel and recognised a kindred spirit. They'd teamed up swapping their own stories of previous abuse and sleeping rough. They were on the lookout for ready cash, to keep the wolf from the door, as her mam would say.

Jay was two years younger than her and had no qualms when she'd taken charge of their setup. He'd readily agreed upon his 40% share of the money. It had been her role to keep look-out and decide which people to thieve from. Therefore, as she'd told him, it was only fair that she should take the bigger split.

Zoe opens the door only far enough open for him to slither inside. At seventeen he's small, painfully thin, and dressed in tatty tracksuit bottoms and a scruffy hoodie. He looks jittery and she wonders if he has had his fix.

His eyes dart around the room. 'Where's it stashed?'

She moves to the bed and lifts back the quilt. 'I'm nearly finished,' she says. 'I've just got the old lady's purse to empty although I doubt there'll be much in that.'

In two fast paces he is at the bed ogling the piles of notes but she's even quicker and shoves him away. 'Get over there until I count and divide this up.'

Zoe opens the old purse. She glances at a medal tucked into the small flap then removes the money and flings the purse into a wastepaper basket in the corner of the room. Keeping her back to Jay she counts out £85 and places it onto the piles smiling secretively. Doing the maths, she quickly calculates his share and counts out £216 then hands it to him.

She'd been good at maths in school and harboured dreams of teaching. All her teachers thought she would get good enough grades for college or university, but this had all been before the silver-haired monster arrived.

Chapter Sixteen

Barbie is home. She'd arrived late last night and after a hot bath we'd not had time to talk before tumbling into bed. But I've just finished my shift in the travel agency and hurried home where we've settled down with coffee and sandwiches to catch up on both our weeks. Although we have spoken on Zoom, we both like to hear all our happenings in full details. I've told her all about Grace, Henry, Matt, Adhar and Binita.

'And, what a coincidence that theirs is our favourite Indian take-away?'

I nod and munch into my delicious cheese and pickle sandwich. 'I know. I couldn't believe it and they were delighted to hear that butter chicken and biriani were our top choices.'

I've changed into my slouch bottoms and T-Shirt so I can chill out. Barbie raises an eyebrow watching me eat. 'I bet you've been eating rubbish all week when I've not been here to cook.'

I place my hand over my chest. 'Ah, my love, I'm mortally wounded that you'd think such a thing.'

She giggles and finishes her sandwich. In her old black tracksuit, she snuggles into my side, and I stroke her hair. 'Well, if I'm honest I have had the odd pasty and sausage roll, but I did cook a burger the other night.'

She nods as if to say whatever, and says, 'It's okay. I've given up nagging you about your unhealthy diet now. And to be honest with working in the kitchen all week at work I can't be bothered to cook tonight. Shall we order something for later?'

I nod and pull out my mobile from my pocket. 'Actually, that's just reminded me that I haven't asked Adhar and Binita the three questions that I've asked the others. So, if I ring and order food for later, I can crack two birds with one stone, as it were.'

I recognise Adhar's voice when he answers the telephone and say, 'Hey there, it's Clive here from the tour office.'

Adhar greets me warmly. 'Ah, hello, Clive. Have you any news from your enquiries?'

I explain briefly about visiting Exhibition Square and the abbey then how I've talked to Grace, Henry, and Matt. 'So, as well as ordering food for later,' I say. 'When I call in to collect our supper, could I ask you the same few questions, if you'll be there of course?'

I can hear whispering and a female voice comes onto the line.

'Hello, Clive. It's Binita here. How nice of you to ring us. Yes, we will be here later, but we'd like to bring the food to you and deliver it ourselves, if that's okay?'

I'm flabbergasted at their kindness. 'Well,' I say. 'That would be kind but only if you have the time? You must be busy with it being Saturday night and I'm more than happy to come.'

Binita tuts kindly and I can imagine her big wide smile. 'We have a free evening today as my brother and his wife are working in the take-a-way and when you rang, we were just discussing where to go for dinner tonight.'

An idea pops into my mind and I ask, 'Hey, why not come to our home and eat with us when you bring the food,' I say. 'We'd love to have you as our guests and my girlfriend, Barbie is here.'

I hear Binita take in a deep breath, and I hope I haven't offended her in any way. I suppose it's cheeky of me to ask people for dinner and expect them to bring their own food. And I'm not sure if I'll have shaken-up their traditions by doing this.

'Dear, Clive,' she says. 'We'd be honoured to join you as your guests. And along with your usual order I will bring some extra Indian treats that I'm sure you'll enjoy.'

We arrange a time and I hang up looking at Barbie who is grinning.

What?' I say and raise my eyebrow. Should I have checked with Barbie first? She might not want strangers here on her first night at home. I bite my lip and look at her.

She laughs now and shakes her head. 'Nothing, it's just that I think you're one of the kindest people I've ever met, Clive Thompson.'

Barbie is setting our small table in the corner of the lounge. It's a circular glass table with just enough room for the small rickety old dining chairs. We've talked about renewing it with something a little bigger but it's on that list of things that we never seem to get around to doing.

Of course, in the past, Sarah and I didn't entertain, so it was perfect. But now Barbie and I have her family around and our friends here, it is a little small. Since she moved in with me, we've had Tina and Jane to dinner, two of her friends from Durham, and of course her family on many occasions. I reckon Barbie is thinking the same while she sets placemats, glasses, cutlery, and napkins on the table.

'The first thing we are going to do tomorrow, Clive is shop for a bigger table,' she says, and I grab her from behind and wrap my arms around her waist.

'I hear you, loud and clear, boss,' I say into her ear and kiss her neck, to which she laughs.

Barbie heads into the kitchen saying, 'I'm just wondering if we should chill a bottle of wine, or maybe they don't drink alcohol? But I've got some strawberry sparkly water if they don't.'

This is a question I can't answer and putting plates into the warming oven I search Google on my phone. 'Ah, it says, consumption of alcohol is not recommended in Hinduism, but it is begrudgingly allowed for special occasions and occupations.'

Barbie nods, 'Okay, and if they're Christian or Muslim then we are covered whichever they decide to drink.'

We have both changed and Barbie is wearing a green skirt and jumper which she really suits. I hear the front doorbell ring and hurry along the hall shooing Spot out of the way to open the door.

Adhar and Binita are on the doorstep smiling.

'Come in,' I call excitedly. 'It's great to see you both.'

Adhar steps inside and hands me three large brown paper bags. The aroma swirling up from the food is amazing and I grin. 'Gosh, this smells good. Come and meet Barbie.'

Binita follows her husband into the hall and Barbie pops her head around the lounge door. 'Hellooo,' she says. 'Come in and let me take your coats.'
Binita removes a long black coat to reveal a gold glittery Sari and I gasp. She looks stunning. Her chocolate brown eyes seem to be dancing as she beams at us both.
Barbie takes her hand while they walk into the lounge and complements her Sari. 'That dress is gorgeous,' she says. 'I'd love to wear something like that!'
Adhar shakes my hand again. 'It's so nice to be invited to your home,' he says.
'You're more than welcome - we are the ones that are honoured to have you and your fantastic food.'
Barbie pours drinks for us all as we sit at the table, but I notice she is the only one drinking wine. We three all opt for water.
Binita begins to open the bags. 'I did bring your favourites, but I've cooked some extras which I hope you'll enjoy,' she says shyly.
'Oh, great,' I say. 'We both love to try new dishes.'
The women open containers filling serving dishes while I crunch into a poppadom and talk with Adhar.
He explains that when they first married his father bought them the take-a-way business to get them going. 'And, not to be big-headed, but we've made an enormous success of it so far. But, going forward, I would like to buy a restaurant. I have great plans for the future.'
We all begin to nibble on the paneer pinwheel and poppadom scoops appetisers. I gush over each one

while Barbie asks the names and how easy they are to cook. The women get along together very well, but I figure my Barbie would get along with anyone. I smile at her. She has put the new guests completely at ease in our home and I like the sound of this phrase. I store it in the back of my mind to add to my notes later.

Our home sounds permanent. And of course, it is our home now. It's not the house I shared with Sarah because that has long gone. Although Barbie hasn't made materialistic changes, she has filled the house with her love and warmth. I look around the room at her favourite photographs which make it feel more homely. As opposed to the stark plain walls before which made the room feel empty and echoey.

I shake myself back to the conversation as Binita is telling us about her background.

'Well, I came to England aged twelve and stayed with my cousins at first until I met Adhar, and we got married,' she says looking starry-eyed at her husband. 'And of course, I want the same things as him with a new restaurant, but I'd also like a baby to start our family. So, that's why I'm reading and writing more to improve my English.'

'But your English is excellent now,' Barbie tells her, and Binita blushes.

We all tuck into the delicious main course dishes they've brought and Barbie raves about the flavours, asking what spices are in each one. The variations on my favourite biriani are great and the smell from all the chicken dishes with different sauces and vegetables is amazing. Barbie takes a pen and finds an old bill to scribble down the names of them.

'Now,' she says. 'In the future I'll know what to ask for when we ring up.'

We all eat and talk then I push myself a little back from the table and rub my stomach. 'Okay, that's me stuffed now. I couldn't eat another thing; it was absolutely scrumptious!'

Binita smiles. 'You see, that is a word I will need to look up in the dictionary to find out the meaning?'

Barbie gets up from the table collecting empty containers together and affectionately squeezes her shoulder. 'It's just another word for delicious,' she says.

We all settle in the lounge area while Barbie heads into the kitchen to make coffee. Spot jumps up onto Binita's lap and begins to purr when she strokes the length of her back.

I nod. 'Oh, you've made a friend there,' I say. 'She's usually shy amongst new people in the house.'

While we relax in the comfortable chairs and chat, I ask them the three questions. Adhar answers mostly and explains the word, loitering to Binita. They both shake their heads and unfortunately didn't notice anyone without a specific purpose in the graveyard. There were no definite smells amongst the crowds as they walked around. And neither of them spoke to another person in the time they spent at the Abbey. I sigh.

'I'm so annoyed with myself,' Adhar says. 'More than anything else £400 is a lot of money to lose.'

I nod in agreement. 'I know, but don't beat yourself up about it,' I say. 'It wasn't until I had my money pinched that I knew Barbie was right and the back pocket of my jeans is a stupid place to carry money.'

Both the women nod, as if to agree and reprimand us while I think, how come women are savvier about these things than we men are?

I ask, 'And you haven't seen anyone suspicious around your business premises?'

Adhar shakes his head. 'Nope, that was the first thing the police asked us, but I just know the theft took place in the graveyard. This has nothing to do with our business.'

I smile feeling glad that I'm thinking along the same lines as our local police officers and our new friends get up to leave. Barbie helps Binita on with her coat and gives her a hug.

'You must come to our home next?' Binita says and follows Adhar out of the front door.

Chapter Seventeen

The following week I arrive early at the café to meet everyone. I order a coffee and decide it is warmer to sit inside than hang around the streets in the cold drizzle. I sit at one of the bigger tables and am glad of my choice when Matt arrives, and the waitress opens the door wide for him to wheel his chair inside.

She gives him a friendly smile and I jump up to move aside one of the small plastic chairs so he can wheel himself right up to the table.

'Hey,' he says. 'I thought I was going to be first to arrive, but I see you've beat me to it?'

I nod and order him a coffee. 'Do you want cake?'

He shakes his head. 'Nah,' he says. 'I'm putting too much weight on, and my girlfriend reckons she's going to leave me if I get fat.'

I can see he's joking, and I laugh. 'Ah, I can't believe that?'

He pushes his floppy blonde hair from his eyes. 'Nah, she wouldn't do now. If she were going to walk away it would have been when I came off my bike and we realised that I was paralysed. And, although I told her repeatedly to go and find herself a guy who could walk, she wouldn't. She's stuck to me like glue!'

I look at this young guy and am filled with admiration. How would I even contemplate getting through an accident like that with all the trauma and upset. He must have felt that his entire world had crashed down around him. The adjustments in his lifestyle have been huge and I'm not sure I'd be brave enough to meet something like that head-on.

I think of Barbie and know she'd be just like his girlfriend. As many times as I'd tell her to go, she would purse those lips of hers and stand fast. Which was something I had never been certain about with Sarah. I sigh knowing I'd been proven right as the temptation of a better life with Chuck in the USA had her packing the suitcase.

Thinking of Barbie now I say, 'Aah, my girlfriend nags me, too. She's always telling me off for eating junk food,' I say eyeing the strawberry cheesecake. 'Although, I don't think cake is sooo bad, is it?'

He grins. 'Probably not as healthy as a crunchy green apple.'

The waitress places his coffee mug down and he digs into his jean pocket and pays her. I'm wondering about his girlfriend now and realise out of the group I haven't had time to talk to Matt.

'So, where do you live,' I ask, 'in the city?'

He nods. 'Yeah, we've got a flat up at Peasholme near The Black Swan pub which is a great location and wheelchair friendly. The guy we bought the flat from had done all the alterations because he was in a wheelchair, so it was a good purchase, and we haven't had to do much to the property other than live there.'

'Oh, that's good, have you been together long?'

He rubs his jaw. 'About six years, I think. And that's another thing she'd give me earache about because I can never remember anniversaries and important dates!'

'Tell me about it,' I say. 'We've just had our first anniversary last weekend, and I did remember although if you ask me again in five years' time, I'll probably be the same as you and forget.'

Matt sips his coffee. 'You'd think I'd be good about dates, facts and figures with working part time in the library but I'm not. Although I do know important ones like, The Battle of Hastings in 1066 and how it was on the 14th of October.'

I laugh now and am intrigued to know about the library. I launch into my writing career so far and the book I've got listed on Amazon. I can tell he is genuinely interested about my novel, and I explain about self-publishing the book.

'Oh, God, so you're an author, a crime writer?'

And no matter how many times people say this to me I want to turn around and see if James Patterson or Peter James are behind me. They're what I think of as proper authors, not little old me bumbling my way through things.

I can feel my cheeks flush, and I shuffle on the chair. 'Well, I don't know if I can be called an author, I mean I don't have a traditional publisher in the sense of the word.'

'Hey,' he says. 'You've written a book, haven't you?'

'Er, well, yes, but…'

He shrugs his shoulders. 'In that case you're an author.'

I pull my shoulders back and pull out a business card from my flying jacket pocket. I give it to him and am delighted when he reads the details and admires the cover of my book.

Matt asks, 'So, have we got it in our library catalogue because I could look out for the book. I'd enjoy this, it sounds like my kind of read.'

I shake my head. I don't know anything about catalogues in libraries. 'Er, I don't think so,' I say. 'Am I allowed to put my book into the libraries and how do I go about that?'

Matt leans forward now and I see his eyes brighten. This is clearly something he knows well, and I can see his genuine wish to help people in the job he does. Obviously, he's what we call a people's person now-a-days and I liken to him all the more.

'Yes, of course, you can. If you find our website, PLR, which stands for Public Lending Right. The British Library runs the service and if you upload your book onto the system then library managers can order it,' he says. 'And I think you get a little payment each time the book is borrowed although, I'm not sure about that but all the details will be there.'

I sit back and whistle through my teeth. 'Well, as they say, you learn something new every day. I had no idea, and thanks for letting me know, Matt. I'll look into that tomorrow.'

I look up to see Grace and Henry walk through the door.

'Cooee, boys,' Grace says and plonks herself down into the chair near Matt. She pats his arm resting on the side of the wheelchair. 'And how are you both?'

Henry goes to the counter and orders their coffees just as Adhar opens the door and Binita walks through behind him.

'Clive, hello, how are you?' Binita asks and greets Grace who takes her hand and rubs it between her own.
I smile at the five of them sensing that they all know one another now and are interacting as a group of friends rather than complete strangers.
We all settle down with drinks and the two ladies tuck into a slice of strawberry cheesecake. I lick my lips wishing I'd had some now. There are discussions about the emails they've sent each other from the general introductory one I'd copied everyone onto.
I'm impressed that Grace and Henry have joined in as well because of their age. Barbie has told me in the past that I'm being ageist when I think along these lines. Even her eighty-eight-year-old mother texts on her mobile and I correct myself.
I know it's my task to bring the group to order now because I arranged this follow up meeting. I start by telling them what I've done so far but haven't seen anyone suspicious in the main attraction areas, and about the three questions I'd asked them all.
'I only have one slither of a lead that luckily Henry has remembered. Of course, this might not be related to pick pocketers, but you never know, it could lead to something.'
I explain about the girl in The Shambles asking for directions but that she might not have anything to do with the thefts.
Grace licks the strawberry jelly from her lips and delves into her handbag. She produces a photograph of her son's medal and shows it to Matt.

He looks at it and says, 'He was so brave, and you must miss him dreadfully?'
Grace nods and gives it to Adhar who tuts his annoyance. 'How can anyone steal this from you - it's appalling!'
I nod and watch Binita look over his shoulder. Her big eyes water and I hope she isn't going to get upset.
Matt brings out a photo of his wallet and hands it around to everyone. 'This was my wallet that was taken. I have a photograph because it was a birthday present from my girlfriend,' he says. 'I wish now that I hadn't left it in my jacket and carelessly hung it on the back of my chair. It was stupid of me, but I never dreamt I'd be robbed.'
'Bloody scoundrels!' Henry exclaims.
Grace pats his arm. 'Don't fire yourself up, love, think of your blood pressure.'
I watch the old man take a deep breath and he sips his coffee. 'I know, but really what is the world coming to when they thieve from a young lad confined to a wheelchair.'
Adhar says, 'You're right, its dreadful. And we've double checked everything at our take-a-way and have nothing suspicious around the premises to report. No strangers have been seen; therefore, I'm convinced it was pick pocketers in the graveyard.'
I sit back in my chair and look at this group of people with a strong bond between them. I'm determined more than ever to help and not give up until I can find some retribution for them all.

***

Barbie has gone to see her mam for the day, and I've seen her safely onto the early train to Durham. She'll be back this evening and I wander down through the city feeling deflated. Not because Barbie isn't with me because I know how much she loves to see her family but more the fact that I'm not getting anywhere with the pick pocketers and my little group of victims.

I frown, do I call them victims? I decide the answer is yes because all of them have been wounded in one way or another. I hadn't wanted to think of myself as a victim and in my own way I'd fought back against the mugger. But when I think of the hurt in Grace's face and the loss in Matt's eyes, I know they are sufferers too. I grind my back teeth and think of how Barbie wouldn't let me give up with the restaurant list until I'd found Tim and pull my shoulders back. I must keep going even if my trailing around the main attractions proves fruitless.

I've arranged more tours for this week and am talking regularly with Charles and the other leaders. So far, we've all drawn a blank.

'Of course,' Charles had said. 'These robberies could simply be an isolated case, and something committed by an out of towner.'

After I'd ended the call, I had thought of the phrase, out of towner, and knew that strictly speaking, it didn't fit because York is a city.

I pick up my pace planning to visit another three main attractions to look for suspicious people in the crowds around Monks Bar, Peasholme Green, and Clifford Tower. If I've covered these today, then it only leaves

The Shambles and The Jorvik Museum which I'll be doing tomorrow on a tour.

I head down towards Deangate and reach Monks Bar standing still to marvel at the sight. It's early in the morning and not many people are about so I enjoy the space to delight in the old building. I take a few photos with my phone as the sun comes up behind the old stonework.

York has more miles of intact city-wall than any other place in England. The walls are two miles long and it is known to take two hours to walk the length of them. They are sometimes known as the Bar Walls and the four gatehouses are known as Bars. Monks Bar is from the 14th century and used to be a self-contained fortress. It is thought to be over seven hundred years old.

On the front of the bar is an archway with murder-holes through which missiles and boiling water was often poured down onto attackers. The rooms above the gateway have had various uses over the years including a jail for rebellious Catholics in the 16th century.

I often ask on my tour if people can image pouring hot water out of the holes and down onto the protestant's underneath? It's at this stage there's usually a heated discussion about how religion played such an important part of our history. And to some extent, is still doing so, with which I must agree.

I decide it's not the best time to be on surveillance and smile at the use of the word. I imagine myself as the super sleuth Barbie calls me and chuckle while I Google the definition of private investigator. It tells me, they search for information about legal, financial, and personal matters. They offer services, such as verifying people's backgrounds and statements, finding missing persons, and investigating computer crimes.

Hmm, I muse, I'm quite good at collecting information and observing people like a PI would do but I'd draw the line at taking photographs of them. I think this would be an invasion of their privacy unless of course, I caught them in the act of breaking the law. Then I wouldn't hesitate.

I suppose pick pocketers don't come out onto the streets until there are crowds of people to blend in with and as it's quiet this morning, I'm probably not going to achieve anything. I am not due into the travel agency for another hour, so I head up to Peasholme Green.

This was an area originally known as a water meadow where peas were grown. Hence the name. I wander around knowing that Matt doesn't live far and wonder where his flat is in the area.

I stand outside The Black Swan Inn and remember Charles telling me the story about a woman called, Margaret Clitherow.

Margaret was an English saint and martyr of the Roman Catholic church, known as The Pearl of York. She was born in 1556 and married John Clitherow, a wealthy butcher and chamberlain of the city. She bore him three children and the family lived in The Shambles. John is not to be confused with the other butcher in The Shambles who killed his wife and her lover. Margaret converted to Roman Catholicism in 1574, although John belonged to the established church, he was supportive because his brother was a Roman Catholic priest. He was a kind man and paid her fines for not attending church services. She was first imprisoned in 1577 and then another twice at York Castle followed. Her third child, William was born in prison. Margaret risked her life by harbouring priests. Local tradition holds that she housed her clerical guests here in the Black Swan Inn where the Queen's agents were lodged.

I smile now and reckon for most men it's not a bad place to be hidden with beer and good food all day and night. And they sell a homemade beer called, Ghost Ale. Unfortunately, Margaret was sentenced to death. Although pregnant with her fourth child, she was executed on Lady Day in 1586, which also happened to be a Good Friday. It was in the Toll Booth at Ouse Bridge, where she was crushed to death by her own door which was the standard inducement to force a plea from prisoners.

I shiver thinking of this barbaric punishment and notice how quiet the green is today, and because I can't see anything or anyone suspicious, I walk back down to Tower Street where Clifford's Tower is situated in the city centre.

Clifford's Tower is one of best loved landmarks in the city. It is an old, fortified complex consisting of a sequence of castles, prisons, law courts and other buildings which were built over the last nine centuries on the south side of the river Foss. It is the largest remaining part of York Castle which was once the centre of government for the north of England.

If I reach this spot on my tours, I usually tell my customers, 'York is the most haunted city in the country, and you can read all about Dick Turpin in the museum here at the castle grounds.'

Today, I can't venture up the high grassy bank to the top because it is covered with scaffolding. English Heritage are putting a roof onto the tower which it has never had to preserve the building for the future. There are boards up surrounding the tower with diagrams of what the intended development will consist of and hopefully what it'll look like. The old steps up to the top will be secured and a wood roof will allow people to walk around on the top enjoying the panoramic views across the city and river which will be awesome.

Smiling, I know this will allow people in the city to do something York residents couldn't do seven hundred years ago. And this is definite progress, I think admiring the drawings and feel grateful to English Heritage for undertaking this mammoth restoration in our city.

I look around the front of the old museum and the law courts but there aren't many people around to observe. However, I do know that later in the day it'll be busy with families and tourists.

Turning the corner, I head down to the travel agency ready to start my shift. My head is still whirling with thoughts of the group and the pick pocketers, but I push these thoughts aside as I open the door and call out greetings to Jane and Tina.

Chapter Eighteen

I'm standing with my tour group of customers the following afternoon just after three. We've had a slight flurry of snowflakes this morning which has now stopped but it's very cold. I hadn't expected all twelve people to turn up, but they have and I'm glad that it hasn't been a wasted afternoon.

It's dusk already and I think of the sentence, these are the dark days before Christmas, which apparently is an old northern proverb.

There is one oldish couple with us, mid to late sixties, at a guess, and so far, they've been fit enough to keep up with our brisk pace through the city. They introduced themselves as Sally and Mike. I look at them and say, 'If I'm walking too fast just let me know, but I figure today is soooo cold it's best to keep on the move.'

Everyone is well-wrapped up against the cold in thick coats, boots, scarves, gloves, and hats. I wonder idly while I gather the people into a huddle how much revenue is made in the northeast from outerwear than in the south of the country.

Sally is wearing a bright red duffle coat and I remember Barbie saying last week how she'd love a new one because the toggles and straps on hers are worn out. I wonder, would this make a nice surprise gift for Christmas? Although we've decided, small gifts only, I'll have to give her a present on Christmas morning but is a duffle too practical? Would a piece of costume jewellery be better?

I shake my thoughts aside and concentrate on the group when Sally and Mike arrive last to our huddle. We've made our way down from St. Mary's Abbey into one of the quiet snickleways which will be my last chance to talk without crowds of people.

'I thought I'd stop here to tell you all about the Jorvik Museum as this will be our last stop on the tour and there's always lots of people in the queue for tickets,' I say and stomp my boots on the cobbles. Even with extra thick socks my toes are still cold. 'And I know some of you have already said that you have tickets to go inside when we finish.'

Three young women in their twenties nod and I wonder why they're not in the pubs doing what all the other twenty years olds do in the city. I shrug and begin.

'The Jorvik Viking Centre is a museum and visitor attraction which holds lifelike mannequins and life-size dioramas depicting Viking life in the city. And for those of you going inside it's true to life as it was back then even down to the realistic smells of grass and manure! So, hold a peg over your noses when you go around. You'll be taken through the dioramas in a small carriage equipped with speakers which takes sixteen minutes. The centre was created by the York Archaeological Trust in 1984 and is one of our most popular attractions especially for school children,' I say. 'But there shouldn't be too many schoolkids at this time of year. They'll be in classrooms making Christmas decorations or rehearsing for pantomimes.'

One of the young women says, ‘Well, that’s why we are going inside because we’re doing teacher training.’

‘Oh, right,’ I say. ‘Well, you’ll be travelling around recreated Viking streets where archaeology is brought to life in this unique underground centre. I hope none of you are claustrophobic?’

The three women smile, and I look past them getting ready to move everyone down the snickleway and across to the Jorvik. And that’s when I see two youngsters hovering at the end.

The girl, I’d guess looks about eighteen to twenty. An arty-student type with black spikey hair and a yellow head band. She’s wearing an old Afghan coat which looks like it’s seen better days. The coat skims her knees in black jeans, and she is wearing dirty long brown boots. She is tall and has her head lowered towards a much younger lad obviously talking to him. She’s waving her arms around and flapping her hands as though she is telling him off.

He is scruffy and must be very cold in a grey fleece hoodie jacket and torn tracksuit bottoms. His trainers are dirty too and I wonder why they’ve both got muddy footwear. I frown and walk slowly towards them with my group following behind me.

A flashing memory pings into my mind, and I remember seeing them earlier. I’m almost sure they’d been in St. Mary’s Abbey when I’d stopped to talk to the group. With the fall of sleety snow, the grassy paths had been wet and muddy.

I need to keep my eye on these two and lead everyone past the couple who are still arguing although not as noisily as before.

I walk everyone across the road, and we stop outside the ticket office area in front of the Jorvik. A queue of about fifteen people is waiting to buy tickets within the barriers outside the brick archways. The street is busy with shoppers bustling around each other laden with bags. I look up to the overhead Christmas streetlights twinkling and decide to halt the tour outside the gift shop.

'Can we just stop here,' I say. 'Well, everyone that's it for today and I hope you've all enjoyed our tour.'

I do my usual low bow and receive a ripple of applause. One by one they head towards me and press notes into my hand which I gratefully receive. Out of the corner of my eye I'm watching Sally and Mike at the back of the group then see arty student approach them.

I see her smile at Sally and start to talk to her although I'm too far away to hear her exact words. Then I see the young lad move stealthily up behind Sally.

Sally has one of those tote bags like Barbie. It's quite big and doesn't have any fasteners other than a pair of wood parallel handles on either side. Barbie reckons it's meant to serve as an easy carryall.

I'm stepping towards them now and my heart begins to thump. Oh, my, God, these look dodgy, and they could be after Sally's bag. I move forwards quickly sidestepping a woman pushing a buggy. No, I fume, they're not going to get away with Sally's purse like they did with Grace's. I must stop them.

My pulse is banging in my ears as I rush towards them but I'm not quick enough to stop hoodie lift Sally's purse from the top of her bag. 'Sally! Mike!' I yell. 'Lookout – he's got your purse!'

Hoodie dashes off down the path but knowing I'd never catch him I shout at the top of my voice, 'Stop him in the grey hoodie - he's a thief!'

Four men wearing rugby shorts turn the corner onto the street. As Hoodie now starts to run, two of the men tackle him to the ground. Mike chases down to them and I see the rugby men take Sally's purse from Hoodie and thrust it into Mike's hands who clasps it safely to his chest.

I rush to arty student and take her firmly by the arm. Sally pulls her mobile out of her duffle coat and rings the police.

'Get off me you bloody pervert,' Arty student shouts. 'It's got nothing to do with me!'

I'm not sure how to arrest someone but she is yelling at me and trying to pull away. I know I must do something. Suddenly, I remember a late-night drama I'd watched with a scene in London. I reckon if it's okay to do this in London then it should work here in York.

I take in a deep breath and feel myself begin to calm down. My heart stops thumping, and I'm more in control of the situation. I lift my chin and say quite clearly, 'I'm making a citizen's arrest and I will hold you until the police arrive.'

Arty student continues to struggle against me as I'm holding both her arms. I am trying not to use too much force because she is a girl, and I wouldn't like to hurt her. But she kicks out at my shins with her heavy boot, and I yelp.

Sally comes to my defence and grabs her shoulder. She shakes her hard and shouts, 'Stop kicking him, you thieving little toe-rag!'

A crowd have gathered around us and an old woman yells, 'Shame on you, lass!'

The young woman with the buggy stands in front of us and her baby begins to howl.

A middle-aged man with two big shopping bags places them down on the pavement and shouts, 'Well done you - it's about time somebody stood up to these bloody villains.'

Arty student is still screaming, 'I'm not a thief – I didn't do anything – leave me alone!'

Thankfully, I hear a siren in the distance and know the police will soon be here.

'Please don't kick me like that,' I say. 'Just stand still until the police arrive then I'll let you go. You can cooperate with them although I don't think they'll like you kicking out at people.'

Soon, the police are with us, and two policewomen have taken hold of arty student. Another two police officers are arresting Hoodie further down the street. They march him up to us and Mike hurries along behind them.

Within minutes they are both taken down the road to the police van and I let out a huge sigh of relief.

'Good, God, I can't believe that happened,' Sally cries when Mike reaches us and hands her the purse.

He's red in the face and bends forwards with his hands on his knees taking deep breaths then puffs, 'You'd better check to see if anything is missing?'

I lean against the streetlamp and catch my breath. Although there's nothing to say for definite that it was these two who robbed Grace, Adhar, and Matt, I've a sneaking suspicion that it is them. I want to whoop with joy. And even if it isn't them at least I've stopped Sally being robbed and this duo will be off the streets for a while.

I feel Mike grasping and shaking my hand firmly. 'Thanks, mate,' he says. 'You've been great. I really appreciate what you've done to help us.'

I shrug my shoulders and want to say, oh, it was nothing but instead I grin like an idiot knowing that, yes, it was something. I feel the same warm glow inside that I'd felt the day Charles and I had pinned Tim to the ground. And without sounding overly dramatic, I think we're fighting back against these crooks. I turn to the police officer to give him a statement.

Chapter Nineteen

Sitting in the police station, Zoe's first thoughts were that she'd get chucked out of the hostel. She had hoped to stay there until the council gave her a flat because out of all the places she'd moved through since leaving home, she liked York the most.

But now of course, because she had broken the hostels rules and been caught thieving, she would have to move on once more. She knew the police would raid her room and find the hidden money then she would be back to square one. Penniless, alone, and scared.

She trembled and pulled the old Afghan coat around her chest staring at her reflection in the glass window. With her black spikey hair and yellow hair band she looked nothing like the tall gangly girl with long blonde curls who had fled from her home late at night.

The memories of her last night at home filled her mind and she lifted her chin. Being here in the police station was scary, but she wasn't as frightened as she had been back then.

Her mam had gone off to an overnight hen party in Glasgow and she'd been in the house alone with the silver-haired monster. He'd pounced upon her in the kitchen and pinned her up against the old pantry.

He was extremely fast for an oldish guy and his hands seemed to be everywhere on her body. Grasping, pummelling, and tearing at the front of her top. She'd been terrified and tried to fight back, but he'd been twice the size of her. He had pulled down her jogger bottoms and she had known what was going to happen.

In one final effort she howled like an animal and grabbed a glass from the nearby bench then hit him over the head. He'd staggered back in shock, and she had run. She had run as though the devil himself was behind her.

Chapter Twenty

Barbie and I are walking hand in hand down to the café to meet the group. I've emailed them to arrange the get-together and told them I have good news. I haven't gone into details until I'd spoken to the police but can't help having a spring in my step now as we walk.

Barbie has insisted upon coming with me and she swings ours hands backwards and forwards as though we were kids in a schoolyard.

'Ah, Clive, let me come with you? I'm the girlfriend of our local hero and I want to celebrate with your friends.'

I'd protested, 'But Barbie, I'm not a hero.'

She had pouted. 'Well, you are to me and everyone who knows us. You should be proud about what you've done for Grace, Adhar, and Matt.'

I had looked into those warm soft eyes and relented. 'Okay, you can come along, but don't keep calling me a hero.'

Yesterday, I'd felt like I did after stopping Charles from being mugged. Tina and Jane had rung, and Barbie's family, but still I had been uncomfortable with the praise and compliments. Sally had posted on Twitter about the pick pocketers arrest and thanked me profusely. She'd said lovely complimentary words about Tommy and his tour company. Of course, he'd been cock-a-hoop when I saw him later about the brilliant publicity.

I think his words had been, 'You're a valued member of staff, Clive.'

I'd hoped he would follow his words with the offer of a pay rise, but he didn't. There'd been whisperings from the other tour leaders calling an increase in wages, danger money and I was concerned. In fact, it had sent shivers up my back because I don't want to be finished from the job. Although my intentions have been good and I'd helped people that were victimised, I don't want a reputation for someone who is always surrounded by trouble. Tommy might not like the police being at the business on a regular basis, although it had only happened twice.

I'd sloped off into the bathroom, but Barbie had followed not giving up on our conversation.

'Clive, it's just because it's a new experience for you to feel proud about your achievements. But you must let people show their gratitude. And I can't see what the difference is from reading great tributes and praise in reviews for your book on Amazon? You love that don't you?'

I had thought about her words while deliberating in the shower. I decided that yes, it was true. I loved to hear people's accolades on Amazon, so maybe it was a good comparison and the way to think of it going forwards.

When I'd got out of the shower, she had been sitting on the closed toilet seat and raised an eyebrow. 'So?'

'Well, yes, of course, I love reading the reviews,' I'd said towelling myself dry. 'But that's on a screen and not face to face with people or talking on the telephone. It seems different somehow.'

However, when I'd come downstairs this morning dressed in my good jeans and Fisherman's blue sweater, she was waiting for me in the hall. She had on those tight-fitting jeans and long boots that I love with a pink fluffy sweater, and I'd melted inside. I didn't think I would ever be able to refuse this woman a thing. And really, I mused, why would I never want her with me?

I push open the door to the café now and gasp. A long table has been placed down the back of the room and the group are sitting there all smiling at me. There's a chair at the top of the table with a blue helium balloon tied to it saying, THANK YOU, in capital letters.

Barbie claps her hands in delight and Binita hurries to us and gives her a big hug. I'm flabbergasted and walk slowly towards them feeling my cheeks flush. Henry and Adhar jump up and shake my hand heartily and Matt gives me a thumbs up sign.

I walk around the table to him and shake his hand too.

The table is set with a white cloth. There are two cafetieres of coffee and a teapot on the table with what looks like a proper tea service not just the usual mugs. Two tall cake stands are in the centre laden with slices of different lemon, chocolate cake, and Victoria sponge slices.

'Ah, folks, you didn't need to do all this,' I say. My voice sounds and feels choked with emotion when I sit down at the head of the table.

Barbie sits next to Binita who introduces her to Grace, Henry, and Matt.

While tea and coffee are poured and Binita hands around cakes, I look at everyone. This is alien to me and can't believe they've done all of this. I've never had a celebratory meal or party of any kind in my honour.

When growing up, my schoolfriends friends never came to our house in Doncaster because it was known as a drug den to get a quick fix, and their parents boycotted us.

And, of course, Sarah had been given these celebratory occasions but that had been from her friends at the hospital because she'd done important things helping patients so deserved all the congratulations.

However, it doesn't matter how many times Barbie calls me a hero, I can't see that I deserve this. The drinks and cakes are lovely, and I keep a smile planted firmly on my face while I tuck into a slice of sponge. I remember Grace telling me that her niece knew the manageress and I figure she's arranged everything. I wonder if they all chipped in to pay for this special tea, and if they did, it worries me that they've spent money on a situation which has already cost them dearly, not just in cash but in mementoes too.

I look at Grace with a small soft blue hat on the back of her grey hair. She's wearing a pale blue skirt and jacket with a white blouse and sips her tea in a classy ladylike manner.

I wonder if my grandma had money if she would have looked like Grace? She had died when I was eight and my recollections of her are scant. She usually wore old jumpers and slacks with a flowery apron over the top. Her face had been very lined with thin pursed lips, but she did have bright blue eyes that always lit up when I went to see her.

I shuffle in my seat longing to tell Grace that the police have found her sons medal in the purse. I smile and listen to her telling Henry off as he picks a second slice of cake.

Even though the group know I've found the pick pocketers they don't know what the police have done and found out. But I'm waiting until we've all eaten to tell them what I know.

Now, that I can see everyone is nearly finished and the chatter is quietening, I pick up a spoon and gently tap the side of the teapot.

Everyone turns to look at me and I smile. 'I've rather a lot to tell you all, so, I'll get started, shall I?'

Grace and Henry nod. Adhar folds his hands onto the table and leans forwards with Binita looking over his shoulder. Matt beams at me and Barbie gives me a little wink from the corner of her eye, as if to say, go for it you'll be fine.

'Well, for those who didn't see it on social media, I'll explain. I was at the end of my tour outside The Jorvik and had noticed a girl in her twenties and a younger lad hovering behind a couple called, Sally and Mike, who had been on the tour. While the girl kept Sally talking the young lad grabbed her purse from the top of her bag and fled off down the street. Luckily, two men in rugby shirts tackled him to the ground and her husband got her purse back. I kept hold of the girl and did a citizen's arrest until the police arrived and carted them both off.'

'Splendid!' Henry says then chortles. 'And rugby men are just the ones to do a skilful tackle.'

Binita grins at me and Adhar nods his head in approval. 'Well done!'

Matt does a little hand clap and laughs. 'Hey,' he says. 'I'd like to have seen that tackle.'

I nod at them all. 'So, the police have been in touch a few times and the main thing to tell you is that they have raided the hostel where the pick pocketers were staying. I sent them the two photographs that Grace and Matt emailed to me of the medal and Matt's wallet,' I take a deep breath to steady myself. 'And, in the hostel room, although the money has gone from them both, they have found which looks like Matt's wallet and your purse, Grace. They've told me the medal is still inside!'

I'm not prepared for her outburst, but she cries out aloud. 'Ooooh, thank you, Clive.' She bursts into huge sobs. 'God bless you!'

Barbie puts her arm around Grace and comforts her and Henry is up from his seat in a shot. He hurries to me grabbing my hand and shaking it so hard that I'm alarmed at the old man's strength. 'Clive, I… I can't begin to thank you enough!'

His wrinkly eyes are wet, and I can tell he is holding tears at bay. I feel emotional myself and clear my dry throat. 'Er, it's okay,' I say. 'I'm just pleased that I could help.'

Henry nods and wipes his face on the sleeve of his brown cardigan. 'Yes, I know but you didn't give up, and kept looking which the police haven't done,' he stutters. 'W…we'll forever be in your debt.'

I feel as though I should stick up for the police and say, 'Well, I know how busy they are and concentrate upon more serious crimes. And, they might have traced the pick pocketers too, given more time.'

But Henry shakes his head. 'No, I don't think that would have happened, young man,' he says. 'It's been your concentrated effort on the lookout that's won the day.'

He shuffles back around the chairs and takes holds of Grace's hand across the table squeezing it tightly.

Adhar says, 'Well done, Clive, I completely agree with Henry. As we say in cricket, you've played a blinder, and have been such a good friend to us all.'

Binita claps her bird-like hands together. 'Oh yes, you've certainly been that.'

I look at the vibrant red Sari she is wearing today and feel my cheeks flush as crimson as her outfit. I put my cool hands to them. 'Aww, give over,' I say.

Grace comes to me now dry eyed with her arms open. She wraps them around my shoulders and pulls my head into her large chest. I feel like I'm suffocating in her blue jacket but she's so warm and smells of lavender that I feel emotion sweep through me again.

I can hear Barbie giggle and raise my eyes above one of Grace's arms. She's got her hand over her mouth smothering her laughter and I slowly peel myself out of Graces embrace.

'So, to continue,' I say and take Grace's hand now that she has released me. 'The police have given me a contact number for you to ring then you can go and retrieve your valuables. I'm just sorry all your money has gone, especially for Adhar and Binita, it was a lot to lose.'

Grace ambles back to her chair. 'Dear, God, it doesn't matter about the money,' she says. 'Well, not to us anyway, our keepsake is more important.'

Grace sits back down then reaches out to Binita. 'Although, I'm sorry you had all of your hard-earned cash taken.'

Binita nods and smiles her thanks.

Matt speaks up. 'Me too, getting the wallet back that my girlfriend bought me is more important,' he says pushing his floppy fringe from his eyes. 'Where did the police find them? You said it was in a hostel?'

I nod remembering the connection to Matt. 'Oh, yeah, apparently, they've been staying up near Peasholme Green somewhere.'

'No way? Really!' Matt says. 'Jeez, to think I've been living so close to them all of this time and didn't know.'

I can see the shock in his face, and I nod. 'Of course, the police aren't allowed to give out details of exactly where, but I think there's a couple of centres up there?'

Matt nods. 'Yes, there is, but I'm not sure which are for the homeless, and which aren't, nowadays.'

Henry grumps, 'Of course, the crooks in all of this have the right to have their details protected which is an absolute disgrace,' he says. 'And it's poor sods like us that are left to suffer and be short of cash by them.'

I shrug my shoulders not wanting to get into a discussion about Arty student and Hoodie. I know nothing about them and don't particularly want to at this stage. I figure, I've done my bit finding them. Unlike Tim, I don't have anything to gain by investigating more.

My top lip is beginning to sweat, and I squirm in the chair.

Barbie comes around to me and stands behind my chair. I can feel her hands on my shoulders, and she squeezes them in support. I sense that she knows I'm not comfortable talking about the pick pocketers any longer.

'I think it's time we made a move if you are going to make that dentist appointment,' she says.

I know fine well that I have no such appointment but am grateful to her for rescuing me. I glance at my watch. 'Oh yes, we'd better get going now.'

I get up and pull on my jacket then wander around each of my friends in turn with kisses on cheeks and shaking of hands. With promises to stay in touch, Barbie carries the balloon and heads out of the café first. I step outside behind her into the fresh air where I take a huge sigh of relief.

Chapter Twenty-One

Barbie and I are going shopping this morning. I'd seen the determined look in her eye when she announced that we were going to buy a bigger table for the lounge. It was that look as if to say, don't even think about arguing, and I had dressed for the full day out shopping.

The bubble of gorgeousness that is my girlfriend, and just as I say this phrase to myself, I decide we're too old to be saying girl and boyfriend. Of course, I'm hoping soon to be saying, this is my fiancé, or this is my wife.

She pulls on her coat, and I open the front door.

'Shall we look in the big shop on Micklegate,' I say locking the door behind us and stepping onto the pavement. From our house on Victor Street, it is only a short five-minute walk-up Nunnery Lane to the shop.

Barbie shakes her head. 'You're just suggesting that shop because it's the easiest distance and you don't like looking around different places.'

I sigh. She's got me in one, I think, but weakly protest. 'Ah, that's not fair,' I say matching her stride. 'I'm coming along, aren't I?'

She smiles. 'Yeah, but I know you've no interest in shopping whatsoever, and I want to look at everything that's on offer before deciding which to choose.'

We set off in the opposite direction down into the town centre in silence. I don't want today to be quarrelsome, so I drape my arm around her shoulder as we walk, and she grins.

The weather this morning has turned milder and considering we are only a few weeks away from

Christmas, I doubt whether we are going to have a white Christmas that everyone, apart from me, longs for. I tell her this as we stand in M&S home section looking at a couple of tables but although she nods at my comment, I can tell her mind is firmly planted on the task in hand.

I sigh, it's not that I don't like snow because if you're indoors, warm and cosy then to look out of the window at the pretty scene is fine. It's the disruption it causes in and around the city that I dislike.

I break my train of thought when Barbie tugs at my sleeve.

'Do you think, wood or glass,' she murmurs and raises an eyebrow. 'Which do you think would suit the lounge best?'

I'd love to say that I really couldn't care but I smile instead. 'Well, both will stand the test of time I suppose but glass might be a little dangerous when Libby and Jack come to stay?'

The tall young sales assistant launches into his speel about the toughened safety glass that is used now and of course, M&S always use top-end materials from guaranteed suppliers. But when Barbie whips out her tape measure and notes down the length and width on a little jotter pad, I smile at the look on the young man's face. His spiky hair appears to stand up even further from his forehead when he realises exactly what he's dealing with. I give him a small wink and he explains the quality associated with the high price tag and an explanation of a six-week delivery time.

Barbie frowns. 'Ah, I didn't think we'd have to wait so long, Clive. I'd hoped to have it for Christmas when the family come to visit.'

I pull my shoulders back. 'Well, this isn't the only shop, lets continue and see what else is available for delivery now.'

I can't bear to look at her face if she is worried or disheartened. I always like to see her happy and carefree. I take her hand while she drops the tape measure back into her bag and we leave the shop.

Three hours later, after exhausting the other shops with the same message about delivery, we head back and cross over Skeldergate Bridge. The river is still and calm even though there's a stiff breeze blowing, and we hurry across to our side of the bridge.

The bridge is old stonework with beautiful views on either side of the river. Rentable small boats and cruisers are moored further downstream in these winter months. On both sides are old stone steps from the bridge down to the river's edge which is a lovely walk in the summer. My stomach rumbles and I pull Barbie's arm in the direction of Middleton's Hotel on Cromwell Road.

It's a few streets away from our house and en-route to the shop on Micklegate, and we've yet to have a disappointing meal there. Being tucked away down the road, the hotel is not well-known for dining, so it's always easy to get a table and the food is consistently good. I've often thought that if it passes Barbie's test then it's the best recommendation to have. Inside it is

light and airy with simple but good décor and we both tuck into a hearty bowl of beef stew with crusty bread.
I want to tease her about the shop on Micklegate which I'd suggested in the first place but decide this would be unkind, so I joke, 'Well, failing this last shop, there's always Ikea online?'
She laughs and kicks me under the table. 'Em, the old table we are ditching is from Ikea so the answer to that is a resounding, no way!'
I grin seeing her happy face back in place and we leave the hotel heading up Nunnery Lane.

***

The moment we enter the shop I know this is going to be successful. There's a relaxed atmosphere when a woman greets us and asks if she can help. I decide, this is the one-to-one customer service that you don't get in chain stores. And although the price will be more, sometimes I think it is worth paying extra to receive the help and attention. Although I don't know this lady, she fills me with confidence, and I have high hopes we can find a table that Barbie likes and wants.
Barbie pauses at a beautiful wood table with six high-back dining chairs to match and I watch her eyes fill with longing while she lovingly strokes the wood. She explains the measurements we need for a table to fit our lounge space then the issue of delivery before Christmas.
The saleswoman raises a finely pencilled eyebrow. 'Hmm, let's see,' she mutters and hurries to the corner of the large room to the desk and telephone. 'That one you're looking at is too big of course, but we did have a

smaller version and I'm wondering if I can find it in the warehouses. Why not have a browse while I see what I can do.'

I wander behind Barbie mooching around the shop, and she simpers looking at all the glorious soft furnishings. A huge, and I mean huge, chandelier hangs from the ceiling, and I see Barbie stand underneath with the lights twinkling on her soft blonde hair. She looks delightful pointing upwards with a wishful expression on her face. I can tell she is daydreaming about the chandelier, but I shake my head in mock-consternation.

'Don't even think about it!' I say. 'It's far too big for our small lounge.'

She nods and I look across at the saleswoman then raise my eyebrow as if to ask if I may sit on one of the big armchairs.

The woman waves her consent and I sink into the seat gratefully. I must admit the chair is as comfortable as it looks, and I think of our saggy old sofa.

Waiting on my own while Barbie is wandering around stroking fabrics and looking at price tags on throws and cushions, I have a secret wish that I could win the lottery and give her the beautiful home she deserves to live in. She is so special that that I'd love to see her surrounded with classy décor and furniture. Although, I know if I told her this, she'd deny a wish for such materialistic things. But all the same, I would love to be able to give Barbie her heart's desire.

The woman at the desk cries, 'Yes! I've found it!'

Barbie hurries over to her and I can tell by the grin on her face that the table she'd been trying to find is ours for the taking. I breathe a sigh of relief and try not to think of the price tag. When I ease back in the chair, something sticks in my side and pull a leaflet from my pocket.

It had arrived this morning and when we'd left the house, I'd pushed it into the pocket of my coat. The leaflet is from the local neighbourhood watch group and while Barbie is busy paying for the table with her credit card, I begin to read.

With the transaction completed and Barbie grinning at a delivery date of Saturday morning the two women walk towards me.

'Ah,' the saleswoman says. 'I see you live local and have received one of our leaflets?'

I nod. She looks at me and smiles. I reckon she's early sixties at least and very well groomed. Her short grey hair is stylish and her long brown tunic with matching trousers are obviously a good cut and quality.

She says, 'I just live on Tower Street which is around the corner from Friars Terrace where Rodger lives who runs the neighbourhood watch group.'

I smile. 'Oh right, the posh side of the bridge, then,' I say and laugh.

She giggles and looks girl-like. 'Well, I don't know about that because we have to access my house through a long narrow walkway, so I'm definitely not posh but my cottage is small, and it is built with Yorkshire stone.'

I can tell she's proud of our heritage by the way she lifts her shoulders.

She holds out her hand and says, 'I'm Daphne Scott. I own and run the shop.'

I scramble up out of the chair and take her small thin hand. The large diamond in her ring glistens in the sun streaming through the window. I want to gasp at the size of the stone, but I see the look of warning in Barbie's eyes standing behind her. So, I shake her hand and smile back.

'I'm Clive Thompson,' I say. 'And this is, Barbie, we live down on Victor Street.'

She nods. 'Oh, that's a nice little street it always looks secluded and quiet.'

'Yeah, it is, I'm happy living in this area,' I say. 'It's great for getting into the city but far enough away not to be in the hustle and bustle.'

Daphne nods. 'You're right of course, and have you had many burglaries in your street?'

This question takes me completely by surprise. 'Burglaries?'

She frowns. 'Yes, that's why we're holding the meeting tonight. We've had four burglaries in the last two weeks around here so we are all getting together to see if there's anything we can do.'

I shake my head and raise an eyebrow at Barbie. 'I haven't heard of any, have you?'

Barbie shakes her head too. 'No, but there again we don't see much of the neighbours in the winter months to make conversation.'

I decide this situation is something we should be involved with and twirl the leaflet in my hand. 'Okay,'

I say. ‘We’ll come along tonight to Friar Street and see if there’s anything we can do to help.’

Daphne heads over to another customer who has entered the shop door and we leave calling, ‘See you tonight.’

***

Once home, Barbie and I dismantle the old Ikea table ready for Saturday’s delivery of the new one. We decide to keep the old table and fold-up chairs in the garden shed.

Barbie says, ‘You never know, it might come in useful for potting plants when I get the garden sorted.’

She heads into the kitchen to make tea while I sink into our saggy sofa. Bringing our tea back she places the mugs on the coffee table and snuggles up close. I’m reading the leaflet again which is addressed to, Mr. G. C. Thompson, and she looks over my shoulder. ‘I keep forgetting that you don’t use your fist name, Gordon,’ she says.

I smile. ‘I know, it’s daft really but I still have torturous memories from schooldays when the other kids used to call me, Gordon-the-gopher!’

She slides her hand under my brown woolly sweater and tickles my ribs. ‘Ah, I’m so sorry that you had a troubled childhood, Clive. When I think of mine and how I was molly-coddled, it seems grossly unfair.’

I can see her wince but not wanting to talk about something we’ve been through many times before, I shake the memories from my mind.

I read aloud the information on the leaflet. 'Jeez, it's awful to think that we've had these burglaries in the area, and we didn't know anything about it?'

Barbie nods. 'I know I was shocked when Daphne told us that. Although hopefully, we are secure here because we tend to come and go at various times of the day,' she says. 'And we've no set routine like other workers have doing nine till five.'

I think about her words and nod. 'True, but I think it's something that we should bear in mind,' I say. 'So, are you going to come along tonight because I'm definitely going.'

'Yes, like I've said before, Clive, where you go, I follow,' she says and smiles. 'We're a double act now, like it or not.'

I grin. 'Oh, I like it, all right,' I say. 'In fact, I'm loving it.'

I remember my words to Daphne about trying to help our neighbours and decide how great it would be if I could make a difference in the area.

'What?' Barbie asks. 'What's whizzing about in that mind of yours now, my little super sleuth.'

I tut and shake my head then smile at the profession she's given me. 'I'm not a sleuth, and would never want to be a private investigator, but I do like the idea of being a specialist to help victims of crimes,' I say. 'Maybe more of a leading light.'

She laughs. 'Well, Clive, your light will always shine brightly for me, and I'd follow your lead anywhere.'

Barbie begins to kiss the side of my neck and I snuggle further down into the sofa. She wraps one of her legs over my lap and I know where these actions are taking us. I squeeze her tightly and murmur into her hair. ‘In a way it helps me feel better for my misspent youth, Barbie. I think of it as a means of giving something back to society.’

Chapter Twenty-Two

'Come, in! You're very welcome,' says a gentleman who looks and sounds flamboyant.

I've knocked on the correct numbered door on Friars Terrace and Barbie is gripping my hand while we stand on the top step. I look upwards at the three floors to the property and know that estate agents would call this a town house. Barbie whispered to me earlier that it looked very grand and Edwardian in structure. A shiver runs up my back.

'Hello,' I say. 'I'm Clive, and this is Barbara.'

I see and hear Daphne hurrying along the grand hallway towards us calling, 'Oh, Rodger, this is the couple I told you about earlier. They live on Victor Street,' she says.

We are warmly ushered inside by them both along the hall. I gape at the amazing pieces of artwork hung on the walls and the plush red carpet my trainers sink into when I walk slowly behind them.

I can feel Barbie's hand begin to sweat as she too looks around in amazement at the high ceilings and deep coving. I figure the hallway alone is the size of our whole downstairs in Victor Street.

However, this is nothing compared to the huge double-fronted lounge I step into. It completely takes my breath away and I gasp at the spectacular views across and down the river from both windows.

There are another three people sitting on a long, green-leather Chesterfield sofa and I stifle a chortle at the difference to this and our saggy settee at home. A chandelier hangs from the ceiling plaster rose that looks even bigger than the one inside Daphne's shop. I watch Barbie look up to it and grin wondering if Daphne furnished the house for Rodger. Although the man looks more than capable of doing this himself.

I look at our host when he scurries across the room to pour us both a glass of wine. He's short with a flock of grey hair dramatically swept over the top of his head to hide the baldness that is appearing. I guess he is early seventies with a smooth face and deep brown eyes. He has a thin purple scarf draped around his shoulders over a lilac shirt which is open at the neckline. I decide he will make an amazing character for my novel and smile while Rodger introduces us to his partner, Simon.

I shake Simon's hand. Where, Rodger's voice is light and excitable, Simon's is gruff and deep. I figure Simon must be at least twenty years younger than Rodger and when we explain where we live, he tells us that he is a solicitor and works around the corner on Clifford Street.

Simon excuses himself to leave and change out of his work suit while Rodger almost skips in front of the people on the sofa and claps his chubby hands together. I hear the tinkle of two thin bracelets he is wearing.

'Now, this is Clive and Barbara who live on Victor Street.'

I smile at everyone while Rodger introduces each person. 'This is Dorothy Blackwell who lives on Tower Place, and Paul Robbins who lives on Nunnery Lane, and finally, Susan Shepherd who lives on Cromwell Road.'

Barbara smiles at everyone when Daphne steps forwards and tells the group that we've just bought a table and chairs and how she met us in her shop. Daphne sits down on a chaise lounge in front of the window and Barbie joins her.

I perch on the end of a matching green armchair and rub the smoothness of the leather arm rest. I sip my wine while Rodger joins me and squats down onto a green leather stool. Automatically, I offer him the chair because he is an older man, but he waves his arm noncommittally around in the air. 'No, stay where you are,' he says. 'I'm fine here on the pouffe.'

I swallow another chortle down in my throat because I don't think I've ever heard a man say the word pouffe but decide this does suit him rather well.

Rodger smiles. 'I'm so glad you could join us this evening,' he says. 'Especially when Simon told me that he'd discovered you on twitter and you're the tour leader who arrested the mugger and pick-pocketers – well done you!'

I shrug my shoulders not liking that my reputation now comes before me, but at the same time I can't help lifting my chin and smiling at his compliments.

I nod. 'Er, it was more luck than anything else,' I say trying to play down the heroics.

Rodger grins. 'Well, hopefully, you might be able to help us in some small way because we'd like you to fight our corner if you know what I mean? Or at least try to stop more burglaries from happening.'

I sip the wine which is too sweet for my taste and feel my cheeks cringe. I place the crystal glass on a nearby occasional table. I'm thankful for the coaster because I'd hate the glass to leave a circle on the rosewood. It wouldn't matter at our house because the side table we have is veneer, but I reckon this table must have cost a mint.

'So,' I ask. 'Has everyone here been broken into and robbed?'

His bright eyes cloud over, and he nods. 'Yes, we've all been burgled and had things stolen, well, all except Daphne who returned early and disturbed the thieves as they fled out the back door. But they had a sack full of her stuff ready to take,' he says and shakes his head. 'It's such a terrible situation.'

I'm shocked to discover the number of burglaries in our area and ask, 'And this was all during the last two weeks?'

Rodger simpers. 'Y…yes, and you can see that most people around here are not shall we say, Easter chicks anymore. So, it's dreadfully upsetting to think of thieves rifling through your drawers.'

I smile at the connotation but at the same time sympathise totally with him. 'I'm so sorry, did you have much of value taken?'

He frowns. 'Well, as you can see, I'm an art dealer, so to me, yes the paintings they stole held artistic value, but I suppose to others who are not art-lovers, it wouldn't be a great deal,' he says then sucks on his thick bottom lip. 'I had three paintings taken which on a good day at auction would fetch around one to two thousand a piece.'

I whistle through my teeth and shake my head. 'Jeez, but that's terrible!'
Rodger smirks. 'I know, but it shows what heathens they actually were because the painting above the fireplace is worth over ten grand and they didn't take that one.'
I digest this information and tug on my ear lobe. 'So, this tells us that the burglars had no idea of value for certain works of art. Do you think it's the same gang that broke into the other houses?'
'Well, it sounds the same to us all and the police seemed to think so too.'
I look at the other five people in the room who are all middle-aged and upwards, except for Simon, of course, and figure in one way this makes sense because the properties around Clifford Tower are expensive. These neighbours obviously bought their houses years ago before it was known as an upmarket and affluent area in York.
I figure trying to help my neighbours will be a great idea, and smile. As well as making me feel good if we can prevent more robberies taking place, it will benefit us, and we'll feel more secure at home.
'Okay, Rodger,' I say. 'I'll certainly try to help you all, although I'm not sure exactly what I can do about missing art works, but I'll definitely come to your meetings.'
Rodger claps his hands, and his eyes light up once again. 'That's grand,' he says. 'Look, why not mingle around and talk to everyone about their houses while I top up the drinks.'

Rodger hurries over to Dorothy and asks if she'd like another cup of tea.

I can tell that Daphne is giving Barbie a full account of what happened in her house, so I decide to start with Paul Robbins.

'Hi, Paul,' I say as he stands up and shakes my hand. It's only when he is standing that I realise he is quite a short man and I'm much taller than him at five-foot-ten. He has a weather-beaten craggy face with big bushy eyebrows which seem to meet in the middle and give him a foreboding look until he smiles then his whole face softens and changes.

'Nice to meet you, Clive,' he says. 'And good to have some young blood in the group.'

He gives a snorty laugh and I immediately liken to him.

'Ah, well, I don't know about that,' I say and release his hand. 'I just wondered if you could tell me what you told the police about the things you had stolen.'

Paul sits on the edge of the chesterfield sofa and swings his leg. 'Okay, so I was an engineer, but I've taken early retirement. I've lived all my life with my father in the cottage but worked abroad for months and years on end. However, at eighty-eight, Dad is nearly blind now and very deaf, so I look after him.'

I sigh and commiserate. 'Ah, sorry to hear that, it can't be easy?'

'It isn't, but I have promised him that he won't end up in a nursing home, so I do my best,' he says and shakes his head. 'Although, as an ex-army major, sometimes he's a bit of a handful!'

I smile. 'I bet he is, does he get out and about much?'
Paul shakes his head. 'He did up until last year in the lockdowns when he'd got used to being sheltered and staying at home. And now I can't get him to leave the cottage at all. In fact, he used to come along to the neighbourhood meetings because he likes Daphne and Rodger, but now I can't budge him.'

I sigh realising the impact the pandemic has had on people especially the older generation. A thought comes to my mind, and I raise my eyebrow, 'So, was he at home when the burglary took place?'

I can see Paul bite the inside of his cheek and squirm. 'Yeah, and I feel terrible because I'd gone out shopping to the market and he was in the front parlour alone. The burglars had got in through the back door and had been up in our attic while Dad dozed in his chair, and of course he hadn't heard them.'

I know this must be a heavy burden to carry around and my insides churn. Along with everyone else in the country I've see old people on TV that have been beaten for measly amounts of money. I ask, 'Oh, God, they didn't hurt him, did they?'

Paul lets out a noisy breath. 'No, thankfully, but if the police ever do find these villains, they'll have to hold me back! I could tear them limb from limb for putting Dad in such a vulnerable position.'

I nod gravely and understand his feelings. 'And what did they take from your attic?'

'Well, I'd bought a new laptop and a mobile phone as presents for my nephews,' he says. 'They were wrapped up in Christmas paper and hidden in the attic.

The kids often call to see us with my sister, and I'd wanted to keep them away from prying eyes.'

'That's a blow,' I say. 'And could your dad describe anything about the burglars?'

He shakes his head and draws his eyebrows together. 'Nah, all he says is that there was two men. He'd woken with a jolt and seen the back of them running out of the front door carrying the Christmas presents. The only thing he could tell the police was that they were two bulky shadows and two voices shouting.'

When I remember the violation that I'd felt being mugged, another thought comes to my mind. I had remembered smells and sounds and the tattoo, but of course the old gentleman can't see well and is deaf. I decide it's worth a shot. 'Could I come and talk to him?' I ask. 'You never know he might just remember something else?'

Paul smiles now. 'Yes, of course, anytime, if you think it'll help.'

I shrug my shoulders. 'Maybe, and in the meantime can you email me the details or an image of the stolen goods that you might have.'

I pull out one of my business cards and hand it to Paul who nods.

'No problem,' he says reading my card. 'I do have serial numbers which I've given to the police, so I'll send them to you as well.'

Paul wanders off outside to have a cigarette and I take his place next to Dorothy on the sofa. I sit back loving the comfortable, yet firmness of the seat and the old lady turns towards me.

Dorothy smiles as I introduce myself. She is holding a small China cup on its saucer in her old, wrinkled hand. She sips from the cup with her little finger sticking out and I smile. She looks like the perfect old English lady in her blue dress and short bolero jacket. Secretly, I know I'm going to call her, Miss Marple, and I look into her small grey eyes.

'I'm sorry to hear about the break-in, Dorothy,' I say.

She nods. 'Yes, it was an awful day,' she says. 'They took the jewellery box that my husband bought me on our honeymoon.'

I wonder how old Dorothy is, and in her next words she tells me.

'And would you believe,' she says. 'After all the years I've lived here and at eighty-eight-year-old, some horrible people broke into my house and took the jewellery that Thomas had bought me.'

I sigh feeling my insides churn for this dear Miss Marple lookalike. To live all those years in the same house and suddenly have your security stripped away must be unnerving. Although, I think, she does look remarkably robust. I can almost hear Barbie saying, appearances can be deceiving, so I listen carefully while Dorothy tells me more.

'It's nearly ten years since Thomas died, and I still miss him dearly,' she mutters. 'Although in one way, I'm glad he's not here to go through this because it would upset him too much. Thomas had bought me a couple of diamond pieces over the years and a set of pearls which match this brooch,' she says fingering it on the lapel of her jacket. 'But now, they're gone, too.'

I can see the pearls in her brooch look real and of a decent quality with tiny diamonds inset on the edges. Not of course, that I'm an expert on pearls and jewellery, but it looks simple yet classy and very real. I don't think they can be imitation or plastic.

There's a thin wafer biscuit on the side of her saucer, and I marvel at the dexterity in her old fingers as she snaps it in half and dunks it into her tea.

'And, of course,' she says. 'It's the memories as much as the value because he bought them for me in Switzerland on holiday.'

Plans are hatching in my mind while I talk and listen to Dorothy. I'm deciding which would be the best way to help her.

I say, 'Oh, that's awful. I don't suppose you have any way of identifying the pearls or brooches that were stolen?'

Placing the saucer onto the coffee table, she extracts a lace handkerchief from the sleeve of her dress and delicately wipes her mouth. 'Well actually, Simon has a photograph of them because he is our solicitor,' she says. 'Last year, he sorted out my house insurance because we have a valuable sculpture in the hall. Therefore, the jewellery box and its contents and all of our other expensive items were re-valued and recorded.'

'Oh, good, and they didn't take the sculpture?'

Dorothy slowly shakes her head then pushes her rimmed spectacles further up her nose. 'No, I couldn't understand that. We bought it years ago in Rome and Simon has had it valued at £4,000.'

I want to whoop for joy. This is great news because it will give the police and myself something to go on. 'Okay, Dorothy, so with your permission can I get a copy of the photographs from Simon?'

Dorothy smiles. 'Of course, dear, I'm sure Simon will have them on his tinternet.'

I want to laugh at the word, tinternet knowing some older people have no concept whatsoever of being online and all it entails.

Dorothy gets up and heads over to Simon who has returned to the lounge, and I can hear her asking him to send me the details. I turn around to look for Barbie and see she is still chatting with Daphne, and I smile at her.

Turning my head back I notice that Susan has shuffled her way along the sofa towards me.

She introduces herself and says, 'I got a leaflet pushed through my door, so I thought I'd come along, but I don't know anyone else here.'

Susan looks to be in her mid-fifties and is dressed in a black suit with a name badge on the jacket stating her name and Middletons Hotel.

'Hey, I see you work at Middleton's Hotel? We've just been there for lunch today and had an amazing beef stew.'

She nods and pulls back her shoulders. 'Yeah, if I say so myself, we do particularly good food, although I'm not connected to the kitchens or chef in anyway,' she says. 'I work in the office and sometimes stand-in for reception but mainly I beaver away in the background.'

She peeps at me from under a heavy black fringe around her chubby face. I can tell she is a shy woman who would be at her happiest hovering anywhere in the background and never upfront. She is wringing her small hands together as though she is anxious just sitting next to me. I want to put my hands over hers and squeeze them tight to reassure her that she has nothing to fear, but I know now-a-days this is not the done thing.

Susan pulls her tight jacket down at the front over her rounded stomach then says, 'I've just come straight here from work and didn't have time to change.'

I decide to try and make her laugh which might put her at ease then hopefully she'll open up and talk. 'That's okay, we didn't know what to expect, hence the old jeans and trainers,' I say staring down and tapping the scruffy toes together. 'I would have worn my good trainers if I'd known how posh it was.'

It works, she laughs and blushes crimson. Dropping her shoulders slightly she crosses her legs. 'I wonder if I could tell you about my break-in?'

She is the first neighbour I haven't had to ask and is volunteering her information without hesitation. She may have heard me talking to Paul and Dorothy, so knows what details I'm after.

I grin. 'There's nothing I'd like more,' I say and sit back on the sofa.

'Well, I came home from work last Tuesday at seven o'clock and found I'd been burgled. They took the computer from my spare bedroom and six Lladro figurines from the fireplace in the lounge.'

'Oh, I'm sorry,' I say.

She nods. 'And I know Lladro seems trifling compared to the grandness of all this,' she says sweeping her arm around the room. 'But they meant the world to me because my father gave them to me as a wedding gift before he died.'

I sigh, knowing I've at least heard the name, Lladro as millions of other people have. Although I have no idea of the value.

They're probably mid-range, I think, but say, 'Hey, no matter what the value is, they were precious to you which is the most important thing. Have you any identifiable records or photographs?'

Once again, I reach into my pocket and give her a business card, and she promises to email me a photograph of her lounge with the figurines on the bookcase.

I feel incredibly sorry for these new-found neighbours of mine. They've had their belongings and mementos stolen which is grossly unfair. And yes, there's been impersonal materialistic things like computers and money taken but mostly their stolen items have been treasured keepsakes. I can feel my hackles rise like I did with the group from the café who'd been pick-pocketed.

***

Later, as Barbie and I walk home back over Skeldergate Bridge I turn around and look behind. The back of Daphne, Dorothy, and Rodger's properties all look over the museum and Clifford Tower. Is there a connection there? However, as Barbie tugs my arm to hurry me home, I decide that because Paul and Susan's properties are on our side of the bridge it can't be connected. As we walk quickly home in the chilly wind an idea begins to worm its way through my mind and I'm longing to get into my office in the morning.

Chapter Twenty-Three

Pete had arrived home yesterday with another bag full of stolen goods and her heart had sunk. Ashley knew that he would make her list the items online for sale which she hated doing, but because he wasn't IT savvy then she had no choice. Well, not if she wanted rid of it all from their spare bedroom which she did. It didn't do to antagonise Pete especially when he had a drink in him.

She sat on the chair in front of the screen and logged-in to a popular sale room and sighed. How had she got herself involved in all of this? She wasn't sure, but she did love her husband even if she was a little scared of him.

He had lashed out a couple of times in the past when Ashley refused to help but she'd managed to dodge his fist. So, technically speaking, he hadn't hit her, but as her mum used to say, 'It's only a matter of time, dearie.'

Ashley ambled over to the single bed and sat on the edge fingering a set of pearls. She marvelled at the small delicate feel of the pearls as she rolled them between her long fingers. Fastening the clasp around her neck she stood up and looked at them in the mirror. The sight of the clean white pearls lying on her black jumper made her gasp. Oh, God, she'd be in her element if she owned a set of pearls like this.

Knowing Pete would be home soon for dinner, she spaced out the six Lladro figurines on the bed spread to take photographs. Items always sold better with good images, and she was experienced at doing this.

The figurines reminded Ashley of her grannie who'd had a couple of Lladro pieces on the fireplace in her old cottage. Remembering how grannie had polished them with care, Ashley sighed heavily. She shuddered, what would her grannie think of her now dealing in stolen goods?

Ashley frowned and knew the Lladro pieces had been cherished on someone else's fireplace but now they were in her hot clammy hands, and she was about to sell them illegally. She frowned, all this torment for the love of a man.

He was the only man that she'd ever known or been with since she was seventeen. Pete had been twenty-two and she had followed him around like a lap dog until he'd finally taken her to bed. She had fallen pregnant within six months, but he'd made her abort their baby. 'It's just not the right time,' he'd said. 'It'll be better later when we get settled with enough money to raise a family.'

She'd gone along with his reasoning because she had lived in fear of what he'd do if she didn't conform to his way of thinking. Ashley always did what he thought best.

She lifted the jewellery box up and opened the lid. It played a ballerina tune, and a single tear ran down her cheek. Since the abortion, she'd not been able to fall pregnant again and, in her way, she thought of this as God's punishment for her actions.

She took a photograph of the open jewellery box with the twirling ballet dancer knowing this would catch a buyer's eye online. She laid the brooches on the red velvet lining inside the box and took another photograph. It could be sold empty as a box or with the jewellery. She made a note of the name on the bottom of the box and read, made in Switzerland. She smiled; a lucky woman had been to one of the countries she could only ever dream about.

Using one of her fake names, Jane Morrison, she listed them and turned her attention to the carefully wrapped Christmas presents on the bed. She stroked her finger around the Santa face on the glittery paper and sighed. It was bad enough doing this any other time of year, she thought, but at Christmastime it always seemed a hundred times worse.

Unwrapping the presents, she choked back a sob knowing a teenage boy or girl somewhere in York should be doing this on Christmas morning but hearing the front door slam shut, she hurried with her task and used his alias name for electrical goods, Colin Morris.

When he'd come home yesterday with his haul and laughed about the old man sleeping in his chair as they'd climbed up the ladder into the attic, she'd gulped. 'You didn't hurt him, did you?'

Her heart had thumped hard with the thought that Pete or his brother would be capable of beating an old man. She'd cowered and taken a step backwards as he'd pushed his snarling face in front of hers.

'Of course, we didn't!'

Ashley had looked at his ugly face and remembered her mum's words, it's only a matter of time.

Chapter Twenty-Four

The next morning while I sit at my desk, I remember Barbie telling me last night about her long conversation with Daphne. I jot down the facts into an online folder I've made with all five names from the neighbourhood watch group. Daphne, Dorothy, Paul, Susan, and of course, the leader, Rodger, and Simon.

Barbie had said, 'Daphne, as you know lives on Tower Street and had returned earlier than usual from the shop with a headache and had disturbed the burglars. She'd found all her stuff, cheque book, jewellery, laptop, and iPad in a big black sack against the front door. Obviously, the thieves had placed it ready to take but instead when she had put her key in the front door, they'd fled out of the back door.'

I'd asked, 'Okay, and did Daphne say that she knew for certain that there was more than one person running out of the back door?'

Barbie had scrunched up her eyebrows. 'Yes, she'd heard two voices shouting at one another. I think they'd yelled, get the hell out of here!'

I write this down and the following sentence. 'It's just the thought they'd been inside my home which is disturbing,' Daphne had said.

I note the items that were about to be taken in her situation, and her contact details from the shop invoice for our table purchase. Fortunately, the goods hadn't been stolen but all the same I'd like to add them to the list of items the burglars are interested in stealing.

Barbie had made me a coffee and as usual I've been so engrossed it's now lukewarm, but I gulp it down quickly. I type into the Google search box, burglaries in York.

The latest post is from April 2021 which tells me that North Yorkshire Police has reminded residents in York to check their home security following several burglaries around the city over the last few weeks.

From this I note that it has been an ongoing problem for six months but now seems to be targeted in our locality and how these robberies are committed during the daytime.

I remember my conversation with Rodger when he'd been seeing us out of his house last night. He'd said, 'The police did a talk about locks and safety at our last neighbourhood meeting and now we are all up to date. But it's a little like closing the stable door after the horse has bolted, nevertheless, it's been worthwhile.'

'Yes, I'm going to get ours checked, too,' I'd said. 'And you're right, it's better to be safe than sorry.'

I pick up my mobile now and arrange an appointment with a locksmith to come to check ours and replace the old lock on the back door which Barbie agrees needs attention.

I open Susan's folder and make a note of the Lladro figurines and after enlarging and cropping the photograph she has emailed; I attach it to her folder. Then I ring her mobile, but my call goes straight to her voicemail. I decide to leave a message.

'Hi, Susan, it's Clive here from last night. Rodger says, the police did a talk at the group two weeks ago about updating your locks on doors and windows. But like us you wouldn't have been at that meeting. So, I thought

I'd let you know because I've arranged a locksmith to come to us later in the week. I can give you his name and number if you are stuck? Bye for now.'

I think about each person separately, their different houses, the rooms in which the items were stolen and locks on back and front doors and windows. I jot the addresses and house differences down in their folders.

Do the streets where they live have any relevance? Do the burglars choose certain houses because they look easy to break into? Properties like Friar Terrace and Tower Street are old Edwardian dwellings but well maintained. Whereas our Victor Street, Nunnery Lane, and Cromwell Road are cheaper but still old Victorian properties. Do the burglars think that because old people live in these houses the door locks will be timeworn and easy to break?

I think about everyday usual patterns which means that the robbers are watching people and properties knowing exactly when they come and go into their houses. I shiver thinking that right now someone could be watching me sit here at my desk or Barbie who is outside in the rickety old garden shed. It makes me glance out of the window for reassurance and I smile at the sight of Barbie's head bobbing up and down in the shed. The garden is empty and there are no suspicious noises or sights to see. She admitted last night that the meeting had made her feel a little insecure and I know she's right because I feel it too.

These thoughts alone make me feel uncomfortable so I can totally empathise with people who have had intruders. When I think of a stranger in here picking up my precious things on this desk it makes the hairs on the back of my neck stand up. I rub my hand along my hairline.

And yes, it's an old computer, therefore not worth much but it is mine, as is the printer which chugs along and spits out printed sheets of paper. Sometimes it needs a little tap on the side to get it going. I sigh thinking of anyone else bashing away on this keyboard. My keys are well worn especially the enter bar which is flattened down on one side because of the way I type. But I'm used to it and have happy memories of sitting here writing especially when I finished my novel and typed the words, The End.

I look at the pot full of various pens and pencils remembering where I bought each one or if it was given to me as a gift. These things are personal to me. Other people might think them worthless rubbish, but they are every bit as precious as the expensive paintings Rodger had stolen.

I decide it is the intrusion of your own privacy that is the most distressing thing about burglaries. Why do burglars think it's acceptable to enter another person's house and rummage around in their belongings? As human beings why do they think they're entitled to do this?

I feel my cheeks flush and bite my lip remembering how I'd stolen a neighbour's purse from a kitchen windowsill in Doncaster and wonder now if I had made the woman feel wary and vulnerable. But of course, way back then these thoughts wouldn't enter a teenager's head. I do remember taking the £22.50 out of the purse in the park. But I'd returned the empty purse to the windowsill with the cards left inside because I hadn't understood how store and credit cards worked. I place my hands onto my warm cheeks and feel them cool down. I'm relieved to think that aged twelve, although my memories of this are scant, I must have had a smattering of decency about myself. Even then.

Shaking the old memories aside, I concentrate on Dorothy's folder, aka Mis Marple, and list the jewellery box, brooches, and pearls that were stolen. Simon has sent me the insurance details with photographs, and I attach these. Thank God, the dear old lady was out at her tea club. She could have died of shock or worse still been attacked for her personal possessions.

However, I remember Paul's father and if these were the same burglars, they'd at least had the decency not to harm him. Although, I shrug my shoulders, at their elderly ages was the shock enough to bring on a heart attack or stroke? Plus, of course, Daphne had interrupted them so I figure they could have turned upon her once she'd discovered them raiding her home. All three, I figure, have had lucky escapes.

I jot down the Christmas presents that Paul and his father had stolen with the serial numbers of the laptop and mobile in their folder. I click open the email I've received from Paul inviting me to meet his father tomorrow morning at eleven and smile. I decide to try my senses test on the old man including smell, sight, and noises. Of course, I know these will be limited because of his partial blindness and deafness but I figure it's worth a shot. Perhaps a shot in the dark, I write and titter at my own humour.

I wonder at the burglars' stories. Their backgrounds ages, and characters then sigh. Considering York is said to be a cultural lover's dream, these burglars can't know anything about true art values because they didn't take Rodger's most expensive painting nor Dorothy's sculpture. Could they be young like the pick-pocketers? Or from an older age group?

My thoughts are interrupted when Barbie shouts up the stairs, 'Clive, do you want a bacon sandwich?'

I grin, save my notes, jump up from the seat and run downstairs.

***

The next morning, I decide to knock on all my neighbours' doors in the street and ask if they've seen anything suspicious. The street is short with less houses compared to others in the area. All the houses, including ours, have attractive and enclosed fore-courted gardens leading through gates to the front entrance doors. Three houses further down the street have new windows, but mostly, like ours, they are old. smile, knowing that I've thought of the house as ours and not mine. Which I'd always done before Barbie came. She is getting ready to go Christmas shopping when I'm finished. She'd grinned and said, 'I'll wait until you've finished your surveillance.'

I stand outside the blue painted door of my direct neighbour to the right and smile at Barbie's teasing. I'm thinking more of making the house our home in a legal sense now. I've never felt so happy as this for years and imagine carrying her over the threshold on our wedding day. I hadn't done that when I had married Sarah because she'd ran ahead inside before I'd had time to think of the gesture.

There's no answer on my second knock and I figure the firefighter must be at work but just when I walk back down the path, he pulls open the door and we talk. I explain about the burglaries nearby, but he has no knowledge of this happening and agrees to be vigilant. I draw the same dead-end answers at another four neighbours who are at home in the street.

When I return home and tell Barbie this, she squeezes my hand. 'But this is good news because it means our street hasn't been targeted.'

We decide this makes us feel more secure but secretly I hope I can discover something about the burglars.

We set off to the shops in the city with Barbie clutching her Christmas gift list in her pink gloved hand. I hold onto her other hand never wanting to be far away from her.

It's two weeks until Christmas now and I agreed that as I've got this week on holiday from the agency it's an ideal time to go shopping. Our plans are finalised, and we will stay home Christmas Eve then head up to County Durham the next morning to see Jenny and Barbie's mam. We'll stay the night with her mam in the old house which I'm really looking forward to because it'll be a real family Christmas. I'm determined to throw myself into all that the festivities entail although selfishly I'd love to have Barbie to myself. But I remember the saying as I swing her hand happily, love me, love my family and grin.

Chapter Twenty-Five

At 10.45 the next morning I leave our house to go and talk to Paul and his dad at their cottage on Nunnery Lane. I head up our street in the opposite direction to the town centre and pass under the archway on the bar wall which leads me directly onto Nunnery Lane.

While I walk, I decide these properties are not posh like the houses over Skeldergate Bridge. But the two up, two down cottages look presentable and are built in light-coloured old brickwork. The small painted door height would be a challenge for very tall people, I decide, but from what I remember about Paul this won't be a problem.

Barbie has already commented that my visit could be a waste of time, and I sigh. She could well be right. However, he is our only credible witness to the burglars, and although he's already given a statement to the police, I'm hoping he might remember little details after a gentle prod. I know that a lot of elderly people get flustered talking to police officers, although from what Paul has told me about his dads' character, I don't think this will be the case.

I count the door numbers while I walk along the lane, which if I continued would lead me up to the train station. Finally, I stop outside a dark-brown wood door with a square of glass in the top. Before knocking I look at the shiny new handle and five-lever lock system then nod in satisfaction. Paul has obviously been prompt at tightening and renewing their security after the break-in.

I'm welcomed inside the small square lounge and offered a seat on a black leather settee. His dad is settled in a high-back winged armchair and Paul is slumped in a smaller chair on the other side of the old fireplace. I imagine them sitting here of an evening watching TV together or reading the newspapers folded neatly on a small coffee table next to the old man's chair. His glasses are lying on top of the newspapers. He picks them up and puts them on to peer at me.

Paul raises his voice an octave and introduces his dad, and vice versa. I get up and shake the old man's wrinkly hand but flinch slightly in surprise at the strength of his handshake.

Sitting back down I refuse tea and hope to get straight into my questions that I've prepared. I begin by commenting upon the new lock on the front door.

Paul wailed, 'I know, it was unbelievable how the burglary happened,' he said. 'We'd had a talk from the police at Rodgers neighbourhood group. And I'd arranged for a locksmith to come and check everything. But it was sods law that the appointment was for the day after the break in!'

I shake my head and tut. 'That's just blooming typical. If something is going to go wrong then it will, no matter what,' I say. 'We've got a locksmith booked for the end of the week.'

Paul's father looks the same short height with a bald head and a very thin wrinkly face. He has sprightly blue eyes which seem to dart around the room from behind thick lenses in his glasses. I sigh. His face looks so vulnerable sitting in the chair that it makes my head spin with contempt for these robbers who broke into the cottage.

I look at Paul's flushed cheeks while he repeats the fact that he'd only left him for an hour to go shopping into the market, and I shiver. I'd hate the guilty feelings that Paul must have in his head since the robbery and know he is trying to salve his conscience. Which is unnecessary.

When Paul had introduced us, he hadn't said his dad's first name. But I decide it would be bad mannered to use it even if I knew what it was. So, I settle for his full itle and lean towards him raising my voice like Paul had done.

'Major Robbins,' I say, 'is it okay to ask you a couple of questions, please?'

I see the old man pull his frail shoulders back and lift his chin. I figure he's still a proud man even at the age of eighty-eight and he nods his consent.

I smile then continue, 'I know that you've already told he police this, but I heard that you saw two bulky shadows?'

The major clears his throat and answers in a louder voice than I'd expected. 'Yes, I woke up with a jolt and he two men were hot-footing it out there!'

He waves his hand towards the door in the corner of he room, and I smile imagining his voice when he was younger barking out orders across the army parade ground.

I nod then ask, 'So, that door takes you into the kitchen and the back door?'

'It certainly does, young man.'

'Okay,' I say. 'And can you remember anything more about the bulky shadows, I mean, were they both tall? Or both short? Or was one was tall, and the other short?'

He screws his wayward bushy eyebrows together of which Paul has the same. Immediately, I can see what Paul will look like in twenty years' time. As the saying goes, a chip of the old block.

'Ahhh,' the major almost growls. 'I understand now. Well, the first one who ran out stooped to go under the door so I would think he was taller than the second one.'

I lean forwards knowing I've got him thinking about the incident again. 'Great, and if you close your eyes now can you remember any noises at all,' I say looking down at the wood flooring. 'Did you hear heavy boots clumping on the wood floor? Or perhaps they were shouting at each other?'

I turn towards Paul and say, 'Daphne reckoned she heard one of them shouting, let's get out of here!'

Paul nods now. 'Dad, I know you had your hearing aids in that morning so did you hear anything?'

The majors face lights up. 'Well, I'll be damned!' He shouts. 'Yes, now I remember they were laughing, and it was a gruff man's laughter. Not a fancy light chortle like Rodgers, but a real man's thick husky rasp like a smoker has.'

I want to hoot but stifle down the chortle although Paul lets rip and howls at his dad's comparison.

I'm on a role and know I am getting more out of the major than what the police obviously had done. I grin.

'And, one last thing, Major, did you smell anything in the room when they passed through to the kitchen?'

The major nods and claps his old hands together. 'Oh, yes, it was a damp smell as though washing was drying. A clinging humid smell that hung around until Paul came home.'

Once again, I turn to Paul. 'Was it raining that day?'

Paul grins now too. 'Yes,' he says. 'It was tipping down and I got soaked walking back from town.'

'Marvellous,' I shout at the major. 'Well done. I reckon the smell was from their wet coats.'

Paul gets up and I say goodbye to the major and shake his hand once more. I'm ready for the tight shake this time and marvel at him.

When we reach the front door, I thank Paul. 'Your dad is certainly a character all right,' I say. 'But he's a great old guy and I've loved meeting him.'

Paul nods. 'He is, and when I think what could have happened to him, I cringe. He's so defenceless in a way but in another, he's still got his wits about him and full of gusto.'

I step outside onto the pavement and shake his hand. 'Well, thanks, again. I don't know what good, if any, will come out of what he's remembered but you never know.'

Paul smiles. 'Even if nothing comes of it then this will have bucked him up knowing he's remembered a little more and perhaps been some use to the investigation. I'll let the police know as well just in case.'

We say our goodbyes and I head off back home whistling down the lane.

I've spoken to Rodger every day since the meeting. Simon has sent me the details and photographs of the two paintings which were stolen, and I have added them to his folder. I have the predicted value of Dorothy's jewellery and it's not as high as the works of art, therefore, the paintings were the most valuable items stolen.

Although, what I know about art would fit onto a postage stamp, I find Roger fascinating to talk with about anything. Simon is also a great guy and Barbie likes them both immensely.

We'd called into their town house again for drinks last night and thoroughly enjoyed our evening in their company. Simon was fascinated by Barbie's job and wanted to know which food products in M&S she'd developed. He wrote down the names so that he could buy them when next shopping.

And I'd realised that Rodger seemed to love our city as much as I do. When I'd told him about the tours and how I make up historical stories to tell the visitors he was transfixed. Loving an audience as I do, I had stood up, and in my spookiest voice, I'd related the butcher story from The Shambles to a rapturous round of applause.

I'd then explained about my detective novel and Simon had uploaded a copy there and then onto his phone. He proclaimed that he loved a good thriller with a surprise ending and would read it on his lunch break at work.

As we'd left their house, I had stopped in front of a glorious painting in the hall. 'Gosh, this is beautiful,'

I'd said. 'I remember being struck by it when we came here last time. I can just imagine myself on that beach, the blue colours are amazing!'

Rodger had preened. 'Ah, this is from a local artist who lives up in Northumberland. It's not a valuable piece, but like I've said many times, beauty and value is in the eye of the beholder.'

I'd grinned. 'Okay, so if I'd been the burglar that night, I'd have stolen this painting straight away.'

We had all laughed and I'd said, 'In the tour agency, we have a poster of a beach in Thailand which I often dream about, but it's nothing compared to this!'

When we'd waved goodnight at the door Barbie asked them to join us for dinner on Saturday night. 'We can christen our new table,' she'd said and smiled. They'd been delighted and agreed immediately insisting they would bring wine.

***

The table arrives on Saturday afternoon and although the money that Barbie has spent makes me wince, I must admit the wood is sturdy, good quality, and beautifully smooth. The colour is light oak and already I can see her mind working when she looks around the room. 'It's gorgeous but does it look out of place with everything else?'

I smile and grasp her small hands in mine. 'Maybe a little, but we'll get there in time and change the rest of the décor to match it all in together.'

She flings her arms around my neck and simpers, 'I do love you so much, Clive.'

I melt inside and wrap my arms around her waist pulling her into my chest. She's warm cuddly and smells so clean and natural that I catch a sob in my throat. I'll never understand why Barbie loves me like she does but will always be eternally grateful.

'I don't suppose we'll have time for a quick, you know what?'

She throws her head back and laughs. 'Er, no,' she says. 'They'll be here in two hours, and I've loads to prepare for dinner.'

I can't help feeling disappointed and it must show on my face. 'Okay,' I say and shrug my shoulders. 'But it doesn't take that long…'

She cocks her head, and says, 'I'll make it up to you later.'

And that, I decide is certainly something to look forward to.

I'm showered, changed into my black jeans and grey sweater and when I come back downstairs the smell from Beef Bourguignon seems to fill the whole downstairs. To use an old saying, I reckon that I'm on a promise for tonight, because she knows this is my favourite dinner.

I help to prepare broccoli just as the front doorbell rings. I leave Barbie putting potatoes into the oven and hurry along the hall to open the door for our guests.

Rodger and Simon are standing together holding hands. I welcome them inside and take their coats. Simon is like me and dressed in jeans and a fair isle jumper, but Rodger is wearing a black suit, white shirt with a pink scarf draped around his neck.

'Oooh, what a gorgeous smell,' Simon says heading nto the lounge and greeting Barbie.
'Well,' she says. 'I remembered you saying you both oved visiting France and the food, so I've made Beef Bourguignon with plenty of red wine!'
Rodger claps his hands together gleefully and grins. Ah, the perfect hostess, catering to her guests likes,' he ays. 'Well done you.'
He kisses her cheek as does Simon and we all stand in front of the table.
'Ta Da!' I exclaim and we laugh.
Simon places two bottles of red wine onto the table nd says, 'I must have had second sight that red wine would be ideal with your dinner plans, Barbara?'
She thanks him, and I look at her in a simple but igure-hugging blue wool dress. Her eyes are sparkling, nd her cheeks are flushed. She looks beautiful and I grin at her.
While I'd been upstairs Barbie has set the table with ork placemats, cutlery, and our posh wine glasses. I otice she's bought new napkins and a single andlestick for the centre with a red candle. Rodger wanders around stroking and examining the table legs while Simon sits down on one of the high-back chairs with grey upholstery on the seats.
They both compliment us over our choice of design nd quality.
'Well,' I say. 'We had help from Daphne of course nd she was marvellous at getting the table delivered oday before Christmas.'

Rodger's dark eyes are practically dancing when he raves, 'Oh, yes, Daphne is a real star! She has amazing taste and style. And of course, is a dear old friend of mine.'

Simon nods. 'Yes, but it's a shame that she'll soon be retiring and selling up the shop. I've been trying to find someone to buy into her business so she can still be a silent partner, but it doesn't look likely now.'

I tut. 'I think we'll all be suffering from the aftereffects of the pandemic for a few years, yet which is sad.'

Barbie ushers us to our seats and brings a corkscrew for Simon who opens the first bottle of wine and pours us all a glass. Although. I'm not keen on red wine or white for that matter, I decide to take a few sips and let Barbie drink the rest.

I find matches in the kitchen and light the candle then turn down the main ceiling light to subdued and switch on the two standard lamps in each corner. It gives a lovely warm glow to the room, and I sit down happily content at our evening with fabulous food and good company.

Barbie brings the large casserole dish to the centre of the table with a big ladle. We all breathe in deeply the smell of beef chunks happily stewing in wine with carrots mushrooms and garlic. I jump up and help carry through the roast potatoes and vegetables with two batons of French bread. And we all tuck in heartily with ooh's and aah's with each mouthful at the amazing flavours.

Barbie thanks us. 'The secret with Beef Bourguignon is to let it simmer for at least two hours if not longer.'

We all agree with Simon when he says, 'Well, you've got this absolutely perfect, Barbara. I don't think we've had this as good, even in France!'

I chuckle. 'Well, that's something we've beat the French at.'

When we've chatted and devoured all the food, Simon opens the second bottle of wine and pours more for Rodger, Barbie, and himself.

I turn to Rodger and ask, 'So, have you always lived in York?'

Rodger nods. 'Yes, other than when I was sent away to private boarding school then Durham University to study art,' he says. 'I returned and began my own business here in York. My art gallery was on Tower Street up until five years ago when it all became a little too much for me and I retired. And that's when I began to run the neighbourhood watch group and I met Simon, of course.'

Rodger takes Simon's hand across the table and squeezes it tightly. I look at Simon. Until now, I'd decided he had quite an ordinary pleasant face. But when he gazes into Rodgers eyes and smiles his whole face changes. The wide smile from his thin lips turns his appearance into something quite extraordinary. I can see the love for Rodger in every inch of his face and wonder if I look like this when I look at Barbie?

She asks, 'And what was it like at private school, was it all boys?'

A slight cloud passes through Rodgers eyes, and he nods his head. He takes a large gulp of his wine. 'Yes, all boys, and maybe it was just the school I was at, and others might have been different, but I hated every second.'

I can see Barbie bite her lip. 'Oh, sorry, Rodger, I didn't mean to seem nosy and pry. I was just interested to know the difference between that and our local comprehensive where I went.'

Rodger reaches over and rubs her shoulder. 'No need to apologise, my dear,' he says. 'Some boys might have had a great time there, but I was goaded and hounded because of my sexuality which seemed to continue through to university where I was tortured because I was different.'

I gasp and can't help exclaiming, 'Nooo, but that's dreadful!'

'Well,' Rodger says. 'It was a long time ago in the sixties and homosexuality was still illegal back then.'

I shake my head and tut then look at Simon. I raise my eyebrow as if to ask if he'd suffered the same. I'm hoping not but would like to know all the same. Rodger's sexuality is obvious as soon as he speaks, as the major had said this afternoon, but Simon has a throaty voice which isn't as discernible.

I watch Simon squeeze Rodger's hand again. 'Well, I was a little more fortunate because I studied at Oxford in 1994 and things had moved-on a little, although I still felt discriminated against because I wasn't a great sportsman of any type. I hated rugby, rowing, and cricket and was always much happier reading a good book,' he said. 'Which, I suppose is a solitary hobby and I never made a good team member. After university, I moved back to York to look after my mother who was deteriorating with early Alzheimer's. She lived on the end of Cromwell Road and when she died, Rodger came to value a couple of paintings and that's when we met.'

'And the rest is history,' I say and smile. 'But I'm so sorry that both of you have been discriminated against. Thank God, things are getting better now-a-days especially for the younger set.'

A discussion takes place about minority groups, and ethnic changes. I tell them about Adhar and Binita while Barbie clears away our plates.

She brings a wood platter to the table with three different cheeses, crackers, and green grapes. I insist she sits down, and I make coffee for us all.

While nibbling on a chunk of cheese, Simon asks me directly. 'So, how's the investigation going? Have you anything to report?'

I smile. 'Okay, so I'll put on my Sherlock hat to tell you all what I've been trying to figure out,' I say. 'I've wondered if there were any similar factors between the properties that were burgled? And using my powers of deduction these are my findings.'

Barbie giggles and I can see she's enjoying the red wine.

'Number 1, Age of owners. Number 2, Older properties chosen because of timeworn locks which are easily broken. Number 3, Burglars have no knowledge of art values, so are they young?'

Rodger holds up his hand and buts in, 'Er, sorry, Sherlock, but that's a little biased because there are young people who are art lovers and do know the difference between an English Gainsborough and the Mona Lisa.'

I laugh at his reference to Sherlock and Simon chortles too.

But I continue, 'Point taken and noted, Rodger,' I say. 'Number 4, There were two of them. According to Daphne, who heard two voices, and Major Robbins who remembers two bulky shadows, one tall, and one short. And he remembers one of them laughing. It was definitely a gruff man's laughter.'

Barbie holds her small hand up this time and says, 'Sorry, again, Sherlock, but an overweight woman could have a bulky shadow too.'

Rodger claps his hands together and Simon laughs aloud.

I grin. 'And Number 5, all the elderly residents don't look online at markets and salerooms, do they?'

I sit back in my chair and smile at them all and finish with, 'So, thanks to all you, Doctor Watson's, for your helpful contributions. They'll be noted down and acted upon.'

I smile while we all begin chatting and know exactly what I'm going to do tomorrow.

At the end of the night, I collect Rodger and Simon's coats from the hall. When I come back into the lounge Barbie is talking to Rodger standing in front of the fireplace. 'And once we've decorated, I'd like a nice painting to hang above the fireplace. Can you suggest something that'll look well in this room?'

'Leave that one with me,' Rodger says. 'I'll have a look around and see what I can come up with.'

Chapter Twenty-Six

Ashley is going to leave him.

They are planning a big job tonight on Friar Terrace and she wants out of this toxic thing they call a marriage. Pete reckons the house tonight is a treasure trove and ripe for the pickings. Goodness knows what they'll come back with, and she's scared. More scared than she has ever been before.

She double-checks the items for sale in the free marketplace online and frowns. No messages mean no interest and no sales. The boxes are piling up in the spare room and last week's electrical items, jewellery box, and Lladro figurines are still there amongst others from the last haul.

Last year she'd cleared the stock well before Christmas but as she had tried to explain to Pete, 'It's the aftereffects of the pandemic, people don't have a lot of money for this Christmas and aren't buying!'

He'd grabbed her shoulder roughly and wrenched it hard then roared, 'Well make them buy!'

The sneer on his face had distorted what she'd always thought of as his good looks and she had trembled in fear.

Last night Ashley had made her escape plan knowing wherever she fled would have to be far away because he'd come looking for her. He had already said as much last year in lockdown when they'd been arguing. She'd threatened to leave him, and he'd scowled at her 'Ha! Wherever you go – I'll find you and drag you back home then you'll wish that you'd never set foot out of the door!'

She had stared at a photograph of her mam with her arm draped around her sister. Aunty Ivy, who now lived in Spain had invited her to visit on holiday. And that's when Ashley had known exactly where to go. She would head out of the country and simply disappear. Pete didn't have a passport, so it would take him months to trace her. And with her small amount of savings, she could extend her stay and make a new life for herself abroad. She'd bit her lip. But was she strong enough to live without him?

Chapter Twenty-Seven

By the time I've cleared up in the kitchen and put out all the lights I climb the stairs up to our bedroom. I glance outside from the small landing window. All is dark and quiet at twelve midnight. I have taken to doing this since our first night at the neighbourhood group. I like to know there is nothing suspicious going on outside and no one is lurking around in the street.

Barbie is snoring slightly splayed out in our bed. No promise tonight, I think and smile. I lovingly stroke the fringe back from her forehead.

Our first dinner party sitting around the new table has been a triumph and it was mostly down to her. Rodger and Simon had thoroughly enjoyed themselves as we had too. The meal was simply delicious with great discussions and laughter. What else could anyone wish for to fill their Saturday evening.

I roll into bed next to her and spoon her back pulling her close into my chest. I nuzzle my face into her neck and sigh with pleasure. She doesn't wake because of the red wine she's enjoyed. The half glass of wine that I had drunk keeps me awake with my thoughts dancing around in my mind.

I've decided that I'm ready. I am ready to propose to Barbie and ask her to be my wife. But how, where, and when is still the question. Should I ask her during the Christmas holiday? That would be romantic, wouldn't it? Or on the day itself when we are at Jenny's house eating turkey dinner. But I frown, there'll be too much activity amongst present openings. I remember how noisy Libby and Jack are then sigh. I don't want my grand gesture, as Jane calls it, to be muddled in the hullabaloo.

I could wait until we get up to Edinburgh for Hogmanay and ask her then as a new start to 2022 as man and wife. I like the sound of this, man and wife, and hug her closer.

However, my proposal should be made on an ordinary quiet day that we spend together when it'll be an even bigger surprise. I want to see the look of complete astonishment in her small gentle eyes. I want to see her face light up at my words. And surely, as a writer I can come up with meaningful romantic words to say.

I begin trawling the marketplace websites. I want to look for my neighbour's stolen goods. It hadn't been until last night that I'd realised it would be worth doing. You never know I might spot one of Rodger's paintings or the Lladro figurines. Or indeed, Miss Marple's jewellery box.

***

Although Barbie had broken her promise last night, she has certainly made up for it today. With shopping done, and no reason to go out in the cold wintery weather, we decide a pyjama day is well deserved.

'And,' I'd said pulling the duvet over our heads, 'I am on my holidays!'

She'd giggled that deep throaty sound then pulled me on top of her.

'Again?' I'd asked. 'But we've just finished…'

I hadn't spoken another word because she'd kissed me full on my lips and I'd been transported once more into

Barbie la la land which is full of delicious toe-tingling feelings and excitement.

By four in the afternoon, we have at least come downstairs to eat and binge-watch box sets on TV. I'm wearing tracksuit bottoms and a T-shirt, and she is in her pink fluffy onesie cuddled up on the sofa. We're nibbling on the cheese and cracker leftovers from last night.

I look out of the window and sigh. 'Look how dark it is at only four in the afternoon. It's the one thing I hate about winter,' I say and shiver.

My mobile rings and I sigh then reach over to the coffee table to pick it up.

Barbie moans. 'Oh no, we said we weren't going to use mobiles or social media today.'

I nod then look at the name on the screen. 'It's Rodger, shall I answer? It seems bad-mannered not to after last night.'

Barbie nods. 'Yes, you must, they'll be ringing to thank us, no doubt.'

I swipe the screen and say, 'Hello there,' in a cheery voice.

'Clive,' he whispers. 'There's someone in the house next door and they're away on holiday,' he says. 'Simon has set off down to London for a conference tomorrow and I'm on my own!'

Stupidly, I wonder why he is whispering and untangle myself from Barbie. I swing my legs off the sofa and sit upright. 'Oh God,' I say. 'Have you called the police?'

His old feeble voice stutters, 'N…no, not yet. Should I?'

Barbie jumps up too demanding to know what is
appening and I shout into my mobile. 'Yes, Rodger,
ing them now and stay right where you are. I'll be
here as soon as I can.'
I gabble the news to Barbie pulling my fisherman's
weater over my head and run into the hall. Grabbing
ny coat and a torch from the drawer in the hall
upboard, I spin around. 'I'll not be long, stay here and
on't open the door at all!'
I nod at her words to be careful and pull open the front
oor. A freezing wind blasts into the hall but I'm
harged-up and hurry outside.

***

I start to run out through the arch and continue onto
keldergate Bridge. There are a few people milling
round and I dodge in between them in my haste to get
the other side of the river. I suddenly realise that I
on't know which house Rodger meant when he said
ext door. Did he mean to his right or left?
I stop at the end of the bridge to catch my breath. I
ean forwards with my hands on my knees cursing at
ny lack of fitness.
I re-dial Rodgers number and shout into the mobile.
Did you mean the house on your left or right!'
Rodger yells back. 'On the left – it's the green door!'
I nod and stand upright again. 'Okay, I'm on your end
f the bridge, I won't be long. Just stay inside where
's safe.'
I hope he does as I've asked because he's an old man
nd I'd hate anything awful to happen to him. Apart
om the harm to Rodger, I know Simon would be

devastated to think he'd been hurt when he wasn't here to protect him and alone in the house.

My heart is thumping as I run up Tower Street and I can see a couple turn to look at me from across the road. They must think I'm up to no good racing along the street as though someone was chasing me.

I reach the top of the terrace and slow my pace down. My heart is hammering in my ears, and I lick my dry lips. I switch on the torch but hold the light downwards onto the path which is above the road behind decorative iron railings. I walk towards Rodger's house. I look at his lounge windows and see him peering out of the first window. He makes a thumbs up signal and I do the same back.

Looking at the green door next to his I stand still. I see an intermittent single light inside at the window and decide it's from a torch like mine. The streetlights along the river path mean I'm not completely in the dark. There is a full cold moon which is bright and often appears in December when we have the longest nights of the winter solstice. I curse myself for these irrational thoughts and take a deep breath. I know I'll have to go inside to see what's happening. There are three steps up to the green door and I take one step and stand still listening for any noise.

None to hear, I think, and take another step up then wait. Is it possible that the owners have returned early from holiday and are unpacking? These are the noises that Rodger could have heard.

It's still quiet, so I step up onto the top and notice the front door isn't fully shut. From the roadside it looks closed but from here I can see it is ever so slightly ajar.
This is it; I think. Do I go inside or stand here and wait for the police?
I seem to remember from Miss Marple that it had taken a couple of hours for the police to arrive when she was broken into. But that had been after the event. Would they be quicker when something is happening now?
I swallow hard. And it is happening right now at this very moment. The burglars could be stashing stuff and running out of the back door while I stand here deliberating.
I know I must do this and carefully push open the big heavy door just enough to be able to slide around it and stand still in the corner of the hall. I raise the torch and see that the hall is the same width and height as Rodger's house. The walls are empty unlike his array of paintings so I figure whatever the thieves are stealing must be from the upstairs or lounge.
It's obvious there's been no heating on in the house for weeks and I shiver inhaling a slight damp smell. My ears prick and I hear noises coming from the end of the hall which I decide must be the dining room or kitchen.
There is a tall Romanesque type of pillar in the other corner. I creep towards it then hide behind hoping that I'm slim enough not to be seen if they come out into the hall. I crouch down in the corner and place my hand on my chest. I can feel my heartbeat banging and I try to swallow but my mouth has dried.

A loud police siren blasts out and I gasp. Are they coming here? Or are they on Tower Street hurtling towards another incident. I listen carefully and the siren gets louder and louder, so I know it's close to the house. I hear the screech of brakes outside.

Suddenly, two men in balaclavas hurry along hall towards me as I hear the police officers jump from their panda cars down on the roadside. They'll have to run to the end of the terrace to get up onto the path and the front door. Simultaneously, I hear Rodger shouting at the police. 'They're inside now, hurry!'

The burglars might have time to run along the path in the opposite direction by the time police get here. Oh, God, I cry silently. I can't let them get away with the black sack full of valuables and know I must do something to stop them.

The man at the front is reaching the pillar now and I stick my foot out so he trips over it and falls flat onto the floor, growling, 'W…what the!'

Close on his heels, the second man behind skids on the cushioned vinyl flooring and falls over him while the bag is thrown to the side just as the police burst through the door. I stay hidden behind the pillar while the three police officers pull the men to their feet and a policewoman picks up the black sack.

I breathe a sigh of relief when both men are escorted through the front door then I pop my head around the pillar. The policewoman gasps and I introduce myself explaining briefly what I've done. She wipes the sweat from her forehead with the back of her hand looking puzzled.

I hear Rodger's voice again talking to the police outside. 'Clive is one of neighbourhood watch group and has done an excellent job helping with the spate of burglaries in the area.'

I step outside onto the top step with the policewoman behind and Rodger rushes up to me throwing his arms around me. 'Oh Clive, thank God you're okay!'

I'm not accustomed to another man hugging me, so I untangle myself from his embrace and put my hand on his shoulder. My heart rate has calmed back down, and I take a deep breath. 'I'm fine, Rodger,' I say. 'Still a little shaken but I'm okay.'

Chapter Twenty-Eight

I sit at my desk the next day and begin to trawl the online marketplaces and websites which buy and sell goods. It's a busy time before Christmas and I know neither, Paul, Susan, Rodger, or Dorothy would have done this to see if any of their valuables are listed. They don't realise that stolen things are available online these days to buy.

I'm quite relieved this time not to have anything to do with the police because as leader of neighbourhood watch group, Rodger is dealing with the burglary last night. Although I did make a statement, but this is all I've been asked to contribute.

Last night after I'd returned home Barbie had practically hugged the life out of me. We'd sat together and she had Googled on her iPad, sentences for burglars.

She'd read aloud the fact that, 'Burglary cases are viewed as serious crimes and often carry considerable sentences. It's not unusual to serve a custodial sentence for any form of burglary and the three strikes rule means that, for a third offence of domestic burglary, there is a mandatory three-year minimum sentence.'

I re-think this now and suppose if the police can prove they committed the other four neighbour's offences, then this should fit into the three strikes. Hopefully, the burglars will be locked-up so they can't, at least for the moment, cause anymore anguish to our neighbours, or indeed, us.

I remember the first man's gruff growl as he'd fallen lat on his face which corresponds with what Daphne eported. However, lots of men have brusque voices, so his is not concrete evidence. Also, the man I'd tripped p was tall and the second man that fell over him was horter, as the major had said. But this too, is not exact roof.

And of course, I didn't see their faces wearing the alaclavas, but luckily, they hadn't seen mine either vhich was the reason I'd stayed hidden behind the illar until they'd been taken away. I don't want any eprisals in the future.

Trawling through the websites is long and laborious. 've printed out the photographs of the Lladro, ewellery, and electrical serial numbers, and have them tuck on the lid of my laptop. I try to pin-point esemblances to the valuables and just as I'm about to ive up after two hours, I cry aloud, 'Eureka!'

There is a jewellery box that I'm sure is the same as he one, Dorothy, aka Miss Marple had stolen. I zoom n and enlarge the photograph on my screen. Yep, I hink, that's definitely hers and although the pearls and rooches might have already gone, she should at least et the jewellery box back her husband bought in witzerland.

I pick up my mobile and call Rodger. 'Hey, I've got ome great news,' I say and tell him what I've found. I opy and paste the link to his mobile so he can forward to the police.

'Oh, Clive, that's absolutely fabulous,' he cries aloud. imagine him swishing his scarf around his neck and smile. It's strange how quickly I've gotten used to his little quirks and endearments as Simon calls them.

He asks, 'So, what's the name of the person selling it?'

I smile knowing Rodger won't understand the implications of using false names online, but I console myself with the fact that Simon will explain it all to him. 'Well, she's called, Jane Morrison, but this could well be an alias name that she is using.'

'Dear, Lord, it's a woman,' he says. 'Fancy a lady being involved in all of this = it's diabolical!'

I smile. 'Not necessarily, Rodger, it could be a man selling but using a female name.'

I hear him tut and know he'll be shaking his head in disbelief as will Dorothy when she finds out.

'Will you let Dorothy know,' I ask. 'And then arrange everything with the police?'

Rodger gladly agrees and I continue trawling through to look for the other things.

Barbie comes into my office and stands behind me massaging my shoulders. I tell her about Dorothy's jewellery box, and she's thrilled, so much so she dance a little jig around my desk.

'Come, on,' she says. 'Have a break, you'll be bog-eyed soon.'

I nod and she stands beside me covering my hand on the mouse with hers. I lean into her shoulder and feel a wave of tiredness sweep through my body. She's right and I should take a break. A nap would be nice because I hadn't slept well after my run through the streets and the burglary. I'd felt charged-up for hours afterwards even though I had been filled with self-satisfaction and wellbeing.

Suddenly, she shouts, 'No, way!'

She crouches forward and peers closer at the screen. I push my face into her chest and rub my nose in her fluffy soft sweater moaning with pleasure.

'What?' I murmur loving the smell of her new shower gel.

'Look, there!' She says, 'I think those Lladro figurines are like the ones in the photos. Most of them are priced at £40-£50 but it says that the dancing woman figurine is worth £250 and they're willing to sell for £175!'

I jerk upright and zoom in enlarging the photograph fully. We both look backwards and forwards from the screen to the photographs.

I yell, 'Yippee! You're right, I'm sure that's the same dancing woman on Susan's bookshelf!'

'Ah, Barbie, you clever gorgeous girl, it's the same figurines,' I say. 'Susan is going to be delighted because they mean so much to her.'

This time, I text Rodger the news that Barbie has spotted the figurines on a different website with the link to send to the police.

I smile reading his reply. 'Well done, Barbara. That's absolutely splendiferous!'

Barbie's success spurs me on and later in the afternoon I match the serial number with Paul's computer on an electrical goods website listed under the name of Colin Morris. Unfortunately, there's no trace of the mobile, but one out of two isn't bad and breathe a sigh of relief that I've at least managed to retrieve some of the stolen goods.

***

The next morning, I ask Barbie, 'Do you fancy a run out to Harrogate on the train? It's my last day off work and although it's cold, I'd like some fresh air and a change of scene.'

She happily agrees and we head off into town. I know there are a fair number of art shops in York and the surrounding areas, and I'm determined to look for Rodger's paintings.

We begin our search in Petergate and then Castlegate at the art galleries. I've printed out the two images Simon sent me and am clutching them in my hand while we wander around looking at paintings that hang in the galleries.

Barbie sidles up to me. 'We must look like true art connoisseurs looking at these paintings as if we knew what we're talking about,' she says. 'When really we are clueless.'

I squeeze her hand and chortle. 'I know, it's a hoot really because I don't know a Rembrandt from a Vermeer.'

We leave the area having drawn a blank and Barbie stands still looking around the street. 'Maybe we're barking up the wrong tree here, Clive,' she says. 'I mean, the thieves obviously don't realise the value of the paintings and they could have sold them to anyone for a couple of pounds.'

I think about her words and nod. 'Yeah, you're right, and I suppose if they tried to sell them to an upper-class gallery this would raise suspicions as to where they'd come from. I've heard Rodger say that art theft and reproductions is big business.'

She puts her head onto one side and grins. 'So, maybe we come down a notch to second-hand shops which might be more of their market for trade,' she says. 'That's the place where we've found the other stuff online.'

I grin and whistle through my teeth. 'You're a star, Barbie,' I say and touch the side of her cheek with my hand. We head up to Boroughbridge Road but can't find any paintings that look remotely like the images and continue up to the train station.

***

Settled on the train, I take Barbie's hand. 'This is going to be a lovely journey for us both because it's where we spent our first full day and night together.'

She smiles and tucks her head into my shoulder. 'Oh yes, it's where I took the plunge and dragged you kicking and screaming back to my hotel room.'

I laugh. 'Well, that's not how I remember the day and I was more than willing to hot-foot back to the hotel with you.'

And, I wonder: would this be a good place to propose? We'd be surrounded with great memories, and I could check us into the same hotel and ask for the same room 203. I could take her to the places we went that day, lunch at Betty's, drinks at The Rose and Crown where I'd told her all about Agatha Christie hiding, and the jewellery shop where I bought her earrings. But is that too cheesy? I suppose wherever I take her we'll make new memories, and she might want to see other places in Yorkshire.

An hour later we jump off the train and head down to the main street and square. The town is busy with a Christmassy air amongst people shopping and collecting gifts. I sigh at the queue length outside Betty's because it is the week before Christmas, so we settle for a sandwich in a small café tucked away up a side street.

There's a Christmas market underway and I see Barbie's eyes light up, but I take her hand. 'Let's see what time we've got left after we've been to the arty shops then we can browse.'

She nods in agreement, and we head up to Eleanor Road. Sitting on the train, I'd Googled the shops in Harrogate, so I know there's a couple of places around and about this area. One is called, Pre-Loved Corner, which I think is a great name for a shop selling cast-offs. And, A Trading Post, which sells mostly furniture, but we look anyway. I'm tempted to go inside a second-hand book shop, aptly named, Books For All, but Barbie expertly guides me past and on our way.

It is in an Aladdin's cave type of shop that we strike lucky. Entering the shop, I smile. It seems like every inch of the place is stuffed full of things. I wander around browsing at old furniture and paintings that are hung on overcrowded walls then inhale the usual damp musty smell that second-hand places have. However, I turn around and see Barbie walk straight up to the man behind the counter and show him the images.

Even without hearing what she is saying, I can tell
he's excited. She is shuffling her black boots together
nd running a hand through her hair. I walk back over
› them as she loosens the top toggle on her brown
uffle coat and her cheeks are glowing.
'Oh, that would be great,' I hear her say as I approach
1em.
She swings around to me grinning like the proverbial
'heshire cat. 'Great news, Clive,' she gabbles, 'This
1an knows Rodger from way back and is sure he's
een these paintings over the weekend!'
I grin and clasp her gloved hands in mine. 'OMG!' I
xclaim then lower my voice and whisper, 'So, what's
e doing now?'
'Well, he won't tell me where he saw them because
's not the done thing,' she says and taps her nose. 'But
e's ringing the shop owner to see if they're still there.'
I guffaw at her tapping nose expression and decide it
ounds like the art dealer's secret society. The man
oks like Del-boy from, Only Fools and Horses, and I
ote his appearance. Especially, the tweed peaked cap. I
ckon, he'll make another character for one of my
ovels.
'Okay,' the man says ending the call. 'Yep, I think
ve found them but of course, I'm not at liberty to tell
ou where they are. However, if Rodger has the same
1obile number, I'll ring him to explain, and he can
ace them himself - how about that?'
'That would be amazing,' I say, and reach across to
1ake his hand firmly. 'But just in case his number is

different I can ring him now and you can talk to him or my phone.'

The man pulls his peak cap down a little further and lifts his rugged chin. 'Even better,' he says.

Quickly, I dial Rodgers number praying he will answer, and he does. I explain the situation and hand over my mobile.

Barbie and I practically skip out of the shop but not before she makes a donation into his cancer charity tin on the counter.

'It was just a small gesture to thank him for his help,' she says. I throw my arms around her and swing her up into the air. We hurry down to the Christmas market and nibble on warm salted-caramel cashew nuts while we look at the old market stalls filled with Christmas gifts and tree decorations.

We browse at an old charity shop where three's a battered briefcase is in the window.

Barbie says, 'Now, that's the perfect gift for a super sleuth!'

She strides into the shop, and I follow her. I agree it has a certain worn, lived-in look and she opens her purse then hands over a tenner. I grin and spot a black, trilby hat. It's a perfect fit and I pull the front down over my brow then nod. She grins and I give the shopkeeper a fiver. I wear the hat and carry the briefcase while we saunter down through the square. It feels warm on my head against the cold wind, and I pu my shoulders back walking with a certain swagger.

Carols are playing and I feel like bursting with happiness. Not just because I've got this wonderful woman with me but also because it looks like Rodger will get his treasured possessions back like the others will.

We stop at one stall filled with every coloured bauble and scene that I can imagine and grin. ‘Remember the bauble I bought you last year,’ I say, and she smiles linking my arm.

‘Oh yes, of York Minster. I’ll be hanging it up again this year on our tree alongside the one you gave me for our anniversary.’

‘So, how about you choose another one now?’

She smiles and I watch her eyes roaming along the rows of choices. She stops at a scene of The Shambles in gold and green. ‘I’ll have this one,’ she says wistfully. ‘It’s beautiful, and after all, it’s where I first met you.’

Chapter Twenty-Nine

'So, that's your cruise to Bahamas all booked for January,' I say to a middle-aged couple sitting across from my desk in the travel agency. They get up to leave and thank me for my help. While I call goodbye, I glance down at my mobile and see a text message from Rodger.

'I know it's short notice, but I've called an impromptu neighbourhood watch meeting at three this afternoon because a police community support officer is attending to bring us all up to date with the happenings. I so hope you and Barbara can make it?'

Immediately, I ring Barbie and she agrees to meet me for lunch when I finish work and come along to the meeting. We've walked up to Tower Street around the museum and Clifford Tower. I can't help remembering running down here two nights ago with my heart thumping full of adrenalin not knowing what was going to happen.

But today, we are taking a leisurely stroll because we're a little early for the meeting. Rodger had rung twice last night. Once on the train coming back from Harrogate thanking us generously and again at eight when we'd finished eating. On this second call, Simon had joined in our conversation thanking us too.

'They're such nice people,' I say to Barbie when we turn onto Friar Terrace. I spot a police car down on the street below the railings. 'Ah, the support officer must be here already.'

We hurry along the path and Simon opens the door greeting us warmly. He takes our coats and ushers us inside where everyone is seated. The officer is standing in front of the huge marble fireplace with her feet splayed apart and her hands clasped behind her back. She looks young with long blonde hair scraped back from her face under a flat peaked cap.

Rodger is standing beside her and claps his hands. 'That's it, officer, we are all here now,' he says.

She begins to explain exactly what happened at next doors burglary and because I've first-hand knowledge of this I look around the room.

I gasp in surprise when I look at the single armchair in the corner to see Mayor Robbins sitting with Paul standing behind him. I hold my hand up in a wave and he nods at me. Seated on the long Chesterfield sofa is Susan, Daphne, and Dorothy who is proudly clutching the jewellery box on her knee. I catch her eye, and she beams at me.

I tune back into what the officer is saying now, and the gist of her news is that the burglars have been detained and will more than likely be given custodial sentences because they've been linked to many other crimes in different areas of York. Also, one of the burglars' wives has been charged with selling illegal stolen goods online, along with a fine for the owner of the website.'

The officer takes a step towards me. 'I hear that you're the man to thank for helping to secure their arrest, Mr Thompson.'

I can feel my cheeks flush red and think, oh here we go again. When, if ever, will I get used to accepting gratitude and compliments. I nod. 'Well,' I say. 'I didn't do much really.'

Rodger, dressed in red trousers and a pink shirt protests loudly. 'Oh yes, you did! You dropped everything and ran here then confronted the burglars which ultimately brought about their downfall.'

The officer frowns and looks at everyone. 'I must say that tackling burglars when you are alone is not something we advise and it's best to ring for us to come then wait.'

My hackles rise a little at her words. 'Well, knowing the layout here where the path is behind railings and above street level, I knew that by the time the policemen ran to the end of the terrace to come up and along the path the burglars could have run the opposite way and escaped,' I say. 'And I didn't tackle them at all I simply put my foot out, so they'd trip over and hoped this would gain a few valuable seconds for the policemen to get to the door.'

I feel Barbie next to me take my hand in hers and squeeze it tightly. I know she is telling me to take a deep breath, and all will be well.

Rodger claps his hands together and shouts, 'Bravo!'

And to my surprise all the others begin to clap too. The officer politely refuses a glass of mulled wine or a warm mince pie which Rodger offers and takes her leave wishing us all a merry Christmas.

Simon takes her back along the hall. In the lounge, everyone begins to talk at once. Rodger hands me and Barbie a cup of mulled wine. I inhale the cinnamon aroma from the small China cup. Dorothy takes a mince

ie from the plate and lays it neatly on her white lace
andkerchief.

I head straight over to the major. 'Hey, it's great to see
ou here,' I say.

As the old man takes my hand, I brace myself for the
rm handshake and this time I don't wince.

He says, 'I wanted to come and thank you myself for
ll that you've done. It's great to see the blighters
rested and get their comeuppance for creeping around
y house uninvited.'

'Ah,' I say. 'But like I told the officer all I did was
ick my foot out.'

'Well, you've made an old man happy and if I'd been
venty years younger, I'd have tackled the scoundrels
yself!'

Paul shakes my hand next. 'Yeah, and thanks so much
r the message about the computer and matching the
rial numbers. I'm going to the station to collect it
morrow.'

I nod. 'It's a shame there's no trace of the mobile but
ou could still keep looking yourself. You never know
might pop up somewhere online or in a second-hand
op somewhere.'

feel a tap on the shoulder and spin around to see
usan grinning at me. Her cheeks are pink, but she
veeps her fringe aside and gushes over the return of
er Lladro figurines. 'I can't believe they're back on
y bookshelf where they belong and have sat for
ears,' she says. 'Thank you so much.'

Knowing this discovery is not mine alone, I call Barbie over and explain again that it was my girlfriend who spotted them online.

Susan smiles. 'Well, whichever one of you did it then thanks again. I'm so grateful that you took the time to do this, in fact, we all are.'

Just as we are getting to the end of all the gushing gratitude, I see Dorothy hobbling towards me and sigh inwardly. I plaster a smile onto my face.

'My dear, boy!' Dorothy cries. 'How can I ever thank you.'

'It's okay…' I start to say.

But in a second, she has me clasped in a bear hug and promptly bursts into tears. I can feel her thin frame and arms around my back while she sobs. I raise my head above her shoulder pleading at Barbie to come rescue me, which she does admirably by leading Miss Marple back to the sofa. Once seated, Dorothy removes her glasses and dabs her eyes with the handkerchief while stand in front of her and admire the jewellery box on the coffee table.

Barbie soothes her and I sip the mulled wine then perch on the pouffe.

I jump up again when Rodger approaches carrying a large parcel wrapped in brown paper.

'Now, Clive,' he says, and everyone stops talking. 'This is just a small token of my gratitude for tracing my two paintings. I'd like you and Barbara to have it for your home.'

I gasp and Barbie hurries over to my side.

'What?' I say dumbfounded.

Barbie turns pink and begins to open the paper. She gasps now, and I stare at the painting from his hallway of the beach.

'But we can't accept this,' I cry. 'It's from your hall.'

Rodger waves his arm nonchalantly. 'Dearest, Clive, I have hundreds of paintings in the attic and won't miss this one. But I know you love and appreciate the artwork, therefore, it's my gift that you must accept gracefully.'

I'm gobsmacked and look at Barbie who throws her arms around Rodger and hugs him. 'Oh, thank you, we'll hang it above the fireplace where it'll take pride of place.'

I decide if Barbie can happily accept this gift, then so can I and shake his hand.

Rodger raises his glass and says, 'A toast to Clive, a pillar of the community!'

Everyone joins him and shouts, 'To Clive.'

I grin from ear to ear and Barbie hugs me tight with pride and love shining from her eyes.

Chapter Thirty

The travel agency is busy this morning because Jane has the day off, and I arrange one booking after another until lunchtime when there's a lull in customers. Tina and I have agreed to have lunch at our desks. I usually like to leave the office and at least stretch my legs, but I also know Tina gets a little anxious left on her own, so this is not a problem.

Barbie has packed a poached salmon bap and an apple into a lunchbox. I smile when I open it knowing she's determined to make me eat healthier. This is another small gestures that she does for me on a daily basis. I try to think of the things I do for her and figure loving her comes top of the list. Along with taking my turn cleaning, washing, ironing, and doing the rubbish bins every week.

I reckon Barbie is up to something today. Something secretive, because I know her evasive look when I'd asked, 'So, what are you up to today?'

She'd shrugged her shoulders. 'Oh, not much.'

However, she had been wearing what I know is her working gear which consists of old tracksuit bottoms and a bobbly stained jumper. She can't be doing things in the garden; I reckon looking out at the pouring rain and wind. I munch into the sandwich and lick my lips at the delicate salmon flavour. Although salmon may be more expensive than tuna it certainly tastes so much better.

I finish the sandwich just as Tina has made us both a mug of tea and places it on my desk. She's been quiet today which isn't like her. Usually, she is bubbly and chats easily about anything and loves a bit of gossip. Jane tends to be the quieter of the two women and often doesn't talk unless the conversation is about an important issue.

I look up at her face while she hovers by my side. 'You, okay, Tina?'

She smiles but it's a half-hearted attempt that doesn't reach her pale blue eyes. Tina has her hair tied up into a long ponytail which makes her slender face seem very thin. She shrugs her shoulders in a long-sleeved green T-shirt. 'I'm sort of okay,' she says.

I smile and move a pile of booking forms from the end of my desk onto the other side. She nods knowing it is an invitation to sit - which she does. Her long legs are clad in brown trousers, and she shuffles back onto the desk from the edge.

'Trouble with the boyfriend or boyfriends?' I ask. 'How many are on the go now?'

She shakes her head and the ponytail swishes from side to side. 'Oh no, it's not about my boyfriend and I'm only seeing one now. He's called, Alex and he's fab!'

I nod. 'Great, so, why the long face?'

She wraps her fingers around the mug and sips the hot tea. 'Well, can I tell you something in confidence?'

I lift my shoulders and raise an eyebrow. 'Tina, we've worked together for nearly two years now,' I say. 'I'm surprised you even have to ask that?'

'I know,' she says. 'But it's about Jane and she'd be furious with me if she knew I was saying this.'

My mind races. Is there trouble between them? Is it about work and her job here? I know Jane thinks she's great and has picked things up very quickly. Quicker than I did at first. She has a natural friendly relationship with the customers and often feels responsible for arranging their trips which shows how conscientious she is at her job.

I ask, 'Is Jane unhappy with your work because I'd find that hard to believe?'

Tina shakes her head and looks down at her hands holding the mug. 'No, it's about Jane's new boyfriend, or should I say manfriend because he's the same age as her.'

This is news because I didn't know Jane had met somebody. I figure being caught up with my sleuthing escapades and off on holiday last week, I've missed out on happenings.

During the years I've worked here, Jane has always been on her own. I knew she'd been engaged ten years ago but they'd split up when he went to Saudi to work, and she refused to join him.

'Oh right,' I say. 'I didn't know Jane was seeing someone?'

'Well, she swore me to secrecy three weeks ago because she feels embarrassed about him.'

Now my mind is racing. 'Embarrassed? Why, what's wrong with him?'

'There's nothing wrong with him as such, or so she says, but it's the fact that she met him on a dating site that she's self-conscious about.'

My shoulders slump and I shake my head at Jane's
lly notion. 'But that's daft, loads of people meet on
ating sites now-a-days, don't they?'
Tina smiles. 'Yes, of course they do, and I've told her
at but all the same she feels embarrassed that she has
sorted to this way of introduction rather than the usual
eet up in a pub or nightclub.'
'Well,' I say and shrug. 'Considering Jane doesn't
equent pubs and nightclubs that would be difficult.'
Tina nods. 'But it's not that which is causing me
ncern,' she says and bites her bottom lip. 'It's him
at I'm worried about.'
I lean further towards Tina in a conspiratorially
anner. 'Ah, so what's wrong with him?'
Tina whips her head around to look at the door as if
xpecting Jane to walk through at any minute. She
ghs with obvious relief and looks at me again. 'I think
ere's something not quite right about what he's told
ne - it just doesn't add up.'
raise an eyebrow and ask, 'As in what?'
She licks her lips, 'Well, he's told Jane that he's a
usiness partner at The Chocolate Story Shop and they
eed more money to add another aspect of the tour.
nd she's been drawing money out of her account to
ve him.'
Oh, God,' I say. 'Do you know how much she's
ven him so far?'
Tina nods, 'I know she's taken £150 out twice now
d she's seeing him again tonight. His name is Rob,
d I just hope she hasn't drawn out more money
day.'

My whole insides slump, and I think about Tina's words. Although, I'm not a businessman, I figure to ad a whole new tour with renovations would cost much more than £300. I shake my head. How can Jane be so gullible as to believe this?

'Okay, Tina,' I say. 'Well, I'm in agreement with you here. This excuse to borrow money, stinks to high-heavens!'

I can see the genuine distress in Tina's eyes. 'Rob has said, he'll be paying her back in a few weeks,' she says 'But will he?'

I try to comfort her. 'Well,' I say patting her shoulder 'I hope so, for Jane's sake because that's a lot of mone to lose.'

Tina drains the tea from her mug. 'And I just wondered, well, now that you're a bit of private investigator, would you be able to find out more about him,' she says. 'I mean, perhaps you could follow Rob and see what he's up to?'

I shudder at the request. Is this something I want to ge involved with? I don't know the first thing about following people and have already decided I wouldn't feel comfortable about doing this. The invasion of someone's privacy is a different thing altogether.

'Er, Tina, I'm not a private investigator and the things I've been doing were to help my colleagues at the tour company and neighbours.'

'Oh, right,' she says and pouts. 'So, Jane isn't a colleague because she works here and not at the tour company?'

I feel bad and try to make my hesitancy sound better. 'Nooo, I didn't mean that! Of course, Jane is a colleague and a friend. But Tina, although I know you have her best interests at heart will Jane see this as interference?'

Tina slides gracefully up from my desk. She nods. 'Maybe you're right, Clive, but I just want to do something to help her.'

I smile and know I've got some soul-searching to do because after all, it's Jane who I've known for eight years, and have always classed as a friend. 'Look, leave it with me and I'll think about it tonight then see what I come up with to help.'

Tina squeezes my shoulder as she heads back to her desk, and I give her a weak smile.

Chapter Thirty-One

I can smell the paint as soon as I walk through our front door. I grin, what has my delectable bundle of joy been doing?

Barbie pokes her head around the lounge door as I hang up my coat.

She grins, 'Hey, I'm pleased you're not late because I've got a surprise for you.'

I walk towards her and kiss her warm lips then drape my arm along her shoulder as we saunter into the lounge. I gasp in genuine surprise at her handy work. Where the walls had been a dull murky beige colour, now they are light cream.

'Wow, this looks amazing!' I say and smile. 'It's so much brighter and the room looks much bigger.'

Barbie nods. 'I know, the paint is called, Ice Cream,' she says and lifts her chin. 'I started as soon as you left this morning and have just pushed all the furniture back into place.'

I hug her tight. 'Ah, you should have waited for me to help with the lifting, but it's fantastic, just like you are,' I say. 'I didn't know you could paint as well as everything else. Is this another of your hidden talents?'

She giggles. 'Oh, yeah, decorating is my second profession that I've kept hidden from you.'

I sniff the air and decide it's not just paint I can smell. 'Are you cooking, too?'

'Yep, I've a pot of chilli in the oven.'

I shake my head in awe of this amazing woman and rub my cold hands together. 'Lush, that'll warm me up, it's freezing out. I think we might get snow tonight.'

Barbie heads into the kitchen and I follow her.
'Shall I lay our new table,' I ask. 'Or are we keeping that just for visitors?'
She smiles. 'No, Clive, I think we should use it and stop eating off trays on our knees, do you?'
'Anything to make you happy, babe.'
She lifts the pot out of the oven and turns to me. 'Er, aren't I a bit old to be your babe,' she asks. 'And where did you get that expression?'
I lift placemats out of the cupboard and cutlery from the drawer. 'I've been in the agency with Tina today and some of her expressions rub off on me.'
Barbie smiles and we chat about our days as we sit together at the table. The chilli is warming and hearty with our favourite warm pitta breads and I sigh with pleasure.
I'm not sure if it is caveman type of attitude to admit this, but it's great to come home on a cold dark winter day to a warm inviting home, great food, and a loving partner. Clive Thompson, you're a lucky guy.
Barbie tears a pitta bread in half then stares at me. 'Somethings going around in that mind of yours,' she says. 'I can see it in your face and eyes, do you want to share it with me?'
How does she do it, I wonder. How can she read my mind like this? I've probably got one of those faces which shows everything I'm thinking and feeling. I shrug my shoulders. Whatever it is, I want to tell her all about Jane because her opinion is always good to know.
Barbie gapes at me. 'Jane!' She cries, 'Jane has been taken in by a conman on a dating site?' She shakes her

head brusquely. 'I can't believe that. She's so sensible and down to earth.'

I nod and lay my fork into the empty bowl. 'I know, but now I'm in the position where I do want to help but I'm also wary at the same time.'

She takes my hand. 'It's a tricky one because you'll be doing it behind her back. It would have been different if she had asked you to investigate Rob, but because it's come from Tina, and Jane doesn't know then it could be difficult.'

I frown at her words knowing she's right. 'That's true. If Jane knew, I'd feel much happier about investigating, as you call it, and then there's the outcome to think about, too.'

Barbie frowns. 'As in?'

'Well,' I say fiddling with the end of my fork. 'What if I discover something terrible about Rob. How am I going to tell her? Will she be furious that Tina and I have done this behind her back? Often in life, people don't want to hear sad things - they like to stick their heads in the sand and pretend it isn't happening.'

Barbie nods. 'Yeah, I see your point, but I don't think Jane is the type of woman to shove her head in the sand,' she says. 'But there again, I wouldn't have thought her the type of woman to be taken in by a man and hand over money to him, but she has. Love does strange things to people, don't you think?'

I think over her words and know what she means. Love alters the way we live our lives or hope to in the future. Look at the difference in me since I met Barbie. I know she's changed me and, all for the better. But

ove doesn't always change things for the best and
ometimes it can be detrimental in relationships.
I lean over and kiss her. 'It certainly does. I think
ou've bewitched me from the first day I met you!'
She grins and takes my hand. 'Think it over first
efore you commit to helping Tina. But because I'm
ke the good witch, Glinda, from The Wizard of Oz,
m sure you'll make the decision that's right for you.'
I chortle and look around the clean bright walls which
ake our new table look even better than it did before.
Jane could be feeling the same happiness with her new
uy, Rob in her apartment for all I know. And who am I
interfere or cast doubts upon her choice of partner.
ut then I remember reading an article online and
own. 'I hope to God, Jane hasn't got herself mixed up
one of these online fake-love scams,' I say. 'I've read
bout the rise in cases of people, especially men, who
ave been robbed of their money during the pandemic
ue to loneliness and isolation. The scammers have
xploited these vulnerable, confused widows and
idowers and took thousands from them in false
ardship stories. They often start by pleading for small
nounts which increases the more they get to know the
ictim. It's reported that the root of most cases is set in
hana and the police there are working with other
rces around the world, especially the English police,
arrest them and retrieve the victim's money.'
Barbie begins to clear away the dishes and I jump up
help.
She sighs heading into the kitchen. 'Well, in Jane's
ase, she knows this guy. And he's local so she's not

posting money online to false organisations, but all the same, I think it would be a good thing if you did look out for her, Clive.'

I wash the dishes and head upstairs to my office for a hour while Barbie rings her mam and Jenny to discuss Christmas arrangements. I log in and write up my conversation with Tina making notes and using her few words.

I usually tell my customers on the tours that chocolate features heavily in the history of York although there's been changes during the years. Chocolate and coffee became a leisure or pleasure pursuit amongst the wealthy Georgians. This paragraph usually serves me well, but I sigh, in future, I will tell them more because it is an important part of our city's history.

I decide to start with Rob's request for money and Google, The Chocolate Story Shop in York.

I read, York's Chocolate Story is a visitor attraction and chocolate museum on King's Square, in York. It opened in March 2012 and shows the history of chocolate making in York, including the Rowntree's factory which opened in 1890 but has been owned since 1988 by Nestlé.

So, I figure sitting back in my chair, the shop has been open for nine years but it tells me that it's run by Continuum Attractions Group which makes me pause for thought.

Could Rob simply work in the shop doing tours or selling chocolate? He can't be a partner in this big group because he wouldn't be asking for small amounts of money. However, this could just be a starter for Rob and his lies. He might move on and request larger sums like the scammers do? I shudder.

I try to remember if Jane has ever told me about her financial status and shake my head knowing she hasn't. I do recall one day that she told me there was only her and a brother because their parents were killed in a fire on a caravan site when they were teenagers. Did they have life insurance, I wonder, and has Jane got a nest egg somewhere? And, does Rob know about this?

I figure I'm simply guessing and close down the computer then head back downstairs.

Barbie is clicking off her mobile and she smiles then walks towards me.

'I think we should hang it up now because the paint is dry.'

I raise my eyebrow. 'Hang what?'

'The painting from Rodger,' she says and picks up a hook and the hammer from the top of the fire surround. 'Do you want to do the honours?'

I grin. 'It would be my pleasure.'

With Barbie behind me saying, 'Left a little, and down an inch.' I successfully hammer the hook in place then lift the painting onto the wall.

We both stand back, and I slide my arm around her waist. The blue colours of the sea and the sandy beach on the artwork look amazing against the bright cream wall.

I smile. 'It looks absolutely beautiful,' I say. We step backwards and sit onto our squashy sofa looking up at the painting. 'I could sit on that beach right now!'

I feel like this is becoming our new home together now, and I pray that she'll agree to be Mrs Thompson when I do propose.

Chapter Thirty-Two

There's a strange atmosphere in the office the next day. I can't help thinking about Jane and keep looking at her as if she's grown another head overnight. How can she believe Rob's story about where he works and what he does? Or does she know and isn't bothered by his obvious lies.

I've never known a more level-headed, organised woman than Jane. And if I use the words, control-freak, I mean them in a kindly way because she is a very considerate person.

When the restrictions of lock-down hit us all, I swear she was more upset about Tina and me than herself. We'd been furloughed at home for months, but she'd done a call-in to us both every Friday morning so that we all stayed in touch. She had made us talk about our worries quite openly and contributed herself with her own concerns about the future and what it would hold. I'd grown quite used to the Friday calls and found them reassuring and comforting. In a way, it had made me feel as though I wasn't alone in the frightening new pandemic world that we'd suddenly all been thrust into.

Before Jane arrived at work this morning, I'd told Tina what I had found out so far about The Chocolate Story Shop in King's square. Her big naïve eyes had widened in shock. But then visible relief flooded her face when I'd told her that I intend to help Jane if possible. Tina had hugged me tight in her response and we'd just pulled apart before Jane entered.

The rest of the day up until three in the afternoon is busy with customers and exchanging money at the bureau. While Jane makes an afternoon cuppa, Tina winks at me behind her back.

Tina asks, 'So, Jane did you see your fella last night?'

Jane swings around to face us both as she drops a teaspoon into her own mug. And there it is. There is the look of being loved-up that I know so well and often see in Barbie's face. I can see it shine in Jane's eyes when she shyly nods, and a dreamy expression fills her whole persona. I notice she has curled her usual straight hair and it softens her face.

'Oh, yeah,' she says. 'We had a lovely night.'

I raise an eyebrow at her and play dumb as though I know nothing about him. 'Ah, Jane, so you have a new guy on the scene, what's he called?'

Jane pours hot water onto her tea bag and swishes it around with the spoon. She has her back to me so I can't judge her expression, but I can hear the tenderness in her voice.

'Yes, Clive,' she says. 'I do have a new partner and he's called, Rob.'

I give an exaggerated little clap with my hands while she walks to Tina and places her mug on the desk.

Tina grins. 'And he's soooo good-looking, isn't he, Jane?'

She titters at Tina's remark, and I can tell by the light in her eyes that Jane is loving the compliments. 'Yes, Tina, he is an attractive man.'

Jane pours milk into my tea and walks towards me smiling. She places my mug onto my desk, and I touch the side of her arm. 'Well, I hope he knows how lucky he is to have met you.'

Jane waves her arm nonchalantly as if to say, away
'ith yourself, and I grin at her pink cheeks.
'We had a lovely meal and drinks up at Middletons
Iotel,' Jane says. 'And it was every bit as good as you
ecommended, Clive.'
I gasp in imaginary surprise. 'Ah, Jane if you were up
ear us, you could have called in to see me and
arbie?'
She pulls her shoulders back in a confident stance.
We will next time.'
Jane almost swaggers back to her desk as though she
nows without a moments doubt that she will be seeing
im again. I decide that she must feel secure in their
elationship and is thinking of them as a couple.
I watch Jane sip her hot tea while looking at her
omputer screen. But I can see at an angle that there is
othing on it only her desktop photograph. I figure she
ust be daydreaming about Rob last night. When I
ink of him telling her lies so soon into their
elationship, my heart goes out to her. I can tell she's
oing to be terribly upset when, and if, it all falls apart.
Tina interrupts. 'So, are you seeing him again tonight,
ane?'
Jane nods. 'Yeah, just for an hour after work at 6pm
ecause he's got a late conference call.'
Tina looks directly at me and nods as if to say, this is
hat we've been waiting for. I give her a tiny wink
om the corner of my eye. With being so young and
rly, Tina can get away with this direct questioning to
ne, whereas, if I'd asked the same question, it would
ave looked as though I was being nosey.

I smile and text Barbie. 'Going to be a little late tonight. I'm going to hang around when Jane meets this new guy at 6pm and see what happens?'

A reply immediately pings back. 'Okay, take care, do you want me to come?'

I reply with a simple, 'No' and a smiley emoji.

***

I left the office a few minutes before Jane which I hope won't raise any suspicions. I'm standing in a doorway three shops down the agency. It is cold but dı and I turn up the collar of my coat and shiver. It's my first time covertly following someone, and I'd read tip from the internet last night.

As soon as he arrives, I'm to memorise his appearanc and hope he doesn't have a car, or I'll be sunk. I must keep my distance and learn the side streets. This will b easy, I reckon because I know York well. I need to fin out about his habits and actions which should be okay as I already know where he claims to work. And if I watch him for a while, I'll get to know his schedule.

The article I read told me that trailing is much easier the suspect doesn't recognise me and I'm not to wear clothing that will stand out. Hence, I've left my flying jacket at home and my thick winter coat is black. If my suspect knows me, which he doesn't, it's best to consider wearing items like, a baseball cap, dark sunglasses, a reversible jacket, or a wig.

Yes, it's from an American website and the sunglasse and baseball cap won't work here in York in the middl of winter. But I smile, if I do need to trail someone in the future, I've got the information ready, and I could try the other items in the summer.

I'm to be prepared for anything, including being noticed, and must have a cover story ready so that it sounds convincing. Props or appearing occupied, like talking on a mobile can also help my story if needed. I could, in the future, bring a dog for walking, prepare a fake name, or pretend to be an estate agent and carry a business card.

I start to shuffle my feet together to keep warm and decide I'm more at risk of being noticed by Jane than Rob. Although, if she is still as starry-eyed as she's been today, Jane might not even notice my presence.

With a jolt from my thoughts, I see a man approach the front of the travel agency just as Jane steps outside. I reckon, he's over six foot with brown cropped hair and from a distance has dark hooded eyes. The suit is certainly not Armani and I figure it looks cheap, as if it could be shiny and well-worn.

Jane raises herself up on her tiptoes and kisses him while he snakes his arm around her waist and pulls her into him. She looks cute and cosy in a grey fur jacket with her long hair falling around her upturned expectant face.

Already, I'm annoyed and know I am using detrimental verbs to describe Rob. I don't like him for misleading my friend. They head off down the street and I follow discreetly at a distance that I judge is long enough not to be seen but short enough if they suddenly quicken their pace, I'll be able to keep up with them.

I smile at my reflection in a shop window enjoying myself and decide that next time I'll wear my trilby hat and be like Del-boy in Harrogate so I can pull it down over my eyes.

Jane and Rob hurry inside The Duke of York pub while I hover behind a red telephone box on the edge of Kings Square. I figure, the hanging around is going to be the worst part of surveillance and hope they only have one drink. I don't class myself as an impatient man but I'm not someone that likes to loiter aimlessly. I always have a plan or route in mind, so I sigh and push my hands deep into the coat pockets.

I look at the pub sign and remember this was somewhere I'd taken Barbie for a drink when we first met. I ring her now and she is languishing in a hot bath. I tell her I wish I were in there with her.

'Just think of Jane, and how you might be able to stop her getting hurt or robbed of all her money,' she says.

I agree and smile. She's my voice of reason, I think, and we chat about her day.

A taxi pulls up at the end of the lane and I end my call to Barbie. Jane hurries out then hops into the back of the taxi closely followed by Rob. However, he waves to her, turns and walks briskly down the street.

Okay, pal, I think, let's see where you are going for your conference call. He is heading towards the Chocolate Story Shop but then veers off and I follow him at my safe distance. We head up towards the train station and onto Leeman Road which takes us around the back and left onto Bismarck Street.

Rob walks at a fast pace and I lengthen my stride to keep up. My senses are heightened and I'm buzzing mainly because I don't know where I am going. It's a little like a magical mystery tour, although I check myself and remember the serious side of what I'm doing. I pause behind the trunk of a big tree and peer around to see Rob stop and take a set of keys from his trouser pocket.

He walks up to the middle house with a red door and goes inside. I pull out my mobile and take a close-up photograph of the door hoping I'll be able to see the house number later. Lights had already been on in the house before Rob entered which makes me think someone else is inside. Or he could be security conscious and leave on lights like Barbie often does when we are out.

I take more photographs of the cul-de-sac and decide they don't look privately owned properties but are too well-maintained to be council. Perhaps they are housing association properties? I smile knowing I can Google the street when I get home. The houses are obviously two or three-bedroom family homes. In the garden of the house Rob has entered is a trampoline and a small bike lying next to an old garden shed. Is he a family man and married with children?

I decide to hang around for a while to make sure he doesn't leave again, after all, he could just be visiting someone. I sigh knowing I could well be jumping to conclusions and my assumptions might not be right. But I hope for Jane's sake, I'm wrong.

Chapter Thirty-Three

Rob Taylor loved women. He simply couldn't help it. He loved their smell, the feel of their soft skin, their shapes, and moulds of flesh. No matter their size or age, it was immaterial to him. He loved everything that a woman was.

At the age of thirty-five he'd long since given up fighting against this fixation and decided it was simply the way he was. He had loved his wife when they first married and in some ways he still did. But since the kids came along, she'd changed. Their every wish came before his needs now and he'd never been able to rid himself of her neglect when they were born. He had been cast aside to make room for them.

When he'd moaned to his mother, she'd been furious, and her words had resounded in his ears. 'You're so shallow and pathetic just like your father!'

His wife had told him that she loved the kids more than him and always would. This had been the final straw and he'd left.

The fact that she had found him with a young girl in bed before she'd said this didn't register with Rob. He couldn't see what all the fuss was about. Sex was a basic need and act, and just because the girl was only eighteen it had made the situation a hundred times worse to his wife.

'You're a selfish liar!' She'd yelled at him. 'You are a cheat, and don't care about anyone else but yourself.'

He'd disputed this because he did care. He cared deeply about a woman's body and worshipped it with the love, attention, and adoration it deserved.

However, his wife had taken him back because the ds had cried, 'Daddy come home!'

Rob had seen her melt before his very eyes. This was eat because money wasn't just tight, it was in dire eed. However, he smiled, there was always, Jane.

Chapter Thirty-Four

My alarm tinkles the next morning at six and I throw back the covers. Barbie groggily asks what time it is, and I kiss her forehead then she falls back to sleep. I creep around the bedroom collecting clothes and shoes and head into the bathroom to shower and dress.

I'd decided last night that Rob may well leave home early to go to work in The Chocolate Story Shop and have decided to loiter outside his house from seven. It could be a waste of time; I think hurrying up past Micklegate and around to the back of the station because he might not start work until nine. But I don't want to miss him leaving this house. If, of course, he's still in there from last night.

If he were only visiting someone then he might not even be there, and I could have stayed in bed. Crunching into a cereal bar, I walk along Bismarck Street and position myself again behind the wide tree trunk.

When I'd told Barbie last night about my findings, she'd suggested that he may well be married with kids but also that Jane could possibly know this. I think of her words now and wonder if Barbie is right? I can't think Jane would have an affair with a married man bu also know, as Barbie has told me before, I'm gullible when it comes to women and their wily ways.

The red door opens and Rob steps outside. I dart bac behind the tree trunk but have enough space to watch and confirm that it is him. He's certainly dressed a gre deal differently to last night. This morning he is in scruffy track suit bottoms and an old parker coat. Whe he hurries down the path, he pulls up the hood. I shiver but fall into step behind him.

There's no one around at this time in the morning and I feel more vulnerable than I did last night. Which, I decide, is silly but the dark morning seems more eerie. Rob walks briskly back along Leeman Road and onto Station Avenue where he halts abruptly at a bus stop.

Damn, I curse, I'd not thought of this. I had comforted myself last night that he didn't have a car but hadn't thought about public transport. I stand at the back of a short queue of people awaiting the number 40 bus. I listen to two women complaining about the bus never running on time and being late for their shift.

While I'm waiting, I fumble around in my pockets for loose change not really knowing where I am going and how much the fare will be. All I know now is that I must follow him. Whether its blatant curiosity or the need to get to the bottom of exactly who he is and what he's doing, I'm determined to find out about his situation.

I look at the sign on the bus stop and decide to ask for the final destination when I climb aboard. This way, if Rob gets off the bus before the end of the route, I can ump off behind him. The bus arrives and everyone ncluding Rob shuffles inside paying their fares. I take a seat two rows behind him and feel my heart begin to pound. I'm finding the chase and my unknown whereabouts and destination exciting.

Not wanting to draw any attention to myself, I copy he other passengers and stare down at my mobile. It's strange how this is everyone's past time now, whereas not so long-ago people would have read a newspaper when travelling.

Every time the bus pulls up at a stop, I brace myself and stare at the back of Rob waiting for him to get up and alight. Finally, after around thirty minutes I see him reach up and press the button to request the next stop.

I'm ready and fall in behind him and the two women as we alight the bus. The other few people also get off here and I look up to the bus stop sign which tells me this is Huxley Road. I fall in behind Rob again and cross the road to a big factory with the huge sign saying, Nestle.

I frown and slow my pace down like Rob has done. Does he work here and not at The Chocolate Story Shop? Maybe he has two jobs? Could this business partner malarky be just a made-up story to tell Jane.

I hear and see an older man approach Rob at the turnstile swing gates into the factory. I stand still wanting to be near enough to hear their conversation but not to be recognised as someone that is snooping. I reach for my mobile phone and look down at it as though I've received a message.

The older man is dressed much the same as Rob in old scruffy jeans and a donkey jacket. He calls to him, 'Hey, Rob, how you doing?'

Rob shouts back. 'Okay, another day, another dollar, as they say.'

Donkey jacket man asks, 'You still on the Kit-Kat line?'

Rob chortles. 'Aye, are you still supervising the chocolate orange brigade?'

'Yeah, but I won't be complaining as long as I'm not amongst the ninety-eight poor suckers about to lose their jobs - I should be okay, but it's a tough time to be laid off, just before Christmas, isn't it?'

I hear Rob sigh and watch him shuffle his feet in heavy black boots. 'Tell me about it, I might be one of them because as they say, last in, first out, so who's to know? The missus will be livid if I do get paid off because we've got nought saved for Christmas stuff and she's just taken me back!'

Donkey jacket lowers his voice. 'Ah, well, let's hope you'll be kept on,' he says. 'How's the wife and kids?'

Rob moves towards the turnstile swing gates and pulls out a pass card. 'Ah, they're fine, thanks,' he shouts and manoeuvres himself through the gates. 'See you later.'

I watch Rob hurry down the factory walkway and donkey jacket pass through the turnstile then head off in the opposite direction.

I whistle between my teeth and shake my head. This guy is something else. He's a real jerk and I'm not sure how to spell the expletives I've got spinning around in my head. I turn back and cross over to the bus stop then flag down the number 40 when it comes along the road.

Settled on the bus in the same seat as when I came, I frown. Is Barbie right and does Jane knows that he's a family man - it could be something that she's accepted.

But what if she doesn't know? Hmm, I grimace and sigh. So much for the reason to borrow money that's needed to pour into The Chocolate Story Shop. Could Jane really be that naïve to believe this? I shrug, as

Barbie says, love does strange things to people, and she obviously adores him.

While the bus takes me back into the city, I try to see my findings about him in a different way. I remember his words and how his wife had taken him back. So, he could have met Jane when he was parted from his wife which doesn't sound quite so bad. But if this is true, now that he is back in the family home, has he told Jane?

Whichever way I try to look at this situation it's not good. I think of Jane's excited face and the look of love in her eyes yesterday when she'd talked about Rob and sigh heavily. I reckon finding this out today is the easy bit. Now all I have to do is tell her.

Chapter Thirty-Five

I'm not due into the agency until twelve and with a hot ·acon bap I sit at my desk gazing around my home ffice. Barbie has gone off to a garden centre to buy wo Christmas gifts for Geoff and Jenny.
I look at my shelves full of books and my own novel itting proudly in the centre. I still love the cover and now during the last few weeks my writing has taken a ack seat. I'm itching to get back to drafting my next ovel. I have my notes ready with each chapter mapped ut in scenes and the all-important plot. There are some riters who just open a page and write free flow but 'm not like this. I like to know where I am going in the :art, middle, and end of my story.
I've already decided to make my detective a happily iarried man as opposed to the usual Rebus type of epressive character. A shiver runs up my back then rin as I write, Chapter One.
Here we go, I think then continue to type. Jim Scott new what side his bread was buttered on. He loved is wife to distraction. Married for nine years now she 'as as beautiful to him as the first day he'd clapped yes on her. Clever, with a heart as big as a lion and a appy-go-lucky attitude to life, she was behind him at very turn. She was his reason for living and gave him a ense of purpose.
While I type the last few words, I know I'm thinking f my Barbie and smile. What am I waiting for? And ıddenly, it comes to me. Christmas Eve. That is the ıy I'm going to propose to her. It'll be the last day we ıve to ourselves and I'm going to make it special to

us. I'll get down on one knee in The Shambles where we met and ask her to be my wife. I shake my head not knowing why I've been dithering for weeks. I rub my chin and suppose that's just the way I am.

I've four days left to sort out the ring and I jump up from the chair and hurry into our bedroom. I sit at the dressing table and carefully open her jewellery box. Although I know she's not home, I look furtively over my shoulder and lick my lips. It feels like I'm snooping into her personal things, but I want to get this right.

I figure if I take her pearl ring which I know is a perfect fit to a jeweller then I'll be able to choose the engagement ring at the correct size. I slip the ring into the pocket of my trousers and hope there'll be time late this afternoon to look around the jewellery shops.

Rushing downstairs, I hunt in the bureau for my ISA account details. I know there is around £2K which was the residue when Sarah left, and her American boyfriend settled with money. I've managed not to spend a penny of it throughout furlough and the pandemic. I grin knowing this will be the most expensive gift I'll ever give Barbie and decide she is worth every penny. I decide to donate at least half of the money to her engagement ring.

***

This will be the good part of the day; I think sauntering up to work. The awful news I've to tell Jane will be the bad part of the day. I brighten remembering Barbie's words this morning when I'd told her about my surveillance and what I had found out.

'Look,' she'd said. 'Jane might take it better than you think and if she already knows he's lied about being married then it's up to her what she does with your information. And remember you have her best interests at heart about the money. At least she'll know and if she continues to give Rob money then that's up to her. You've done your bit to help which is all you can do.'

I'd nodded. But now when I turn onto King's Square, I rehearse in my mind how to say the words.

'Just state the facts,' Barbie had said. 'There's no point in trying to gloss it over even though you want it to sound less hurtful. She needs to know the truth.'

I breeze into the office calling hello and settle at my desk. There's just one old man sitting at Jane's desk patiently waiting for her to book up his staycation to visit a cousin in Bristol.

I glance over at Jane. She's dressed in a black suit, and I see the confident organised look on her face as she chats to the gentleman. While I wait for my computer to boot-up, I look at Tina who is standing at our display of brochures near my desk.

She is pretending to organise the brochures into the correct piles, but I see the expectant look on her young face while she stares at me. I'd been tempted to text her when I had arrived home this morning but then decided to wait. I give her a small nod and a little wink hoping to convey the fact that I've been successful.

The old man leaves the shop and Jane smiles at me.

'Hi, Clive,' she says. 'Enjoyed your lie in this morning?'

I nod. 'Yeah, thanks' I say, and although I have been up since six, I continue the charade. 'How was your drink last night with Rob?'

Jane nods even though she doesn't seem to have the same dreamy expression as yesterday. Her shoulders look a little stiff. Maybe I've hit a raw nerve, as the saying goes, and she shuffles papers together on her desk. 'Yes, it was nice, thanks.'

Should I tell her now? But what if a customer comes into the shop? If Jane is going to react badly to my information about Rob, then she'll be mortified at getting upset in front of customers. I rub my jaw. Perhaps waiting until we close for the day will be best, I decide.

My telephone extension rings and while I take the call, I see Tina making us a cuppa.

She places the mug on my desk and asks, 'Had any more thoughts about proposing to Barbie?'

'Well, actually, yes. I'm hoping to sort it out later today,' I say, and pull-out Barbie's ring from my pocket. 'I'm going to propose to her on Christmas Eve and I've borrowed her pearl ring to take it to a jeweller and get it sized.'

Tina squeals with delight and I see Jane grin too.

'Ooooh, how romantic,' Tina sighs heavily. 'I'd so love a man to do that for me!'

I smile at her eager young face and say, 'Your time will come, Tina, I'm sure of that.'

Jane gets up and walks towards me then looks down at the ring in the palm of my hand. She looks a little wishful and I can see her eyes have clouded over. I curse myself for being thoughtless. This isn't the best of days to talk about love and marriage. My stomach churns and I wonder if I should tell Jane my news tomorrow. But I hear Barbie's voice in my ear saying, don't put off the inevitable just get it sorted.

'So,' Jane asks. 'What type of wedding are you going to have when Barbie says yes?'

This takes me by surprise because I haven't thought that far ahead yet. I was just hoping to get through the engagement bit first. I answer truthfully. 'Well, it'll be second time around for both of us, so I don't suppose Barbie will want the big affair with white dress, flowers, and bridesmaids, will she?'

Jane smiles. 'Hmm, maybe not. She might just want a registry office with close friends and family.'

I nod. 'Possibly, she's not a showy person much like myself, but I do want her to enjoy our special day together.'

Jane raises an eyebrow. 'And what type of wedding do you want, Clive?'

I sip my tea and stare up at my favourite poster of the beach in Bali. 'I'd love to marry Barbie standing right on that beach,' I say, and point to the poster. 'It's been my favourite scene from the first day I started here.'

Tina snorts. 'Oh, now that would be a dream come true.'

I tell them about the painting Rodger gave to us and how it is hanging above the fireplace.

Jane smiles. 'So, a wedding on a beach sounds like something you'd both love. Well, best of luck, Clive and if you need any help or advice about the ring just let me know. I'll be glad to help.'

Jane heads back to the desk and her cuppa while I take a deep breath and an idea formulates in my mind. If I ask Jane to come with me to the jewellers, then I could ask her for a coffee afterwards and tell her about Rob.

But I don't get the chance to do this because at five o'clock while Jane turns around the shop sign from open to closed, she stands with her back against the door. 'Okay, both of you, I want to know what's going on?'

I sigh and look at Tina who looks down fiddling with her mouse.

Jane folds her arms and sighs. 'There's been a funny atmosphere in here all day, and I know something's not right.'

This is it. I've got to get it all out now. I can't put off the dreaded deed any further and take a deep breath. 'Please sit down, Jane,' I say nodding towards her desk.

Jane heads to her desk and perches on the edge with her arms still folded in a defensive manner. First, I tell her about Tina being concerned and then slowly and carefully I relate everything I've discovered about Rob.

I see the colour drain from her face and notice her hands trembling as she unfolds her arms and clasps them together in front of her chest. Her eyes have filled with unshed tears, and she mumbles, 'Dear, God!'

From behind me, I hear Tina burst into loud sobs. 'Ooooh, Jane, I'm so sorry!'

Jane doesn't move. I walk over to Tina and place my hand on her shoulder. 'Tina only told me because she as really worried about you, Jane,' I say. 'As we both ere.'

So, w…what are you going to d…do?' Tina wails.

head towards Jane, but she holds her hand up in front me as if to say, do not come any closer. I see her pull ıck her shoulders and lift her chin. The tears don't fall om her eyes. She swipes at them with the back of her ınd. 'It's okay, I was thinking of finishing with the eep anyway!'

My stomach churns and I take another step towards er holding open my hands. 'Look, I could try to help ou get your money back,' I say. 'Shall I come with ou and demand he pays it back, or we could threaten involve the police?'

No!' She shouts. 'I'm perfectly capable of sorting this ıt myself!'

Chapter Thirty-Six

It's Christmas Eve and I can hardly contain myself. Bubbles of excitement keep filling my stomach and I want to laugh aloud. I have all my plans in place to propose to Barbie with help from Jane and Tina.

Barbie is getting ready upstairs because I've told her I'm taking her out for lunch. Of course, she wants to know where I am taking her, but I have refused to tell which is adding to the surprise I have planned.

After I'd told Jane about Rob, I had worried that her bolshie reaction would affect our friendship but thankfully, it hasn't. Jane told Tina and I the next day that she'd met with Rob and ended the relationship. H had apologised and reassured Jane that he will pay he the money back monthly on condition that she didn't inform the police. Jane explained that if he had a cour case for theft against him, he would lose his job at Nestle and sensibly had decided that situation wouldn help anyone.

Tina and I congratulated her, and they both joined m at the jewellers to give their opinion on the ring I have chosen for Barbie. Both women swooned at my choic and told me they'd love to be given a ring like this which was a comfort to know that I've chosen well.

When I'd arrived home last night, Barbie had ordere an Indian take out meal and we were both delighted when Adhar himself delivered the food. We exchange news and Binita had added her home-made extras which made an amazing banquet of food laid out on o new table.

I'd looked around the lounge with our Christmas decorations and helped Barbie attach her two new baubles to the tree then reach up and place the silver star on the top. We'd both whooped and laughed when I'd turned on the lights. The red, green, and gold tinsel shimmered in the glow of our lamps, and I had hugged her tight. It was a wonderful sight.

She had stood our Christmas cards up on the mantelpiece and I read a big glittery card from Tim and Rosa. They'd written how the restaurant was going from strength to strength, and they hoped to see us over the holiday period.

Barbie had giggled then said, 'We've made some nice friends during your sleuthing escapades.'

To which, I'd agreed and picked her up then carried her upstairs laughing into the bedroom.

***

Now, I'm dressed in my navy-blue suit and grey shirt. When she joins me, I help her on with her white wool coat and we set off into town arm in arm. I steer us towards The Shambles.

'Oh,' she says. 'Are we calling in to see Jane and Tina?'

I smile and tuck her arm further into the crook of my arm. 'Well, we can after lunch,' I say. 'Let's see what time we've got left later in the day.'

Ordinarily, there's no reason to book a table at Shambles Tavern but I have done and asked for the small round table in the corner by the roaring fire. It's where we sat on our first date, and I want us to relieve our memories before I ask her.

I'm just about to pull open the tavern door when I hear someone call out, 'Hello, Clive!'

I swing around to see Pamela and Charles walking up to the tour office and I wave. 'Hey, Merry Christmas, guys,' I shout across the street.

Barbie waves too, then I whisk her inside and we are shown to our table.

'Ah, Clive, we haven't been here for ages,' she says while I ease the coat from her shoulders.

'I know, but I was thinking of it the other day and remembering our first date here,' I say. 'As it's Christmas Eve I could have booked somewhere more upmarket like, The Starre Inn, but knew we'd be just as happy in here.'

She nods and smiles. 'You chose just the right place.'

The fire is roaring, and I look around the small quaint room. The brown wood chairs and tables are old and could do with updating but it's cosy and the food is always great. There are gold glittery streamers hanging everywhere with a big tree in the corner. The tinsel and baubles are gold and red and I smile. It certainly is a magical time of year.

'I'm starving,' Barbie says. 'But one thing I'm not going to have is turkey because we'll be having that tomorrow at Jenny's.'

I grin. 'When we came here the first time you had steak & kidney pie with fresh vegetables and I had ham egg & chips,' I say. 'So, I don't know about you but I'm going to have the same now.'

The waiter come to the table, and she says, 'I'll have the steak pie with vegetables, please.'

I laugh and order mine then we sit back and sip our drinks. The tiny sequins on her back cocktail dress are sparkling under the overhead lights. The fire is creating a little glow around her face, and I hold her cheeks between my hands. 'You've no idea how much I love you, Barbie.'

She smiles and kisses the palm of my right hand. 'Oh yes, I do because I love you just as much.'

Piped music is playing Christmas songs and I hum along to, Last Christmas I Gave You My Heart, by George Michael and decide the song is more than apt.

Our food arrives and we tuck in while discussing the gifts we've bought for all her family. Soon to be my family, I think and grin.

'Em, is it just because it's Christmas that you seem very excitable and OTT or is something else churning you up?'

Ah, here she goes again reading my mind, I think, but smile and shake my head. 'Nope, I'm out with my gorgeous girlfriend who I love from the bottom of my heart, so what more can I ask for?'

We wrap up again in our coats and scarfs, and my heart begins to beat a little faster. It's nearly time, I think knowing I'm going to ask her as soon as we walk down the cobbles to where we bumped into each other last year. I step outside first and hold the door back for her. As if like magic small light snowflakes begin to fall.

'Oh, Clive, it's snowing,' she whispers.

I look up and a flake lands on her nose. I wipe it away and hold her gloved hand while we walk down the cobbles. At the top of The Shambles are a group of churchgoers singing the carol, Good King Wenceslas, and I hear Barbie hum along.

I feel like I'm about to climb a mountain. My chest swells and a light film of perspiration forms along my top lip. I am buzzing and can't wait to give her the ring. Ripples of pleasure surge through my chest then I stop outside a tiny shop doorway. I tap my coat pocket to make sure the small red box is there and take a deep breath.

'Barbie,' I say and swing her around to face me. 'Last year I bumped into you in this exact spot, and you've changed me and my life around. I can't imagine ever being without you.'

She grins at me and nods.

I drop down onto one knee and pull out the box. I try to flip open the top but with my gloves on it's tricky and I curse under my breath. Suddenly my knee slides on the sleety cobble and I stumble to the side.

She bursts out laughing and bends down to help me scramble back up onto my knee then cries, 'You're just like the wayward tin of beans!'

I laugh too but try to compose myself after the slip.

All is not lost; I think and pull off my glove with my teeth. I manage to open the box and ask, 'Will you marry me, Barbie.'

I see her eyes widen in surprise and delight then visibly melt when she looks down at the ring. I can tell she loves it and I grin when she whispers, 'Oh yes, Clive, I'd love to.'

f you have enjoyed this story - A review on amazon.co.uk
ould be greatly appreciated.

'ou can find more Christmas stories from Susan Willis
re:
he novella – prequel to this novel is, Christmas Shambles
York https://amzn.to/3ggrluK

he Christmas Tasters https://amzn.to/3jITooL
he Man Who Loved Women https://amzn.to/3A1X7Uv
he Guest for Christmas Lunch https://amzn.to/3EcyGcy

Website www.susanwillis.co.uk
witter @SusanWillis69
acebook m.me/AUTHORSusanWillis
nstagram susansuspenseauthor

Printed in Great Britain
by Amazon